Lines in the Sand

Book Three

The Lone Star Series

by

Bobby Akart

Copyright Information

Other Works by Bestselling Author Bobby Akart

The Lone Star Series

Axis of Evil

Beyond Borders

Lines in the Sand

Texas Strong

Fifth Column

Suicide Six

The Pandemic Series

Beginnings

The Innocents

Level 6

Quietus

The Blackout Series

36 Hours

Zero Hour

Turning Point

Shiloh Ranch

Hornet's Nest

Devil's Homecoming

The Boston Brahmin Series

The Loyal Nine

Cyber Attack

Martial Law

False Flag

The Mechanics

Choose Freedom

Patriot's Farewell

Seeds of Liberty (Companion Guide)

The Prepping for Tomorrow Series

Cyber Warfare

EMP: Electromagnetic Pulse

Economic Collapse

DEDICATIONS

Every day, I wake up to a beautiful world filled with the undying love of my wife and the loyalty of our pups. Without them, none of my books would be possible. I wish every family could have what we have.

The Lone Star Series is dedicated to the love and support of my family. I will always protect you from anything that would disrupt our happiness..

Acknowledgements

Writing a book that is both informative and entertaining requires a tremendous team effort. Writing is the easy part. For their efforts in making the Lone Star series, a reality, I would like to thank Hristo Argirov Kovatliev for his incredible cover art, Pauline Nolet for her editorial prowess, Stef Mcdaid for making this manuscript decipherable in so many formats, Sean Runnette and the folks at Audible Studios for producing the incredible narration, and the Team—Shirley, Denise, Joe, and Jim, whose advice, friendship and attention to detail is priceless.

A special thank-you to Kevin Baron and the team at *Defense One* for providing invaluable insight into the North Korean threat and how we'd defend against it. Also, thank you to Michaela Dodge, senior policy analyst at the Heritage Foundation, Center for National Defense, for her extensive background material on missile defense, nuclear weapons modernization and arms control.

Thank you all!
Choose Freedom!

About the Author

Bobby Akart

Bestselling author Bobby Akart has been ranked by Amazon as the #3 Bestselling Religion & Spirituality Author, the #5 Bestselling Science Fiction Author, and the #7 Bestselling Historical Author. He has written nineteen international bestsellers, in forty different fiction and nonfiction genres, including the critically acclaimed Boston Brahmin series, the bestselling Blackout series, the frighteningly realistic Pandemic Series, his highly cited nonfiction Prepping for Tomorrow series and his latest project—the Lone Star series, which has already produced two #1 bestsellers.

Bobby has provided his readers a diverse range of topics that are both informative and entertaining. His attention to detail and impeccable research have allowed him to capture the imaginations of his readers through his fictional works, and bring them valuable knowledge through his nonfiction books.

SIGN UP for Bobby Akart's mailing list to receive special offers, bonus content, and you'll be the first to receive news about new releases in the Lone Star series, updates on his other series, special offers, and bonus content. You can contact Bobby directly by email (BobbyAkart@gmail.com) or through his website:

BobbyAkart.com

FOREWORD

by Dr. Peter Vincent Pry
Chief of Staff,
Congressional EMP Commission

Executive Director, Task Force
on National and Homeland Security

The recent escalating war of words and actions with rogue nations like North Korea and Iran has given rise to a new sense of urgency about threats we face—especially the existential threat that is a nuclear electromagnetic pulse (EMP) attack. I am pleased to write this foreword for author Bobby Akart as he continues to inform his readers, through his works of fiction, about the EMP threat, both man-made and naturally occurring.

With the Lone Star series, you will learn about the potential of nuclear-armed satellites flying over America daily in low Earth orbit, positioned to collapse our power grid, destroy our way of life, and possibly kill up to ninety percent of Americans.

The Congressional EMP Commission warns North Korea may already pose a worldwide threat, not only by ICBM, but by satellites, two of which presently orbit over the United States and every country on Earth.

A single satellite, if nuclear-armed, detonated at high-altitude would generate an EMP capable of blacking out power grids and life-sustaining critical infrastructure.

Yet, after massive intelligence failures grossly underestimating North Korea's nuclear capabilities, their biggest threat to the U.S. and the world remains unacknowledged—nuclear EMP attack.

The EMP threat continues to be low priority and largely ignored, even though on September 2, 2017, North Korea confirmed the EMP Commission's assessment by testing an H-Bomb that could make a devastating EMP attack.

Two days after their H-Bomb test, on September 4, Pyongyang also released a technical report "The EMP Might of Nuclear Weapons" accurately describing a "super-EMP" weapon generating 100,000 volts/meter.

North Korea's development of a super-EMP weapon that generates 100,000 volts/meter is a technological watershed more threatening than the development of an H-Bomb and ICBM because even the U.S. nuclear deterrent, the best-protected U.S. military forces, are EMP hardened to survive only 50,000 volts/meter.

My colleague EMP Commission Chairman William Robert Graham warned Congress in 2008 that Russia had developed super-EMP weapons and most likely transferred that technology to North Korea allegedly *by accident*, according to Russian generals.

The result of this newly discovered relationship between Russia and North Korea is that the DPRK now has the technology to win a nuclear war. At the very least, a North Korean EMP attack could paralyze the U.S. nuclear deterrent and prevent U.S. retaliation, perhaps even by U.S. submarines at sea that cannot launch missiles without receiving an Emergency Action Message from the president.

However, the warning signs have gone largely ignored. Although North Korea, Russia, and China have all made nuclear threats against the United States recently, in the case of North Korea and Russia repeatedly, most analysts dismiss the war of words as *mere bluster* and *nuclear sabre rattling*, not to be taken seriously.

In the West, generations of leaders and citizens have been educated that use of nuclear weapons is unthinkable and the ultimate horror. Not so in Russia, China, and North Korea, where their nuclear capabilities are publicly paraded—missile launches and exercises are televised as a show of strength, an important part of national pride.

Then there is the issue of an EMP attack. An electromagnetic pulse attack would be perfect for implementing Russia's strategy of "de-escalation," where a conflict with the U.S. and its allies would be won by limited nuclear use. It's their version of "shock and awe" to cow the U.S. into submission. The same kind of attack is viewed as an acceptable option by China and North Korea as well.

An EMP attack would be the most militarily effective use of one or a few nuclear weapons, while also being the most acceptable nuclear option in world opinion, the option most likely to be construed in the U.S. and internationally as "restrained" and a "warning shot" without direct loss of life.

Because an electromagnetic pulse destroys electronics instead of blasting cities, even some analysts in Germany and Japan, among the most antinuclear nations, regard EMP attacks as an acceptable use of nuclear weapons. A high-altitude EMP ("HEMP") attack entails detonating a nuclear weapon at 30–400 kilometers altitude—above the atmosphere, in outer space, so high that no nuclear effects, not even the sound of the explosion, would be experienced on the ground, except the resulting EMP.

An EMP attack will kill far more people than nuclear blasting a city through indirect effects—by blacking out electric grids and destroying life-sustaining critical infrastructures like communications, transportation, food and water—in the long run. But the millions of fatalities likely to eventually result from EMP will take months to develop, as slow as starvation.

Thus, a nation hit with an EMP attack will have powerful incentives to cease hostilities, focus on repairing their critical infrastructures while there is still time and opportunity to recover, and avert national extinction.

Indeed, an EMP attack or demonstration made to "de-escalate" a crisis or conflict is very likely to raise a chorus of voices in the West against nuclear escalation and send Western leaders in a panicked search for the first "off ramp."

Axis of Evil and the entire Lone Star series are books of fiction that are based upon historical fact. The geopolitical factors in this series leading up to a potentially catastrophic collapse of America's power grid are based upon real-world scenarios.

Author Bobby Akart has written several fiction and nonfiction books with the intent to raise awareness about the threats we face from an EMP, whether via a massive solar storm or delivered by a nuclear warhead. While many books have been written about the results of nuclear war and EMPs, few have tackled the subject of using satellites as a means of delivering the fatal blow, until now.

The Lone Star series is written to be thought-provoking. It will be a reminder to us all that, as Bobby says, you never know when the day before is the day before. Prepare for tomorrow.

Dr. Peter Vincent Pry
Chief of Staff
Congressional EMP Commission
Executive Director
Task Force on National and Homeland Security

About Dr. Peter Vincent Pry

Dr. Peter Vincent Pry served as chief of staff of Congressional Electromagnetic Pulse (EMP) Commission (2001-2017), and is currently the executive director of the Task Force on National and Homeland Security, a Congressional Advisory Board dedicated to achieving protection of the United States from electromagnetic pulse (EMP), cyber warfare, mass-destruction terrorism and other threats to civilian critical infrastructures, on an accelerated basis. Dr. Pry also is director of the United States Nuclear Strategy Forum, an advisory board to Congress on policies to counter weapons of mass destruction. Foreign governments, including the United Kingdom, Israel, Canada, and Kazakhstan consult with Dr. Pry on EMP, cyber, and other strategic threats.

Dr. Pry served on the staffs of the Congressional Commission on the Strategic Posture of the United States (2008–2009); the Commission on the New Strategic Posture of the United States (2006–2008); and the Commission to Assess the Threat to the United States from Electromagnetic Pulse (EMP) Attack (2001–2008).

Dr. Pry served as professional staff on the House Armed Services Committee (HASC) of the U.S. Congress, with portfolios in nuclear strategy, WMD, Russia, China, NATO, the Middle East, Intelligence, and Terrorism (1995–2001). While serving on the HASC, Dr. Pry was chief advisor to the vice chairman of the House Armed Services Committee and the vice chairman of the House Homeland Security Committee, and to the chairman of the Terrorism Panel. Dr. Pry played a key role: running hearings in Congress that warned terrorists and rogue states could pose EMP and cyber threats, establishing the Congressional EMP Commission, helping the commission develop plans to protect the United States from EMP and cyber warfare, and working closely with senior scientists and the nation's top experts on critical infrastructures, EMP and cyber warfare.

Dr. Pry was an intelligence officer with the Central Intelligence Agency, responsible for analyzing Soviet and Russian nuclear strategy, operational plans, military doctrine, threat perceptions, and developing U.S. paradigms for strategic warning (1985–1995). He also served as a verification analyst at the U.S. Arms Control and Disarmament Agency responsible for assessing Soviet arms control treaty compliance (1984–1985).

Dr. Pry has written numerous books on national security issues, including *Blackout Wars*; *Apocalypse Unknown: The Struggle To Protect America From An Electromagnetic Pulse Catastrophe*; *Electric Armageddon: Civil-Military Preparedness For An Electromagnetic Pulse Catastrophe*; *War Scare: Russia and America on the Nuclear Brink*; *Nuclear Wars: Exchanges and Outcomes*; *The Strategic Nuclear Balance: And Why It Matters*; and *Israel's Nuclear Arsenal*. You may view his canon of work by visiting his Amazon Author page.

Dr. Pry often appears on TV and radio as an expert on national security issues. The BBC made his book *War Scare* into a two-hour TV documentary *Soviet War Scare 1983*, and his book *Electric Armageddon* was the basis for another TV documentary *Electronic Armageddon* made by National Geographic.

EPIGRAPH

In the Law, Moses commanded us to stone such an adulterous woman. So, what do You say?"
They said this to test Him, in order to have a basis for accusing Him.
But Jesus bent down and began to write on the ground with His finger.
When they continued to question Him, He straightened up and said to them, "Whoever is without sin among you, let him be the first to cast a stone at her."
~ John 8:5-7

*****

No matter how big your house is, how your new your car is, or how big your bank account is, all of our graves will be the same size.
~ Anonymous

*****

Now I am become Death, the Destroyer of Worlds.
~ J. Robert Oppenheimer, Physicist & Father of the Atomic Bomb

*****

The living would envy the dead.
~ Nikita Khrushchev, on nuclear war

*****

They will be met with *fire and fury* like the world has never seen.
~ President Donald J. Trump

*****

Sometimes you have to draw a line in the sand and say—*enough is enough*. If you have an unspoken policy to move the line, know this …
What you allow is what will continue.
~ your most humble servant

PREFACE

The phrase *line in the sand* has been used for centuries in several historical and military contexts. From the days of the Roman Empire until the present geopolitical strife between the United States and North Korea, a *line in the sand* has been used both figuratively and physically to describe a point of no return—a metaphor for an event or moment in time beyond which the decision and its resulting consequences are permanently decided and irreversible.

As early as 168 BC, history shows that one Roman leader, in an effort to convince an adversary to concede his demands, slowly walked around the king and drew a line in the form of a circle. "Before you cross this circle, I want you to give me a reply for the Roman senate," the Roman consul demanded. The king, who was occupying Roman lands in Egypt, was warned to acquiesce or be destroyed. Staying within the circle, the king nodded his agreement and extended his hand to the Roman consul. Only then did the Roman consul shake it and remove the line with his foot.

Typically used in a military context, one of the most famous instances in American history occurred at the Alamo in 1836. Colonel William "Buck" Travis had just been named commander of the newly constituted Republic of Texas on March 2, 1836.

In the final days of the Battle of the Alamo, with the famed Mexican General Santa Anna surrounding the Texas stronghold, Colonel Travis received an ultimatum from his Mexican counterpart—*surrender or die.*

Colonel Travis consulted with James Bowie, the co-commander of the Alamo. They agreed that their group of less than a hundred defenders were no match for the larger, well-fed Mexican army of fifteen hundred. Nonetheless, Colonel Travis called his men together in the Alamo's open courtyard.

He explained in all honesty that defeat was certain. The letter demanding surrender was read aloud. Colonel Travis proudly announced that he'd rather die than give the Alamo to the enemy. He then removed his sword and drew a line in the sandy soil of the Alamo between himself and his soldiers.

Colonel Travis asked for volunteers to cross over the line in the sand and join him. He made sure they understood their decision was irreversible. All but one man crossed the line to join Colonel Travis in a battle the tales of which will be told for as long as men tell tales. Emboldened by his men's unselfish bravery, Colonel Travis provided Santa Anna his answer—cannon fire.

In recent times, presidents have used the phrase to intimidate world leaders and to rally public support for military initiatives. President George H. W. Bush famously drew a line in the sand when Iraqi dictator Saddam Hussein invaded Kuwait in 1990. As the crisis intensified, President Bush declared this line in the sand was drawn for the purposes of defending Saudi Arabia in the event Iraqi forces advanced beyond Kuwait.

But then, the line shifted as U.S. military forces were used to drive Iraq's Revolutionary Guard out of Kuwait. Many within the Bush administration advocated invading Iraq and removing Hussein from power, but the president elected to work within his United Nations' mandate. A dozen or so years later, the next President George Bush initiated the Iraq war.

In 2012, President Barack Obama declared that the use of chemical weapons by Syrian President Bashar Assad would cross a line that would trigger a U.S. military response.

Following this proclamation, Syrian forces used chemical weapons in Aleppo (March 2013), Damascus, Ghouta, Jobar, and several other Syrian towns throughout August of 2013. The line in the sand had been obliterated by President Assad.

There are consequences to not backing up the line drawn in the sand. After the *red line*, as he called it, was drawn by President Obama, over one hundred thousand Syrians died, many as a result of chemical weapons attacks.

There has been a change in policy toward Syria with the Trump administration.

On April 6, 2017, Syria used chemical weapons again to attack the northwestern Syria town of Khan Sheikhoun. Eighty Syrians were killed and scores more were injured. This prompted the typical United Nation's condemnations but the United States took it a step further. President Trump ordered an attack on the Shayrat air base in central Syria where the chemical attacks originated. Fifty-nine Tomahawk cruise missiles later, the base was reduced to dust and rubble.

On April 9, 2018, Syrian military forces launched another chemical attack on Douma resulting in the deaths of forty-three Syrian civilians. The photographs of dead women and children were horrific.

For the second time in a year, the line in the sand was crossed, and once again, there were repercussions. The U.S.-led attacks on three Syrian chemical weapons facilities were precise, effective, and overwhelming. Over one hundred missiles were fired in total, leaving craters where chemical weapons manufacturing facilities once stood.

This leads us to the present-day conflict with North Korea. For decades, prior administrations from both political parties have drawn lines in the sand concerning the DPRK's nuclear proliferation. Sanctions were imposed, negotiations occurred, and the lines ultimately became blurred or moved altogether.

As a result of America's passive diplomacy in the past, a series of extortionate demands from Pyongyang yielded capitulation by world leaders and an advancement of North Korea's nuclear capability. While the world focused on the DPRK's nuclear and missile programs, the more immediate threat, their conventional forces, had become unacceptably large and dangerous. Kim Jong-un easily spent a third of the nation's feeble gross domestic product on military uses.

For years, the line in the sand for U.S. policymakers has been North Korea's development of an intercontinental ballistic missile capable of reaching the U.S. mainland. North Korea achieved that goal in 2016.

The line in the sand was moved again. The new line was to prevent North Korea's development of a hydrogen bomb. In early 2017, that line was crossed.

Finally, in 2017, the ultimate line in the sand was to demand that North Korea stop development of an ICBM with a nuclear-tipped warhead capable of reaching the U.S. mainland.

In 2017, President Donald Trump stated that *North Korea best not make any more threats to the United States … they will be met with* ***fire and the fury*** *like the world has never seen.* The terminology was different, but the intent was the same. The question remains whether this line in the sand will be blurred and what, exactly, does *fire and fury* look like.

Sometimes, both militarily and in life, you have to draw a line in the sand and say *enough is enough.* Once someone identifies that point of no return—that moment when an adversary has crossed the line—they have to be prepared to back it up. If you have an unspoken policy to move the line, know this …

What you allow is what will continue.

Part One

The Twelve-Hour War

CHAPTER 1

December 1, 2022
North American Aerospace Defense Command (NORAD)
Cheyenne Mountain, Colorado

The dragon that never sleeps.

Native American folklore claimed Colorado's Cheyenne Mountain was a sleeping dragon that saved the Ute Indians from a massive flood that invaded the valley surrounding the mountain. The Utes believed they were being punished by the Great Spirit, but after they repented, the dragon was sent to drink the water. The dragon then fell asleep, became petrified, and thereafter became known as Cheyenne Mountain.

Unlike the legend, Cheyenne Mountain, which was located outside Colorado Springs and just south of Denver, hadn't slept in over half a century. Once made fully operational in the spring of 1966, the country's most important military installation had been home to the North American Aerospace Defense Command, or NORAD.

NORAD was the nerve center of the U.S. military, especially during times of heightened tensions around the world. After the electromagnetic pulse attack of a week ago, the entirety of the nation's defense forces were operating at DEFCON 1, the maximum state of readiness.

Referred to as the *cocked pistol*, military personnel operated at DEFCON 1 around the clock. Around the globe, as well as from space, ground-based sensors and satellites transmitted data to NORAD's unparalleled computer systems for analysis.

Like the operation of a human brain, NORAD collected information from these various sensors and compiled the data in one place for analysis. The personnel within Cheyenne Mountain pulled it together, made sense of it, and then passed it along to the commanders who made the decisions that defended America.

The stress levels in the operations center were high for the airmen whose focus was on detecting and tracking incoming nuclear threats to the U.S., but not from what might happen if a nuclear attack was initiated. The nerve center of NORAD was determined to detect a possible attack in order to give the nation's defense network maximum response time.

Everyone in Cheyenne Mountain knew a nuclear missile fired from North Korea could reach the U.S. mainland in approximately thirty minutes. At DEFCON 1, nerves were frayed, creating an atmosphere of controlled chaos within the operations center.

Lieutenant Colonel Jim Klaus remained within the newly renovated *battle cab*, a dedicated command center and meeting room used by the commander and senior members of his staff. If the operations center was the brain stem that gathered information from the sensors around the globe, the battle cab was the brain, which processed and made decisions based upon the information.

Colonel Klaus was studying the satellite images of North Korea taken by a reconnaissance satellite just four hours ago. Klaus refused to believe the hollow promises of Kim Jong-un that his country had no intention of escalating hostilities following the satellite EMP attack. His job was to trust no one, especially the words of dictators like Kim.

Despite his skepticism, the satellite images continued to tell the same story—the DPRK was, in fact, standing down. There had been troop movements but the opposite of what he'd expected. The DPRK appeared to be thinning their ranks. The number of personnel operating along the border with South Korea had diminished. There were not war games under way. Most importantly, no missile launches seemed to be imminent. The Korean Peninsula was eerily quiet.

Oceangoing vessels had been entering and leaving at a steady pace, with a slight uptick. Their cargo was unknown to Colonel Klaus, although that was beyond the scope of his command anyway. He focused on their nuclear arsenal.

North Korea relied heavily upon its mobile missile launchers created by retrofitting Chinese-made timber haulers into a highly practical transporter erector launch vehicle. These vehicles could be easily camouflaged and moved throughout the country undetected by a satellite's probing cameras.

Colonel Klaus had developed an eye for these vehicles and even employed an old-school magnifying glass to home in on a suspicious-looking truck in the satellite images. Yet there had not appeared to be any concerted effort to redirect the launch vehicles toward the DMZ or North Korea's east coast nearest Japan, which were closer to the United States' targets.

The colonel took a long sip of his black coffee, the first of many on a typical day in the battle cab. He had been warned repeatedly by his cardiologist to cut back on the stimulants, to which he would reply, "I will, as soon as the world cuts back on nuclear bombs."

"Launch detection! Launch detection."

The suddenness of the announcement over the speaker system

within the operation center startled Colonel Klaus, causing him to choke on his coffee and cough repeatedly to recover.

"Repeat. Confirmed launch detection. Coordinates are forty-one degrees, fourteen minutes, nine seconds north latitude and one hundred twenty-eight degrees, thirty-four minutes, thirty-nine seconds east longitude."

His first reaction was to look down at his Casio watch, and he pushed the timer. He knew the next few minutes would be the fastest of his life.

"That's Komdok-san in Mount Komdok," the colonel muttered to himself. "Do you think we were fooled by your phony, beachfront resort?"

Komdok-san was an underground missile base in a northeastern province of North Korea that had been used for Nodong missile tests. Years ago after his successful charm campaign in which his sister wowed the gullible media at the Winter Olympics, Kim had created a tourist area designed to soften their image and encourage international tourists to visit the DPRK. However, it was what lurked underground that was always an area of concern for the colonel and his team.

Two of the colonel's aides rushed into the room, carrying computer printouts. The battle cab was about to get busy.

"Talk to me," Colonel Klaus barked to no one in particular.

"Confirmed by Constant Phoenix," started one of his aides. Constant Phoenix, the Boeing WC-135 aircraft specifically designed and deployed to monitor missile launches, had been deployed to North Korea by Defense Secretary Montgomery Gregg before he left for Texas four days prior. "The missile has been launched from—"

"Deploy defensive measures," Klaus calmly instructed, interrupting the frantic aide. "Get me the acting defense secretary on the horn. Also—"

"Second launch detection. Repeat. Second, no, correction. Second and third launch detections. Confirmed coordinates are thirty-nine degrees, zero-eight minutes, fifty-one seconds north latitude and one-hundred-twenty-seven degrees, twenty-six minutes, forty-six seconds east latitude."

"That's Wonsan Missile base on the eastern side of the peninsula," said one of his aides. "They're using their fixed positions first."

Klaus took a deep breath. This was a high-stakes game of chess, and the next move would have to be made by the president.

"Sir, we have the Defense Secretary on the phone."

Klaus reached for the phone and cupped the mouthpiece with increasingly sweaty palms. His heart was racing; now he understood why he should cut back on the stimulants. The side of his face was growing numb and his left arm began to ache, telltale signs of bad things to come. He encouraged himself to put the anxious thoughts out of his mind.

"Bring these screens up to mirror the ops center. I wanna track these bogeys in real time."

"Yes, sir."

Klaus began to address the new Defense Secretary when his thoughts were interrupted once again.

"Launch detected. Multiple launches detected. Eight. Nine. Strike that. Thirteen. Fourteen. Seventeen."

God help us.

His mind was racing as he processed what was happening. *Very clever, Kim. Exhaust your fixed missile locations first, and then fire off your road-mobile ballistic missiles. I bet the rest are scattering like cockroaches when the light turns on.*

The colonel didn't wait for the final count. He pressed his left index finger into his ear to block out the airman's announcement and turned his attention to the acting Defense Secretary.

"Mr. Secretary, Kim's bringing the house, sir. They're sending everything they've got."

CHAPTER 2

December 1
Raven Rock Mountain Complex
Liberty Township, Pennsylvania

"When was the first launch?" asked President Alani Harman as she entered the Raven Rock operations center. Lieutenant Colonel Baker of the 1111th Signal Battalion was hustling from one computer station to the next, providing instructions to his communications team. The large wall-mounted monitors appeared to be showing a movie in fast-forward as data was displayed and maps constantly changed. The display that caught the president's eyes first was a global satellite image focused on the Pacific Ocean as nearly two dozen flashing red beacons approached the continental U.S., Hawaii, and Guam.

"Six minutes ago," replied her chief of staff, James Acton. "Cheyenne Mountain has initiated nuclear missile defense protocols, but I'm afraid we missed an ICBM headed for Guam. The island will be struck within minutes."

She looked at Acton, dumbfounded. "What? We missed?"

"Yes, Madam President. The focus is now on Hawaii, where the primary target would be Joint Base Pearl Harbor-Hickam, ma'am."

"Can we knock it down?" she asked.

"Intercepts are en route," replied Acton. "There's more on Hawaii, however."

"What?"

"Former President Obama and his family are vacationing on Oahu as well."

"Good God. Has he been warned?"

"Colonel Baker is coordinating that now, Madam President," replied Acton. "It's my understanding the president is golfing, and the rest of the family is shopping at the Ala Moana Center. The entire island has been warned, and necessary measures have been taken to assure them this is not a drill, unlike the 2018 debacle in which Hawaii issued a false alarm."

"James, how many are headed for us?"

"Madam President, we need to have a conversation in the conference room, now," said Acton without providing her a reply.

He gently grasped her by the arm, leading her quickly out of the operations center into the conference room, where they joined Homeland Secretary Carla Pickering, acting Defense Secretary Clayton Evans, and Major Patterson, the keeper of the nuclear football.

Appearing on a large monitor at the end of the room was the chairman of the Joint Chiefs, Admiral Terrence Dasanti. He was located at Cheyenne Mountain and appeared via closed-circuit television. He was standing in front of a wall of televisions with an LED digital clock rolling through seconds and minutes behind him. The president surveyed the display, which showed over eight minutes and counting, referenced the firing of the first nukes.

"Admiral, please tell me our current situation and then your recommendations," the president instructed. As she finished her words, she remembered Top Gun's admonition earlier in the day. *He who hesitates is lost.*

"Madam President, nine minutes ago, two Hwasong-15 ICBMs were detected in liftoff stage from the east coast of North Korea. Trajectory and speed analysis confirm these missiles are destined for our East Coast locations, most likely Washington and New York."

"ETA?"

"Less than thirty minutes, Madam President," Admiral Dasanti replied before continuing. "Two minutes after this initial launch, the DPRK unleashed a barrage of road-mobile ICBMs toward Guam, Hawaii, and points on the mainland. At any moment, based upon trajectory analysis, Guam will be hit near the capital of Hagatna. Our

B-2 Spirits have already been deployed from Guam, with nuclear weaponry awaiting your orders, Madam President."

"Admiral, is there any hope of bringing down the missile destined for Guam?"

"Madam President, we have deployed our F-35 Joint Strike Fighters in an attempt to intercept the missile in midflight. It's a last resort, ma'am."

President Harman let out a deep breath in an attempt to calm her nerves. It didn't work. A glass or two of wine might have helped, she thought to herself, but there wasn't time for that.

Her chief of staff interrupted her thoughts as he asked a question. "Admiral Dasanti, have you deployed all of our missile defense protocols?"

As he answered, a second monitor in the room displayed a graphic depicting the nation's missile defense system. The president had given it a cursory look before, but was now studying it intently.

"Yes, Mr. Acton, we have. The THAAD system and the Aegis ships are prepared to intercept. Our next step is up to the president. A returned nuclear strike, using the B-2 Spirits and our available B-52s, is on its way to the theater. This includes two specially equipped B-2s carrying the B-61 tactical nuclear gravity bombs, ideal for their accuracy and hitting underground targets. We have Ohio-class nuclear submarines awaiting your green light. Naturally, we have our Minuteman IIIs on standby throughout Montana and the Dakotas."

"Have they attacked South Korea or Japan?" asked the president.

"Neither, Madam President. However, six minutes after the first Hwasong-15 launch was initiated, South Korean Defense ordered a retaliatory strike of Hyunmoo II missiles directed at DPRK missile batteries near the DMZ. Their warships and combat aircraft immediately began firing at the North."

"Their attack was unprovoked?" asked DHS Secretary Pickering.

"That is unclear at this time," replied Admiral Dasanti. "They were certainly quick to react."

The president walked closer to the monitor and looked into the high-definition camera. "Admiral, a retaliatory strike, as you've said, will act to destroy their offensive capabilities, am I correct?"

"Madam President, on your order, we can destroy the entire country."

President Harman turned and looked at her advisors in the room. Secretary Pickering spoke first.

"Madam President, total annihilation may not be necessary. There are innocent lives at stake. Perhaps we should focus on high-value military targets."

"No, Carla. Not this time. Kim started this war, and I intend to finish it. I'm sorry for the loss of life of the innocents, but his mobile launchers could be anywhere, and I'm not willing to risk one more ICBM reaching our country."

Major Patterson rose from his seat in the corner of the room, anticipating the president's next request. She nodded to him as he set the briefcase on the conference table.

The president was wearing khaki slacks and a white blouse covered by a blue blazer. She reached into her jacket and pulled out a small card. The acting Defense Secretary inched closer to Major Patterson, who indicated he was ready to begin the authentication process by opening the briefcase known as the nuclear football.

"Ready, Madam President," said Major Patterson.

She read the eight two-letter codes aloud. "OL, HN, MI, BE, XM, OK."

Major Patterson repeated the codes. "The president's identification is confirmed. Admiral Dasanti, the launch codes are accurate and being transmitted to your attention at Cheyenne Mountain."

The president's encrypted launch order included targets, an immediate launch sequence and the necessary authentication codes to unlock missiles by air, sea, and land. Within five minutes, approximately fifteen minutes after the first missiles were fired from North Korea, the United States released thirty-nine nuclear warheads toward the northern half of the Korean Peninsula.

The missiles could not be recalled as they raced toward their military targets and large population centers, not that the president wanted to.

Kim Jong-un had crossed the line in the sand.

CHAPTER 3

December 1
Kingsbury Colony, Montana

"Are those nukes?" Riley screamed his question over the roar of the afterburners from the Minuteman III missiles headed for North Korea. The group was mesmerized by the spectacle of the twelve rockets lifting off into space. Cooper now understood what *shock and awe* felt like. The sheer power and force behind the magnificent missiles forced a nervous laugh out of him despite the ramifications of what was happening.

"If we're firing at them, that means they fired at us first, I think," yelled Cooper. "We've got to take cover."

"Pacheco and I will take the food inside," said Fiorella Schlossmacher, who had been so generous in opening up her home to care for Adriano Morales, who'd been shot. She turned to Eduardo Pacheco, the best friend of Morales and a fellow bull rider of Cooper's. "Let's gather everything and go inside. We have to move your friend to another room."

"Do you have a root cellar or crawl space under any of your buildings?" asked Cooper.

"No, everything is built on a slab, except for the barn, of course," replied Fiorella. "But we've taken some precautions."

"Like what?" asked Palmer.

"I'll tell you inside when we're settled," she replied as Pacheco stacked the trays of food on top of each other and headed toward the house. Fiorella grabbed the drinks and gestured toward the barn. "Go to the barn and retrieve the rolls of plastic and duct tape. It's a thick plastic we keep on hand to protect tender plants in the event of a late spring freeze."

Palmer added, "For the windows, right?"

"Yes. Get all of it, and look in my husband's toolboxes for a handheld staple gun. Hurry. We may not have much time."

Cooper led the way as the trio raced to the barn. It was dark inside and being unfamiliar with it didn't help them. Palmer found the duct tape, and Cooper rustled through the tools until he located two staple guns.

"Check up in the loft," Palmer suggested.

Riley climbed a ladder into the hayloft and found the rolls of plastic. There were four rolls of eight-millimeter-thick plastic sheeting. The label indicated they were ten feet wide and a hundred feet long.

"Watch out, you guys! These suckers are heavy."

Palmer and Cooper backed away from the loft as Riley tossed the seventy-five-pound rolls over the edge. Each time they hit the ground, a combination of straw, dust, and dirt flew throughout the barn, which reminded Cooper to grab a woodworking mask he'd seen on the workbench.

Riley descended the ladder and swept his arms from side to side to wave away the floating debris.

"Come on, grab an end," Cooper said to his brother. He reached down and lifted one side with a lot of effort and a loud grunt.

"Don't bother, Coop," said Riley as he kneeled down next to one of the rolls. "I've got this. The steers I wrestle weigh a lot more than these things."

Riley squatted, gathered a roll up in his arms, and pushed himself upright using his powerful leg muscles. "Let's go. I'll carry in the rolls, and you guys start to cut them to fit. I assume that's what the plan is, right?"

"Yep," replied Palmer. "Can you get the rest?"

"Piece of cake," he replied with a smile as he staggered out of the barn like a clown with oversized shoes. He picked up the pace. "C'mon, I'll race ya."

Palmer and Cooper laughed, temporarily enjoying the lighthearted moment. Riley was the most emotional of the three, but he had a way of making them forget their troubles.

As they approached the front door, Fiorella swung it open and motioned for them to come in. She'd already moved the furniture out of the center of the room with Pacheco's assistance to make room for the project.

"I've turned on the emergency radio to get the broadcast out of Great Falls. It was repeating that mechanical-sounding voice warning. I'm afraid we are being attacked."

The reality hit Palmer, leading to her nervous reaction as Riley set the plastic on the floor with a thud.

"Riley!" she protested, causing her brother to shy away and mutter an apology. She turned her attention to Fiorella. "Any details? You know, targets?"

"Nothing," the woman replied. "The message simply confirmed this was not a drill and warned everyone to immediately take shelter until further notice."

"Ma'am," started a concerned Cooper, "how long have you lived here? I guess, I mean, um, do you think we'd be a target here?"

"Young man, we're surrounded by nuclear missile silos. Nearby Malmstrom Air Force Base controls all of them. That said, I can comfortably say that Kingsbury Colony is not a target, but Malmstrom might be."

Riley patted Cooper on the shoulder and headed out the front door. Before he left, he whispered something their granddaddy, Pops, used to say all the time when the kids were growing up on the Armstrong Ranch. "Talk while you work."

Cooper set the staple guns down and began to unroll the plastic. He continued his thought. "Ma'am, how far is Malmstrom from here?"

Fiorella handed Palmer a notepad and pencil. With a tape measure in hand, she walked toward the first windows near the front door.

"I know what you're thinking," she began to respond. "The base is about a hundred miles from here, toward our southeast. Trust me,

I've thought about this before. If the base got hit, it's not likely we'd suffer damage, but we could potentially be exposed to the radiation fallout. That's why we need to seal up all of the openings in the house. Quickly."

She and Palmer measured the first two windows, and Cooper began to cut the plastic sheeting using sewing shears provided by Fiorella. He added four inches all the way around to allow for both stapling and sealing with the duct tape.

"I wish we had an inside room without external walls," continued Fiorella. "I've read that any fallout that penetrates the outside walls will lose its intensity because it's absorbed. My cloth furniture will help as well."

Riley returned with another roll and immediately headed back to the barn for a third without comment. Cooper cut the first two window coverings and crumpled the excess, trimmed plastic sheeting into a ball.

"Save the scraps," said Fiorella. "We'll use them to cover the air vents to the HVAC system. I don't know if that's necessary, but it won't hurt."

The three of them continued to work together as Cooper thought of another question. "Would we be able to see the explosion if it hit the base?"

"Oh yeah, but we won't be watching for it," said Fiorella. We'll pull my velvet drapes shut to help with blocking the fallout. Besides, I'm pretty sure we'll feel it."

"Like an earthquake?" quipped Palmer as Riley returned with the final roll and, due to exhaustion, dropped the heavy plastic with a thump that shook the floor. "Or from my brother's rude arrival?"

They got a chuckle at Riley's expense and continued the measuring and cutting process. Pacheco rejoined the group, and he began affixing the plastic to the windows with Riley's help. With the group working together, they managed to seal the three exterior doors and twenty-one windows in the small farmhouse in less than twenty minutes. After the air ducts were secured, everyone collapsed into a chair and took a moment to relax.

Fiorella was the first to rise as she pulled her drapes together throughout the home. After the final curtains were closed, she picked up a photo frame with her husband's picture in it and began to cry.

Cooper looked in Palmer's direction and nodded. Palmer hopped off the sofa and went to comfort Fiorella. After a minute, she calmed down.

"I wasn't afraid for my husband until now. His trip home would take him through major cities like Omaha and maybe Denver, depending on which route he chose. He's a strong, smart man. The EMP attack wouldn't faze him. He'd look at the power outage as an annoyance. But nuclear bombs flying around. That's much different."

Cooper rose and joined his sister by Fiorella's side. "Ma'am, we'll pray for his protection. He'll find his way home through all of this. You have to stay strong."

The group heard Morales coughing in the bedroom, so Palmer, Pacheco, and Fiorella rushed in there to check on him. This left Cooper alone with Riley.

Riley looked past Cooper until they were alone, and then he whispered, "Coop, shoot straight with me. Are we screwed?"

"I don't know for certain. It ain't good, that's for sure. We'll know real quick, though."

"How?"

Cooper removed his hat and scruffed his hair. "Oh, we'll feel the earth shake like it's comin' apart at the seams."

CHAPTER 4

December 1
Sixty miles southeast of Hawaii
Pacific Ocean

Duncan Armstrong Jr. comforted his new friend as the two flew out of Yongsan Garrison in Seoul, South Korea, earlier in the day. The last forty-eight hours had been a whirlwind of activity reminiscent of an episode of *24*, one of Duncan's favorite shows as a teen. Sook let out the emotional loss of her family, and despite the third-world conditions she'd lived in, a part of her would always be fond of her familial home in Sinmi-do, North Korea.

Upon their arrival in Guam, Duncan overcame some resistance from Air Force personnel to allowing them a seat on the Boeing C-17 Globemaster destined for San Diego. The large military transport was full to capacity with troops and military supplies returning to the States to help with the EMP-recovery effort.

After a brief argument, the Air Force personnel were called away, allowing Duncan and Sook to board the C-17. Keeping to themselves, the two cuddled in the backseat of a Humvee being returned to the States. The EMP had disabled most operating vehicles, and the military was in dire need of transportation for their personnel.

The C-17 was capable of transporting one hundred thirty-four troops on sidewall seats, together with six armored security vehicles. This flight's payload included two M1117 Armored Security Vehicles and four Humvees. The need for ASVs back home puzzled Duncan when he saw them on board. They were commonly used in war theaters because of their mine-resistant hulls and their weapons capabilities.

Are things so bad in America that we need to use armored vehicles to control people?

His mind wandered as Sook fell asleep in his arms. For the first time since he and Park had entered North Korea with the goal of assassinating Kim Jong-un, he allowed himself to think about his family.

While in the service, like a lot of the guys, he'd carried a picture of his mom and dad, as well as his siblings. Once he entered the black-ops world of the CIA, this was a risk he couldn't afford. Were he to be captured, emotional ties would be used against him to extract information. His possessions, and his mind, had to be devoid of the Armstrong Ranch and his family.

Now, with this incredible young woman by his side, he started to envision a reunion with his folks. He knew they would be accepting of Sook and their relationship, whatever that meant. This was new territory for Duncan. He'd never found time for a steady girlfriend. While other guys his age were focused on hookups and conquests, he was absorbed with his military career and staying alive on the field of battle.

Arriving at Camp Pendleton just north of San Diego would present a challenge for the pair. He wasn't exactly sure how far it was to the ranch, but he guessed a thousand miles would be pretty accurate. There were very few operating vehicles, he'd been told in Guam, and many of those were being confiscated by the government.

His brothers and Palmer would have found a way home on horseback, something he'd shunned as a teen but would quickly embrace now. His mind calculated walking a thousand miles—*two months*. He could do it, but he wasn't sure if Sook had the strength. Plus, the journey would be fraught with danger. If the military was returning ASVs to the U.S. to deal with the EMP's aftermath, then things must be pretty ugly on the streets.

Duncan was weighing the different options and scenarios, including reaching out to his handlers, the same ones who had abandoned him in North Korea. The least they could do was arrange a ride for him back to Texas or some location close by. In exchange, he'd promise not to kill them when he found them. Leaving him and Park in North Korea to die was an unforgivable betrayal, one which he vowed to get revenge for on Park's behalf.

A commotion outside the vehicle startled Duncan, which in turn caused Sook to stir awake. Shouts of *look, look* forced him to scoot up in his seat and poke his head out the Humvee's rear window.

This new BC-17 variant of the Globemaster, initially proposed for civilian operators, had window portals scattered down both sides of the aircraft. Soldiers were huddled along the left side of the plane, taking turns pushing their faces against the window.

Based on his flight-time calculations and the gradual descent in altitude, he placed them nearing the California coast, almost home. He assumed everyone was enjoying a bird's-eye view of their final destination.

Then someone exclaimed, "Oh my god!" Now Duncan had to see what was going on.

It was a cloudless evening, and at their cruising altitude of thirty-eight thousand feet, ordinarily the lights of most large cities could be seen flickering below them. He'd been told much of the continental U.S. had been impacted by the electromagnetic pulse inflicted by the *Axis of Evil.* California and its large population centers of San Francisco, Los Angeles, and San Diego were no exception.

However, it was not California that had garnered the passengers' attention. Duncan took his turn at the window. His eyes were immediately drawn to the anomaly in the darkening sky.

When an object enters Earth's atmosphere, it experiences pressure from gravity and drag. Gravity pulls an object down to Earth's surface, but the particles of air making up the atmosphere rub against the object, creating friction and drag. This friction causes intense heat, which creates the illusion of the object speeding earthward having a brilliant, fiery tail.

What Duncan observed could've been a meteorite, but it wasn't. His eyes strained to make out the landscape miles below their aircraft.

Camp Pendleton's lights were barely visible as they flickered just beyond the Pacific Ocean.

The object continued racing on its downward trajectory as the tension inside the Boeing C-17 grew higher, causing voices to fade away. The object sped up as the gravity of Earth assisted its descent.

Faster. Faster.

Impact.

The concussive blast caused the aircraft to tip from side to side, even from many miles away. What Duncan and the rest of the soldiers onboard the aircraft witnessed brought gasps, prayers, and tears to their eyes.

As the nuclear-tipped warhead made impact in Southern California, the atomic bomb detonated, suddenly releasing a massive amount of heat into the sky. A giant fireball rapidly developed and rose into the air, creating a vacuum effect and forming a mushroom cloud over the California coastline. The visual from above was unmistakable to everyone aboard.

San Diego had been destroyed.

Duncan closed his eyes for a few seconds and reopened them, hoping and praying this was a bad dream. It was not a dream, but it was indeed bad, because another streak of light caught his attention as it invaded the night sky.

"Another one!" someone shouted.

"And another. This can't be!"

Duncan shook his head in disbelief as another streak of light hurtled toward the California coastline and struck Los Angeles and northward toward the Silicon Valley.

In each instance, with rapid succession, the sudden release of energy created temperatures to millions of degrees, similar to the heat on the surface of the sun. The mushroom clouds rose in a crescendo from south to north, leaving millions of dead and total destruction beneath them.

Duncan whispered aloud, "It is done," unknowingly echoing the words of his sister, who was thousands of miles away in Montana.

CHAPTER 5

December 1
Ninety Miles South of San Diego
Pacific Ocean

Battle-hardened soldiers fell into the wooden fold-up seats that lined the C-17 transport and cried like babies. It was impossible to stifle the emotional effect of seeing their country devastated by nuclear weapons. It wasn't glamorous as portrayed in some post-apocalyptic movie. The mushroom clouds represented real death to their fellow Americans, including family and friends who lived in the blast radiuses.

Duncan gave the horizon one last look, immediately wondering if Texas had been hit. His mind processed the geography and demographics of Texas. The Armstrong Ranch was located in proverbial *BFE*, an acronym akin to the middle of nowhere. He doubted the ranch was a target, but points west of there might be, such as Roswell or Albuquerque.

The fallout might impact the ranch as well. Upper-level winds and the jet stream might pull radioactive particles from San Diego or Los Angeles across the desert landscape of Arizona and New Mexico toward Texas. Duncan reminded himself that the fallout would hopefully dissipate over that distance.

He also took comfort in knowing that his parents were attuned to and prepared for this type of catastrophic event. On one occasion, when he'd teased his mother about her preparedness activities, she was quick to admonish him.

She'd said, "Son, prepping is like insurance against a catastrophic event. For years, we've paid Texas Windstorm a premium against hurricane-force winds, and we may never see them in our lifetimes. Prepping works the same way. A catastrophic event may never happen, but if it does, you can rest assured your old parents will be safe. That's peace of mind for us, and for you, son."

Duncan smiled as he reminded himself that mothers were always right.

Sook joined his side and wrapped her arms around his waist. It was also comforting to have her with him as she once again found a way to save him from despair. He turned to her and pulled her back toward the Humvee.

"I know something is bad, yes?" she asked, using her best broken English.

"Sook, we've been attacked. At least three nuclear bombs have hit the west coast in California."

"Duncan, I am so sorry. Dear Leader is horrible man. Are you okay?"

Duncan was about to respond when one of the pilots made an announcement.

"Attention, please. We need everyone to take their seats as we modify our flight plan. Camp Pendleton is no longer available to us, so we'll be diverted to a secondary landing area in either Arizona or Nevada. As we receive further instructions, we'll provide you an update. Also, we do not have details on the attacks I know you witnessed, as we did. Our prayers are with our brothers and sisters on the ground, as well as with those of you who have loved ones in harm's way. God rest their souls."

Duncan gestured toward two seats near one of the windows as the passengers shuffled about looking for a place to settle in for landing. The mood of the soldiers turned from solemn to anger.

Expletives filled the air together with shouts of revenge and war. Racial slurs toward all Asians began to permeate the cargo hold, despite the fact that several of their fellow soldiers were of Asian descent.

One mouthy Marine hurled an insult in Sook's direction, causing her to shy away and bury her head in Duncan's chest. Duncan balled his fists and stared the man down, but held his tongue. If nothing else, Duncan had become a disciplined operative over the years. He knew now was not the time to engage a highly emotional Marine in a fistfight. Duncan allowed his stare to speak for him.

The Marine sat across the fuselage from them and was joined by several others in fatigues bearing the patch of the official seal of Camp Pendleton. These men had just lost their comrades and families. Their anger was expected.

"Sook, we have to be very careful right now. Do you understand?"

She responded by nodding her head.

Duncan explained his concerns. As a teen, he'd studied military history, including the societal reactions to war. Following the attacks on Pearl Harbor in December 1941, tensions ran high across America. Japanese in the States, many of whom were American citizens, were attacked mercilessly as people lashed out in anger.

President Franklin Roosevelt signed an executive order requiring all Japanese-Americans to be relocated away from the West Coast into ten internment camps spread across the country. Approximately one hundred twenty thousand people were held in these camps throughout World War II before being released. It wasn't until March 1946 that the last camp closed.

On the surface, and with the benefit of hindsight, many argued that this was the worst violation of civil liberties in American history. But with rumors of war with Japan spreading, and hatred growing, fueled by racial prejudice against the Asian population, the Roosevelt administration was forced to protect Japanese-Americans by segregating them from the angry mobs that continued to harass them.

Duncan looked at the cross, distraught faces in the low light of the Boeing C-17. He imagined those same looks had permeated the public psyche in those weeks and months after Pearl Harbor. He wondered if the despair following the recent EMP attack would be replaced with a galvanized public ready to lash out at a common enemy—North Koreans, or anyone who looked like them.

Sook's brown eyes met his as he pulled her a little closer to his chest. She was an innocent in this war, just like those who had perished in the nuclear wasteland below them. Somehow, he doubted an angry mob intent on causing Sook harm would give him a chance to explain.

CHAPTER 6

December 1
Air Force Global Strike Command
Barksdale Air Force Base
Near Shreveport, Louisiana

Major Edmee Boudreau had been assigned to the Air Force Global Strike Command, or AFGSC, since being elevated to the rank of major. A New Orleans area native, having been born and raised in the French Quarter, she sought a better life for herself than the one her mother had led working the streets of the inner city. The name given to her by her Cajun mother, pronounced *ed-may*, meant prosperous protection in the archaic form of the French language used by the descendants of French Canadians in the bayou communities.

Major Boudreau's mother, who'd died of a drug overdose many years ago, would have found it ironic that her beautiful baby, whose name meant prosperous protection, was now assigned the task of issuing the commands to deploy the nation's nuclear-capable assets.

Barksdale AFB, located near Shreveport on the border with East Texas, was the home of the Global Strike Command, which controlled two-thirds of the nation's nuclear deterrent. The AFGSC deploys air assets like the B-2 and B-52 aircraft, and as the headquarters for the Eighth Air Force, it stands ready to provide on-alert combat forces to the president. Known as the Mighty Eighth, the unit adopted a motto—*deterrence through strength, global strike on demand.*

Outwardly, Major Boudreau exemplified the attitude of the commanders of the Mighty Eighth. She was known as a no-nonsense, don't-mess-with-me soldier. Cajun women were often portrayed in music and movies as stunningly beautiful heartbreakers who were the source of male frustration and misery.

Major Boudreau fit that mold as well. As a child, she had grown up in rough environs, required to take care of her younger brothers and sisters at an early age. She became immune to the activities of her mother and focused on running a tight household as she raised her siblings. Out of a sense of duty and loyalty to her family, she remained at home until her early twenties when the youngest of the Boudreau brood entered high school. At that point, she felt she could escape the confines of New Orleans.

She never looked back. Always fascinated by the airplanes taking off from Louis Armstrong Airport to the east of downtown New Orleans, she found an Air Force recruiting station and signed up for a new life. Her career was stellar. As part of the Air Force's Affirmative Employment Program, she was given the opportunity for advancement, but Major Boudreau earned her way nonetheless.

Focused on her career, she studied, trained, learned, and impressed as a result. It was her steely nerve and unflappable character that had brought her to the Mighty Eighth. It was the ice running through her veins that had earned her a spot on the console leading to the first nuclear-tipped warheads being deployed by the United States since the atomic bombs were dropped on Japan in August of 1945.

It had only been a few minutes since her commanders had received notice of the nuclear launches being detected from North Korea. Major Boudreau, whose area of responsibility included the 341st Missile Wing at Malmstrom Air Force Base in Montana, scrambled to her station and awaited orders.

The ICBMs within her scope of responsibility were ready every second on any given day. She'd established personal relationships with the commanders of every Minuteman missile silo within the 341st Missile Wing and its support squadrons. This was a day that none of them wished would happen. The deployment of the nation's nuclear assets most likely meant one thing—retaliation. And, as

Major Boudreau reminded herself from time to time, retaliation could logically be equated with incoming nuclear missiles to the United States.

She'd alerted the command at Malmstrom, who were fully aware this was not a drill. They in turn advised the senior officers of the LGM-30G Minuteman III facilities to be at the ready for a launch order. Upon her command, relayed by the President of the United States, the Minuteman III missiles, equipped with the latest variant of the W87 thermonuclear warheads yielding four hundred seventy-five kilotons of destruction, would be launched toward their designated targets.

The operations center designated to the 341st Missile Wing was separate from the areas responsible for similar military bases in Wyoming, North Dakota, and New Mexico. The team sat quietly, focused on their computer screens as they watched data stream in from USSTRATCOM. Major Boudreau was singularly focused on the one that provided her the codes to be authenticated. Consisting of alphabetic characters, the message to her would mean that the president had issued the order the world dreaded most.

Two senior officers stood behind her console. Their job was to confirm the code sequence to absolutely ensure there were no mistakes. They all waited, barely breathing. She hated the so often overused cliché *it's not a matter of if, but when*, but it certainly applied under these circumstances. Everyone in the room knew there were nuclear missiles heading toward the United States. The order would be forthcoming.

Suddenly, her screen illuminated. Her palms became sweaty as the reality set in. She was about to launch nuclear missiles at a country whose citizens were as much in the dark about their fate as Americans were. She silently cursed the people responsible for allowing the hostilities to come to this, yet she steadied her nerves to do her job.

"We have an authentication order," announced the colonel standing behind her without emotion. "Major, please read the code aloud."

Major Boudreau began the process. "Oscar Lima, Hotel November, Mike India, Bravo Echo, X-ray Mike, Oscar Kilo."

The two superior officers standing behind her echoed their confirmation.

"Code authenticated," they said.

Major Boudreau entered the code into a message destined for Malmstrom AFB in Montana. They would also be relayed to an Air Force captain and his team sitting deep underground in a missile silo somewhere in the state of Montana. This team would insert keys into consoles similar to Major Boudreau's. The result would be the liftoff of massive rockets headed into space for a subsequent reentry into North Korean airspace.

With the message prepared, and reviewed by the men behind her, the usually stoic Major Edmee Boudreau slowly pressed the enter key on her keyboard, secretly hoping someone would call off this madness at the last moment.

Edmee allowed a single tear to flow down her cheek as she silently said a prayer of protection for the innocent lives in North Korea.

Heavenly Father, please lift up and protect the people of North Korea, knowing they are surrounded by enemies and a certain death will soon fall upon them. Take them to that secret place on High and shelter them under Your wings to guard and protect them, just as You guard and protect us from danger.

Heavenly Father, protect these people and show them refuge, as You have provided refuge and protection to us. I pray that You provide them the safety of Your fortress because it is You, alone, in Whom we place our trust and salvation.

Lord, I ask this in the name of Jesus Christ, our Lord and Savior. Amen.

CHAPTER 7

December 1
The Armstrong Ranch
Borden County, Texas

Major and Lucy carried out a tray of bread and side dishes to accompany the steaks cooking on the grill. Preacher and Antonio were chatting with a couple of the ranch hands about their day's activities as they huddled around the fire. The evening temperatures had been a tolerable low forties on the Texas Panhandle for the last couple of nights, and Major thought a cookout would provide a perfect opportunity to create a sense of normalcy in an upside-down world.

"Perfect timing, boss!" said Preacher as he gave the meat a final flip to create a crosshatch pattern. Preacher was a throwback to the Old West in many ways. He was an avid reader of James Michener, William Johnstone, and, of course, Louis L'Amour. Despite his rough-around-the-edges appearance and overuse of Texas-speak, as he called it, Preacher was actually an astute, learned individual.

And he was one heckuva storyteller. "Back in the day, after the spring roundups, cowboys would herd their cattle out on the great trails of Texas. They'd leave out of San Angelo for Cheyenne on the Goodnight-Loving Trail. The Chisolm Trail ran from San Antone to Abilene, Kansas. The Shawnee Trail ran from down near the King Ranch all the way to upstate Missour-ah. I'm tellin' ya, cowboys were the eighteen-wheelers of the good old days."

Miss Lucy interrupted to begin handing out the plates to everyone. Major and Antonio stoked a big fire in the center of several cut-up stumps converted to seating. The hands gathered around the hot, dancing flames while Major, Lucy, Preacher, and Antonio set their plates on a nearby picnic table.

After the group filled their plates, Preacher said a brief prayer thanking God for their food and blessings before he continued. "While they were out on the trail, they'd eat meals consisting of beef, biscuits, corn, beans, and coffee that tasted like hot sludge. During the Civil War, the number of cattle drives increased in order to feed soldiers on both sides. As a result, the cooks found it harder and harder to feed the fifteen or twenty men necessary to drive the cattle."

Preacher paused to carve off an oversized bite of steak and began chomping it down as he continued to tell the story.

"Anyhoo, an old Texas Ranger, James Goodnight, who created the Goodnight-Loving Trail, came up with an idea he called the chuckwagon. It was kinda like the mobile kitchens you see in the city that feed them construction workers on the job sites. The chuckwagon and its cooks became the lifeblood of cowboys on the trail. The ranchers wanted their cowboys well fed to ensure their livestock made it to market, so they stocked the chuckwagons with plenty of food.

"Of course, like now in most of the country, they didn't have electricity, so everything was cooked in cast iron over an open fire. Their meals were simple, but filling, just like what we've got here tonight. They'd also have dried fruits, rice, cornmeal, bacon, brown sugar, and everything needed to bake. It made for good cowboy grub."

Preacher paused to dip his bread into the baked beans and took a big bite.

Lucy added, "Back in the day, these men knew how to survive on basic foods that could be prepared without a big fuss. It wasn't a horrible way to live. It was just, well, simple."

The group became quiet as they contemplated life on the cattle trail and enjoyed their dinner. Major looked around at this group of people from diverse backgrounds. The Mexicans had been adopted for all intents and purposes by the Armstrong family. They'd arrived at the ranch alone, sometimes having walked for days after arriving in America.

Eventually, at the Armstrongs' insistence, they became citizens, and then they made arrangements to bring their families to Texas through the proper processes, something Major insisted upon.

Everyone was given a job and a sense of purpose. Nobody got a free ride, including the children. Earlier that day, he and Lucy had laughed at how much their numbers had multiplied over the past few years since Major's retirement from the Texas Rangers. There was no particular reason for the increased number of children on the ranch other than coincidence.

He and Lucy had not been blessed with grandchildren, which was just fine at this stage in their lives, but it was indeed a joy to see the young ones play when they gathered at the barns or up at the barnyard.

Preacher, who was much like a grandfather to all of these kids, enjoyed when the group got together for special occasions like July 4th, Cinco de Mayo, or Christmas. The kids enjoyed playing a game of hide-and-seek with Preacher, or a form of tag in which he was always *it*.

Major and Lucy enjoyed the spectacle, and it did cause them to long for grandkids of their own. Watching Preacher interact with the children was the best part for Major, who referred to the activity as *toddler wrangling*. He'd always been familiar with the phrase *like herding cats*. From Major's perspective, chasing around a bunch of young'uns was more like toddler wrangling, a term that needed no further explanation.

As the group laughed and told jokes, Major finished up the last of his meal and kissed his wife on the cheek. "Thank you for taking care of us, Miss Lucy."

"Honey," she began, "I have to say this is nice. You know, peaceful and relaxing, without the external stresses created by life in general, you know?"

"Yeah, and if our kids could just find their way home, life would be pretty darn good."

Lucy pulled her husband close and whispered in his ear, "There's no doubt in my mind, dear. I've never been as sure of something in my life except for the fact that I've always loved you."

Major smiled and provided her another kiss on the cheek. "I have no doubt whatso—" He finished his statement, but Lucy couldn't hear it.

A thunderous boom cracked high above the ranch, startling everyone, including some of the ranch hands, who instinctively dropped their plates and fell to the ground. All heads were lifted skyward, and their eyes stared at the spectacular flame created by the speeding object above them.

"Asteroid?" asked Preacher.

"Too small, maybe a meteor or something," replied Major.

Several members of the group were now standing and slowly walking toward the east as the object sped across the night sky.

"Where's it headed?" asked Lucy.

"Due east," replied Preacher. "Toward Dallas or even beyond that to Shreveport."

Everyone stood silently as the object became smaller in the sky and disappeared from view. The hands were talking amongst themselves in Spanish when another boom was heard.

Major jumped and turned his head to the south. "Again? Something's wrong, Preach."

Off in the distance toward San Antonio, a similar bright flash was accompanied by an object streaking toward earth.

"That's goin' toward Houston!" exclaimed Preacher. "Major, this ain't no meteor storm. Do you think they're nukin' us now?"

Major ignored the question and grabbed Lucy by the shoulders. "Honey, get the radio and see what you can find out."

"I will. Do we need to go to the bunker?"

"I don't know. Grab the radio."

Major swung around to Preacher. "Tell the hands to wait here. I need you to go down to the bunker and get it ready. Take Antonio with you. By the time you come back, we'll know whether to gather everyone again."

Preacher gave instructions to the men and their wives before hustling off to the underground bunker with Antonio.

Major slowly walked away and stared in the direction of Dallas and Houston. Each city was nearly five hundred miles away, too far for the naked eye to register an explosion even as big as a nuclear strike. As he studied the horizon, he heard the sound of the radio as Lucy ran back outside.

"Major! Major! It's the emergency action notification. Listen!"

She ran toward him, holding the radio in the air, which was playing at full volume. The robotic, text-to-speech voice of ScanSoft Tom repeated the words.

"*We interrupt our programming. This is a national emergency. From the Fusion Center in Austin, stand by for an emergency action notification message issued by President Burnett.*"

The new president's voice came onto the radio. "*My fellow Texans, this is not a drill. We have an emergency situation. It is imperative you take cover and shelter in place. Let me repeat this. The United States and Texas are under attack. This is not a drill. Take cover now and shelter in place until further notice. God bless you all.*"

Major turned to a couple of the hands who spoke the best English. He gave them instructions to gather everyone as quickly as possible and bring them into the shelter like they'd done before. He reminded them to bring their weapons, perishable foods, and a minimum amount of clothing.

His extended family ran for their horses and took off in all directions. Major shook off the night air and the chill that had run up his spine when he heard the notification. He turned to his crying wife and comforted her.

"Listen up, Miss Lucy. We've got this. We've had a dry run, and everyone knows what to do."

Lucy lifted her apron and wiped the tears from her face. "I know. It's the kids, Major. They're out there alone, and that madman is shooting rockets at us. What is wrong with this world?"

She began sobbing again, and Major wrapped his arms around her and whispered a prayer. "Lord, I pray You protect our children. Keep evil far from them and help them through this madness. We trust You to guide them in their decisions and to give them encouragement in the presence of this dangerous time. Help them, Lord. In Jesus' name, Amen."

Lucy began to calm down, and she stood on her toes to kiss Major. They held each other for another moment in silence until Preacher shouted for them.

"Did you hear? We're under attack!"

Major looked down into his wife's eyes, and she smiled back as she nodded. "I'm ready."

"Yeah, we heard," shouted Major.

Preacher ran up to them, arriving out of breath. "Come on, y'all. You two need to get into the bunker."

"Miss Lucy, go on down and get set up. Preacher and I will—" began Major before being interrupted.

"No, both of you," said Preacher. "We'll round everyone up. You guys need to get safe and monitor the radio."

"But—" started Major.

"Boss, no arguments. Please. I don't have time to hog-tie y'all."

Major looked at Lucy, who nodded agreement. "Okay, hurry, Preach. It's not our time to die."

CHAPTER 8

December 1
Kingsbury Colony, Montana

Palmer emerged from the back bedroom and joined her brothers. Cooper and Riley had slipped through the plastic sheeting protecting the kitchen door and loaded up several armfuls of firewood to store inside for the night. They had just finished stoking the fire and sat cross-legged on the floor to absorb the heat when Palmer arrived. Cooper patted the floor between him and Riley with the palm of his hand, indicating Palmer should join them. The boys slid to the side so she could slide in between.

"How is he?" asked Cooper, who'd competed against Pacheco and Morales on several occasions. He knew the Brazilians to be tough *hombres*. That cough, however, didn't sound very good.

"I don't know, y'all," started Palmer. "He's definitely not gettin' better. But he's not dyin' either. He needs a doctor, but obviously that's not gonna happen anytime soon with missiles flyin' around."

"Did Fiorella calm down?" asked Riley.

"Yeah. In a way, takin' care of Morales is good for her. It keeps her mind off her husband being on the road. Pacheco helps too. She's fascinated by Brazil and how both guys' families came to Texas. It passes the time, you know?"

Cooper nodded and leaned in closer to his younger siblings. "Me and Riley have been talkin'. Assuming, of course, we don't get nuked into oblivion tonight, we've gotta make a decision."

Palmer put her hand up. "First off, do you think we might get nuked? Fiorella doesn't seem to think so."

"I don't know, sis," answered Riley. "I've seen a few movies about nuclear wars and stuff. Who knows if they're accurate? It just seems to me that it would have happened by now. I mean, it's been more than an hour since those things flew over our heads. I'm thinkin' North Korea is toast at this point."

"Which means they can't shoot back," added Cooper.

"It also means that any nukes they fired our way would've hit already," Palmer deduced. "I take it y'all think we're in the clear."

"I reckon we'll know for sure in the next hour, but, yeah, I think we're good," said Cooper.

Morales began to cough again, and Pacheco darted through the living room into the kitchen. He could be heard filling up a pitcher of water, and then he moved quickly back to the bedroom without even a glance in their direction.

"What if the Russians or Chinese decide to finish us off or something?" asked Riley before adding, "They could do it, you know."

Cooper shrugged and briefly closed his eyes before commenting. "I suppose they could, but what purpose would it serve? Most times, countries go to war to take the other country's stuff—like gold, oil, or territory. If they reduced America to a nuclear wasteland, what would be the point?"

"They might do it 'cause they hate us," replied Palmer. "I truly believe every country in the world is jealous of us. They'd love to see us knocked down to our knees."

"True, but we've already been knocked down to our knees," said Cooper. "We're the only nation on the planet without electricity."

Riley and Palmer both nodded in agreement. The three sat in silence for a moment as they attempted to overhear Morales discussing his pain with Fiorella. He was looking for pain medications, and she explained that her supply was running low.

"Coop, what were y'all talkin' about when I came out of the bedroom?" asked Palmer.

Cooper leaned forward and confirmed that neither Pacheco nor Fiorella were moving toward the open doorway.

"Palmer, I don't believe we're gonna get hit, and I think that Air Force base down by Great Falls would've been hit already. We've gotta make a decision."

"You know, like the old song," interrupted Riley. "Should I stay or should I go, nah-nah-nah-nah, nah-nah-nah."

Palmer elbowed her brother in the chest, drawing a playful moan in protest.

"Our original plan was to leave at first light," continued Cooper. "Are we jerks to leave these guys alone in the middle of a nuclear war? I've tried to put myself in Pacheco's shoes. Would I be pissed if he and Morales ditched us here?"

"What did you decide?" asked Palmer.

"Truth?" asked Cooper.

"Yeah."

"I'd probably be pissed, but, in the end, I'm glad it's not me being left behind. We've gotta do what's best for us, you know?"

Riley leaned in and whispered, "Family first, you guys. I know Daddy would agree."

Palmer thought quietly for a moment, and she began to rock back and forth before she registered her opinion. "I've kinda thought about this already, but about a different issue."

"What?" asked Cooper.

She continued. "Daddy packed us the IOSAT tablets, the masks and the three RAD stickers to detect radiation. We each have the same package in our backpacks. I thought about whether we should share with them."

Cooper raised his eyebrows. He hadn't thought about that. Once again, he was torn between being selfish and survival.

"I think we should do this," started Riley. "We've got these guys pretty well sealed up in here. Plus, Coop found that woodworking mask over there. They can all stay in here until this passes over, if it even happens. If one of them has to go out, they can use that mask." He pointed toward the side table with the N100 particulate mask sitting on top.

"We could spare one of our RAD stickers so they can check for radiation," added Palmer. "We'd still have two left."

Cooper looked toward his backpack and double-checked to make sure they would not be disturbed. He quickly crawled across the floor, unzipped an outer pocket, and rooted around until he found the RAD sticker. He handed it to Palmer. "Here, you give it to her. You've got the best relationship with her, I think."

Palmer took the small cardboard radiation detector and slipped it into the pocket of her blue-green plaid flannel shirt.

"What about the tablets?" asked Riley. "That's what they'll need to stay alive."

"No!" Palmer and Cooper whispered in unison.

Palmer took the lead. "We can't give those up. Momma told me how the radiation slips into your body and invades your thyroid. Even if the radiation doesn't kill us, we could get cancer and there's all other kinds of ways for our organs to fail."

"Yeah," interjected Cooper. "We've got a long way home. We can't risk giving up something this valuable. It's worth its weight in gold and then some."

Palmer chuckled and whispered to the guys, "Do you know what one of those packs cost?"

"Uh-uh," grunted Riley.

"About eight bucks on Amazon," said Palmer. "Somethin' this cheap can save your life right now."

The three immediately stopped talking and separated slightly as Fiorella returned to the room. Pacheco stayed behind with his friend.

"Did you kids get something to eat?" she asked.

"Oh, no, we totally forgot about the food," replied Cooper, who was telling the truth. He rose off the floor and extended his arms to assist Palmer, then Riley, off the floor. Can we fix you a plate, ma'am?"

"No, thanks. But you three eat. I'm going to fix Pacheco something. I don't think he'll leave his friend's side."

Palmer led the guys toward the kitchen, and Fiorella joined them. Palmer inquired about the condition of their patient, and Fiorella was as unsure of his fate as Palmer was.

The answer to every question posed to Fiorella, including when or if the next bombs would drop, was *time will tell.*

CHAPTER 9

December 1
Raven Rock Mountain Complex
Liberty Township, Pennsylvania

The president insisted upon spending a moment alone with her husband in their living quarters. His words of encouragement fell flat as the gravity of the situation began to crush her psyche. Over his protests, she downed a glass of wine and poured herself another before the gentle tapping at her door forced her to set the glass aside. She couldn't understand why they couldn't just give her a moment. She'd ordered the retaliatory strike. It was now up to the country's missile defenses to do their job and protect them.

"Madam President, we're needed in the situation room," said her chief of staff through the door. "The first damage assessments will be coming through shortly."

President Harman closed her eyes and exhaled. Visions of Hollywood blockbuster movies crossed through her mind—buildings obliterated, bodies melting from heat and radiation, debris from the blast killing countless people, leaving body parts strewn about in its wake.

Why do I need to hear the details? Just get me when it's over.

The knocking started again, this time more forceful. "Ma'am, please. We're needed—"

The president barked her response. "I get it, James. Hold on." She considered knocking back the second glass of wine but opted for some breath mints instead, curiously annoyed that they weren't sugar-free.

Without addressing her husband, she flung the door open and

marched past Acton. She turned slightly, imagining the two men in her life were giving one another *the look*. Lucky for them, they weren't. She was in a mood and not to be trifled with. Her dreams of ascending to the presidency to help the poor had been erased. She now presided over the end of the American empire.

President Harman entered the situation room of Raven Rock without any formal announcement. The pomp and circumstance typically afforded a president was set aside, as more important matters were at hand. The first North Korean ICBMs had struck the U.S. mainland.

"Madam President," started acting Defense Secretary Evans, "we have our first damage reports from the initial launches by the DPRK. Within moments, our THAAD systems will be engaging the final wave of ICBMs as they reenter the atmosphere."

"Before you begin, Clayton, what is the ETA on our rockets?" she asked.

"Nine minutes for the first wave and twenty-two minutes for the wave just launched," he replied.

"Okay, proceed with the damage assessment."

"Guam was the first to be hit, ma'am," began Evans. "Our tertiary measures failed to intercept the first missile launched by the DPRK. The island suffered a direct hit. Based upon our initial analysis, this was a three-hundred-kiloton nuclear warhead, roughly equivalent to our original W87 Minuteman IIIs. All infrastructure on Guam has been destroyed with only a few buildings' skeletal remains visible. Eighty percent of the local population has most likely perished and the remaining injured upon impact."

The president shook her head. "How many dead? Best estimate."

Secretary Evans referred to his notes before responding, "In excess of one hundred thousand dead, with another forty thousand injured or exposed to the radiation."

"That is a huge percentage of the public, are you sure?"

"Ma'am, Guam is a tiny island with a dense population. There's nowhere to hide."

"What about our naval forces?"

"Evacuated, ma'am. They train for such an evac constantly."

She sighed. The president knew Hawaii was next, and the fate of a former president rested in the hands of the U.S. Pacific Command stationed there.

"Hawaii?" she asked.

"Spared, ma'am," responded the newly installed Secretary of Defense, who wouldn't officially take the post until confirmed by Congress, when and if it reconvened. "The Raytheon SM-3 Block IIA missile defense system did its job on the ICBMs. The Pacific Tracker was perfectly positioned for intercept, ma'am."

The six-hundred-sixty-six-foot vessel was designed to have long-range, highly efficient telemetry processing systems to aid missile defense systems like the SM-3 IIA. The SM-3s were part of the forty-four ground-based interceptors in Alaska and California that defended the country against ICBM missiles.

"That's great news!" exclaimed the president, whose enthusiasm wasn't shared by the military leaders who surrounded her. She immediately felt embarrassed and sensed a *but* coming from her Defense Secretary.

"Yes, ma'am, to an extent," continued Secretary Evans. "Without seeming inappropriate, ma'am, but Chairman Kim was shrewd in his tactics."

"What do you mean?"

"The first two missiles fired by the DPRK were from known, fixed locations on the east coast of North Korea. Both were sent to expected targets—Guam and Hawaii."

"So?" The president put her hands on her hips and looked to Acton, who gave her a blank stare in return.

"Madam President, because our past success rate in testing the SM-3 defense system was fifty-fifty, coupled with the fact that only two nukes were detected, we attempted intercept of these two initial missiles with eight of our forty-four SM-3s."

"Leaving us only thirty-six?" she asked.

"Yes. Moments after our release of the intercepts, the DPRK launched twenty-four additional rockets."

"Dammit! Bottom line this for me!" The president was irate.

Secretary Evans referred to his notes. "We can't intercept them all, ma'am. There have already been direct hits in San Diego, Los Angeles, Sacramento, Colorado Springs, outside Houston, and at Barksdale near Shreveport."

The president's knees became weak, and she leaned backward into a wall. Acton moved quickly to grab her arm, preventing an embarrassing collapse to the floor. She became light-headed and suddenly had the urge to run. Run as fast as she could. To anywhere. *Just not here.*

"Have they all hit us?" she said with a tepid voice. She didn't want to hear the answer. She just wanted to run.

"There are still seven en route to the Eastern United States," he replied. "Anticipated targets are Washington, New York, Omaha, Philadelphia, Pittsburgh, and Toledo."

The president looked puzzled and turned her head as if the slight tilt would allow the list of cities to compute in her brain better. "Wait. Toledo? And why Sacramento? Did they miss?"

"No, ma'am. Toledo and Sacramento have between six and eight military installations surrounding their metropolitan areas, not to mention nuclear power plants. While New York City, for example, is a prime target because of its large population and high profile, more strategic targets include cities like Omaha and Philly, which have a number of military bases and nuclear plants as well."

"Have you been in contact with NORTHCOM in Cheyenne Mountain?"

"Yes, ma'am. The city of Colorado Springs took a direct hit, but there was only minor damage within the mountain. The design worked."

"Okay, what else so far?"

Secretary Evans nodded to Colonel Baker of the 1111th Signal Corps, who was in charge of all communications within Raven Rock.

Colonel Baker began. "Madam President, the Global Strike Command center at Barksdale took a direct hit. It's hard to imagine any survivors. All infrastructure on base has been destroyed, and their operations have been delegated to support bases under their command."

"How many service personnel did we lose?" she asked.

"Unknown, but most likely numbered in the thousands. But there is an ancillary aspect to this, ma'am."

The president exhaled, no longer attempting to hide the smell of wine on her breath. She was ready for this to be over. "Go ahead, Colonel."

Baker looked at the Defense Secretary, who nodded for him to continue. "Madam President, Barksdale is next to one of the nation's major data transmission lines, which runs parallel to Interstate 20 into Texas. It's part of the Louisiana Optical Network Initiative, or LONI."

"And?" the president interrupted.

"It appears, Madam President, that the transmission lines have been severed. Raven Rock—and the Pentagon, when the time comes—has been cut off from our military bases in the Southwest."

CHAPTER 10

December 1
Kingsbury Colony, Montana

Another hour had passed and the same emergency message repeated itself on the AM radio. Fiorella went to check on Morales and returned with a Charles Chips potato chip can. It was sealed with an aluminum tape that resembled air-conditioning duct tape. Riley immediately jumped out of his chair to assist her with the load. When she broke his heart by revealing that potato chips were not inside, he set the can on the kitchen table and sulked.

"I'm sorry, Riley," joked Palmer, and then channeled their momma. "Are you not gettin' enough to eat, hon?"

"Whatever, Palmer," he gruffed. "I was just tryin' to help her carry it. That's all."

"Liar!" she said playfully before Riley took a swat at her. Cooper often wondered who would come out of a wrestling match alive if they actually went at it. Riley was strong as an ox, but Palmer had tremendously quick reflexes. Plus, she was slippery. She'd always wrangled out of a choke hold when they played as kids.

Fiorella retrieved a knife from the kitchen drawer and cut the tape, followed by popping the lid. One item at a time, she unloaded the contents from the foam-lined container onto the kitchen table. Each item was wrapped in heavy-duty aluminum foil.

"A Faraday cage," muttered Palmer.

"Very good, young lady," said Fiorella. "They encourage everyone in the colony to have them. Believe it or not, this was a house-warming gift when we moved here. I've got one for my sister-in-law when they arrive as well."

Winnie, the Schlossmachers' English bulldog, slowly emerged from the bedroom in a half-sleepy state, looking for something to eat.

"Let me feed this tummy while you guys find the shortwave radio in this stuff," Fiorella instructed. "There should also be some batteries. The shortwave band will provide you a lot more options to get information. You might even find the Three Percenters."

"Three Percenters?" asked Cooper.

Fiorella pulled a bowl out of the cupboard and provided Winnie a combination of dry dog food and some leftover corn, which she shaved off the cob for a little added flavor.

She replied, "The Three Percenters are a nationwide group that, well, I guess some refer to them as a militia."

"Why are they called the Three Percenters?" asked Palmer.

"Here's what I know," Fiorella began. "During the American Revolution, the number of men fighting against the Brits never really amounted to more than three percent of the colonist population."

"You mean only three percent of the population wanted freedom and independence?" asked Riley.

"No," she began her response. She set the food on a place mat for Winnie, who eagerly chomped it down, passing gas twice during the process. "Only three percent of the colonists took up arms against the British. Today, the Three Percenters identify with those colonists willing to fight, because they were considered the true patriots fighting for freedom from the king."

"Wow, who knew?" said Palmer jokingly. "It kinda shows how powerful a minority can be if they're passionate and stick together."

Fiorella sat down and reached across the table for one of the aluminum-foil-covered bundles. She began to unwrap it and eventually revealed a silver Sangean world-band receiver.

"Here we go. Did you find any double A batteries?"

Riley slid four across the table in her direction.

Fiorella continued. "Anyway, they're what the government commonly refers to as a *militia.* Back in the colonial days, a militia was a normal, accepted form of raising an army. In fact, most of the three percenters were civilians who supplemented the regular Colonial

Army who fought in the Revolution. Today, any group deemed a militia by the government is bad because they are labeled as anti-Washington, pro-freedom, pro-gun, pro-religion, etcetera."

"We've got militia groups in Texas, especially along the Mexican border," said Cooper. "I think they call themselves the United Patriots."

"Three-UP," interjected Fiorella.

Cooper sat up in his chair. "Yeah, that's them—Three-UP. Do you reckon they're the same bunch? I gotta tell ya, in Texas, the ranchers along the border loved them. Until they finished the wall from Brownsville to El Paso, ICE and federal border protection were undermanned and overrun. It was lawless. The United Patriots just had to stand across the river and the illegals would scatter in all directions on the other side."

"That's the same type of organization, or might even be connected, I don't know. I haven't listened to their broadcasts in a long time, but I imagine Three-UP stands for Three Percenter United Patriots."

"Makes sense," said Cooper.

"You mentioned broadcasts," asked Riley. "Do they have a radio station or something?"

Fiorella inserted the batteries and closed up the radio. It powered up immediately, providing a loud static throughout the kitchen.

"Well, it's a long shot, but they might be on the air," she said as she handed the radio to Riley. "They're located all over the mountain west. Plus, they're all preppers. If we had one Faraday can courtesy of Charles Chips, each of their families had five or six."

Palmer and Cooper huddled around the portable radio as Riley thumbed through the digital dials. Fiorella cleaned up after Winnie, and the two of them left for the bedroom to see about the Brazilians.

After they'd left, Palmer asked. "When should we tell her that we're still plannin' on leavin'? She's so nice, y'all."

"Let's see what we can find out on the shortwave, and then we'll sleep on it," replied Cooper. "If nothing else happens, then we'll tell her when we wake up. I hate long goodbyes."

CHAPTER 11

December 1
The Armstrong Ranch
Borden County, Texas

It took thirty minutes to gather everyone in the bunker and seal the hatch. Most of the Armstrong Ranch residents heard the sonic booms and immediately began to gather their things under the assumption they'd be vacating their homes. They lived in a different world now, and situational awareness had become a way of life for everyone on the ranch.

In the first bunker, Major had gathered those who were interested in monitoring the radio for news from around the state. The second bunker was dedicated to the children and anyone who couldn't handle the circumstances happening aboveground. The two bunkers were filled well beyond their capacity, and he didn't want to expose people to the realities of nuclear war unnecessarily.

He and Lucy huddled in their room to scour the internet for information, since HughesNet finally made adjustments following the EMP. Major felt terrible they hadn't monitored the radio more diligently. They'd reached a false sense of security after the president indicated hostilities had ceased based upon the words of Kim Jong-un. Major silently cursed Washington in general, as he held them responsible for this escalation. Then he scolded himself for trusting his better judgment to politicians.

"Here are some details from the BBC," he said to Lucy, who sat in a folding chair alone in the corner. Despite their comforting words to one another, the reality had set in for Lucy when the hatch was closed for the second time in a week. *My kids aren't safe in a bunker.*

"Okay," she murmured her response.

"Apparently the first missiles were launched from North Korea a couple of hours ago. One hit Guam and the other was destroyed heading to Hawaii. We knocked some of them down, but several found their way through."

Lucy became concerned, and she retrieved a U.S. atlas from a plastic bin under the steel-framed bed. She frantically thumbed through the pages until she found the border between Canada and Montana.

"Where did they get through?" she asked hesitantly.

Major replied, "The West Coast in California. Near Denver. Galveston. Near Shreveport. A couple of cities in the Midwest."

"What about Canada?"

"Nope. No locations in Canada were targeted, according to this report."

"Major, could the kids have made it to Denver already?"

Major took a deep breath and let out the air from his lungs. "Honey, I've thought about this every day. I've tried to imagine where the kids are and what they've done so far."

Lucy added, "We've instilled a sense of urgency in them under these types of circumstances. I hazard to say they knew this was an EMP within a minute of it happening. They knew the telltale signs."

"And we taught them the government wouldn't be able to fix things immediately," Major said as he leaned back in his chair and clasped his hands behind his head. He looked up to the ceiling as he performed some mental calculations. "For sake of argument, let's assume they left on horseback that night, or by the next day. It's only been a week."

Lucy interrupted. "Which means they've only made it as far as the middle of Montana or Northern Colorado, which would be a stretch."

"Agreed. They're probably in Montana."

"Were any missiles fired at Montana?" asked Lucy.

Major returned his attention to the article and scanned through the list of targeted locations. He smiled and looked over the top of the screen at his wife.

"Not so far. Also, there's this. The BBC reports that we've retaliated. We fired our nukes back at them."

"Major, will this stop the attacks on us?"

"If we unleashed the hounds, so to speak, there won't be anything left of North Korea. Yes, the attacks would stop."

Lucy began thumbing through the map book again. She traced her index finger from Calgary, along the eastern edge of the Rockies, until she reached Texas. She looked up at Major with a look of concern. "If they take a direct route south, they'll have to travel through, or at least near, Denver. What about the fallout?"

Major set the laptop aside. "I'm sure they have their get-home bags. They have the masks, the IOSAT tablets, and the radiation stamp things. Besides, by the time they reach Denver on horseback, the fallout will be gone."

A gentle knock on the door interrupted the parents' conversation.

"Major, can we talk for a minute?" asked Preacher.

"Yeah, come on in."

Preacher slowly opened the door and slipped inside, quickly closing it behind him. "Listen, they found a Mexican station that is reporting that California got hit. Is that true?"

"Yes, unfortunately. San Diego, LA, and near Frisco. Why?"

Preacher grimaced before answering, "A lot of our people have family in Southern California. What should I tell them?"

Major looked to Lucy for advice.

Lucy had a question. "Major, if we retaliated and that means they can't fire off any more nukes, how long will it be before we can leave the shelter?"

Major closed his left eye in concentration and stared at the ceiling as he thought about the fallout. "Assuming they didn't hit Arizona or New Mexico, which there is no indication that they did, then we could leave whenever we want. The fallout from the West Coast will most likely dissipate before it reaches Texas."

"But we'll still monitor for radiation, right?"

"Absolutely. The emergency radio will be monitored, too. I can promise you that."

Lucy thought for a moment and then addressed Preacher. "All of us should make this decision together, but it sounds like we would be safe if we left the bunker in the morning, after we confirm that North Korea has been wiped off the face of the planet. If that's the case, let's put off telling everyone about the cities that were attacked until we're outside. I realize the unknown breeds anxiety. But the word of lost loved ones to a nuclear bomb will stir them all into a frenzy."

Preacher shrugged. "I hate lying to folks, especially our people. That said, it's the right thing to do under the circumstances. We can't have everyone in a panic. It'll use up all of the oxygen in these buried tin cans."

"Hey, these tin cans, as you call them, got here just in time, don't you think?" asked Major.

"Can't argue with that," said Preacher with a laugh. Then he got a serious look on his face. "When we walk out of here, things will be different. What does our future look like?"

Major stood and patted his friend on the shoulder as he reached for Lucy's hand. "Here's the thing about the future. Every time you look at it, it changes because you looked at it. And that, my friend, changes everything else. We'll take it one day at a time and be thankful for another day after that one is over."

CHAPTER 12

December 1
Grand Canyon West Airport
Peach Springs, Arizona

"This is Captain Doug Thomas speaking. We've been cleared for landing and have begun our descent into Grand Canyon West Airport. The Arizona National Guard and elements of the 58th Operations Group has taken control of GCW. I need everyone buckled up and holding tight, as this runway presents a challenge for this aircraft. You will be briefed further on the ground. That is all."

Grand Canyon West Airport was located sixty miles northwest of the small Arizona town of Peach Springs. From the sky, it appeared abandoned, as it stood on top of a mesa overlooking the Grand Canyon. The runway, which stretched only five thousand feet before it reached the rocky soil, was just long enough to stop the massive Boeing aircraft, which would use every inch of asphalt.

The pilot began his final approach, and the C-17 decelerated as it dropped lower toward the runway. As the one-hundred-seventy-five-foot aircraft touched down, the reverse thrust of the four Pratt & Whitney turbo engines countered the aircraft's forward momentum, causing the passengers to lurch toward the front of the plane.

Duncan did his best to hold his position and not crash into the female soldier to his left, but Sook's groan told him that the passenger next to her was not as polite. In fact, purposefully so.

Duncan had no idea where Peach Springs, Arizona, was, but he knew the Grand Canyon was a long way from home. At least they wouldn't have to battle any large population centers. Their first battle, however, could be with the people who surrounded them.

The aircraft came to an abrupt stop and sat at the end of the runway for an excruciating minute. Despite the darkness, Duncan could feel the eyes upon Sook. He desperately wanted to depart the plane and be on their way, but then he remembered it was the middle of the night.

Within minutes, bright lights were turned on outside the aircraft. Large temporary lights had been installed with generators powering them. Duncan surmised that the runway was purposefully dark except for the landing lights embedded in the pavement. Most likely, they used instrument flying due to the lack of visibility, as they would in poor weather conditions.

With the taxiway now fully illuminated, the aircraft slowly made a left-hand turn and taxied back toward the terminal, Duncan assumed. Others on the plane had removed their shoulder harnesses and began to gather their gear before crowding near the rear mechanical ramp.

Sook and Duncan also unstrapped, but he pushed down on the top of her leg, indicating they should wait. He wanted to assess the potential for a physical altercation before they joined the group to depart.

As the ramp was lowered and the troops began to shuffle out, he noticed the mouthy Marine across the way had ignored them and disembarked. That was fine with Duncan, so he decided to grab their one duffle bag containing his Barrett rifle and a change of clothes given to him at the Andersen base exchange in Guam. Duncan hoped to blend in with the crowd as they entered the terminal for an anticipated debriefing.

The cold wind struck them in the face as they deplaned. The temperatures were near forty, but the wind chill at what seemed like the top of the world at GCW caught them both by surprise. There were several military police personnel guiding the departing passengers toward the small one-story terminal of the airport. To their left was a tent city surrounded by military vehicles. The orangish glow of lanterns illuminated the desert storm camouflaged tents, which were lined up by the dozens.

The group shuffled under a canopy supported by four-by-four posts toward the entry of the terminal, which held a sign greeting passengers with a hearty *gamyu*, which meant hello in the native tongue of the Hualapai Tribe.

The airport was owned and operated by the Hualapai Indians. Their reservation, which spans three counties in Northern Arizona, included their tribal capital of Peach Springs, which was a small town on historic Route 66.

As Duncan and Sook entered the terminal full of uniformed military personnel, he immediately noticed there were no Hualapais in sight, nor were there any other civilians. He immediately became concerned about how the two of them would be treated considering their identification put them within the Defense Department, but not active-duty military.

"Everyone gather around, please," shouted an MP who stood near the ticket counter for a helicopter tour of the Grand Canyon. "Attention! Please gather around and give the colonel your full attention."

The group crowded the ticket counter and began to settle down as the colonel spoke.

"My name is Colonel Jacobs with the 58th Operations Group from Luke Air Force Base in the southern part of the state. You have touched down at Grand Canyon West, one hundred miles west of Flagstaff, Arizona, and also a hundred miles or so southeast of Vegas.

"This is a civilian airport, and we are here as guests of the Hualapai Indian Tribe due to developing circumstances around the country. First, and I'm not gonna sugarcoat this, let me get the bad news out of the way as we know it. Several hours ago, NORTHCOM notified the president that several ICBMs were inbound from the Korean Peninsula. Initial targets included Guam and Hawaii.

"Our defenses were successful in Hawaii, but not Guam. This aircraft departed just hours before Guam was hit. When you consider what lies ahead for you in this post-nuclear world, remember how close you were to a certain death.

"Since those initial attacks, and I know that you are aware of this, California was hit as well. San Diego, Los Angeles, and an area east of San Francisco all took direct hits. Several other warheads were intercepted, but these three slipped through. The country has faced additional devastation. Here's the list based upon the information relayed to me at this time.

"Colorado Springs, New York, Omaha, Toledo, Ohio, Galveston, and Barksdale Air Force Base in Shreveport have all been hit so far. Now, before anyone jumps to conclusions about the fate of your families, know this. The cities I have mentioned are fairly large metropolitan areas. The death toll varies depending upon someone's proximity to ground zero. I urge all of you to keep your families in your prayers. Do not give up hope.

"Let me explain the situation for you tonight. GCW and Peach Springs are potentially in the fallout path of the Los Angeles attack, but more so the San Francisco attack, which is located six hundred plus miles to our northwest. Let me explain to you what fallout means.

"After a nuclear blast, radioactive material is thrown into the upper atmosphere as the mushroom cloud rises upward. The radioactive dust and ash mixes with air particles that become highly charged with radiation.

"The prevailing winds, following the jet stream, greatly influence the fallout pattern. The winds help carry the fallout longer distances, but they also serve to diminish the radiation levels. As time passes, the radiation levels decrease, and your exposure is less likely to result in your death.

"Let me bottom line it for you. Radioactive fallout decays relatively quickly with time. Most areas become safe for travel in three to five weeks within the area surrounding the blast zone. For areas like ours, some six hundred miles away, the likelihood of receiving radiation poisoning is very low.

"Tonight, all of us are safe from nuclear fallout. By the end of the day tomorrow, if the radiation travels under perfect meteorological conditions, low doses of radiation will appear on our monitoring devices.

"As protection against the effects of the radiation, we are going to issue each of you the following items."

The colonel paused to retrieve a ziplock plastic bag from the table behind him. He pulled out a package of tablets and showed them to the group. "This is a blister pack containing a fourteen-day supply of IOSAT tabs, which is potassium iodide. It is a full-strength radiation-protective medication designed to block the nuclear radiation from entering your thyroid."

He reached into the bag again and retrieved a yellow, postage-stamp-sized card and showed it to the group. "This is a RADTriage card, or a RAD sticker. It's a personal dosimeter that will instantly detect radiation exposure. When you first detect radiation using the RAD sticker, you should seek protective shelter. Once in a protective shelter, or regardless, you should begin taking the KI regimen. As for me, I plan on starting the potassium iodide tomorrow and run it for the entire fourteen-day dosage.

"Ladies and Gentlemen, we know the radiation will come this way. The question is how much punch it will pack on arrival, which leads me to the logistical problem we have. Needless to say, your arrival was unexpected, and you may not be the only flight redirected to GCW.

"Sadly, that means you can't stay here except for tonight. You are welcome to bunk in here, but we'd prefer you not interact with the troops assigned to this detail, who are sleeping in the tents outside. Their deployment orders can change by the hour. We'll get you fed, but we have nothing in the way of bedding. Tomorrow morning at oh seven hundred, we'll get you some chow, and then you'll be loaded up on M35s and delivered to Peach Springs. Unfortunately, you'll be on your own after that."

Sook looked to Duncan, and he shrugged. "Tonight, we'll get some sleep here. Tomorrow, we head home. How does that sound?"

She simply smiled and wrapped her arm through his. He liked this soft, gentle side of Sook. He just hoped she could turn on her survival instincts when the time came.

CHAPTER 13

December 1
Raven Rock Mountain Complex
Liberty Township, Pennsylvania

"Sir." A serviceman dressed in his fatigues approached Colonel Baker, who was still deep in thought. He was more concerned by the loss of the transmission lines to the west than he'd let on to President Harman. He was continuing to communicate with former Defense Secretary Gregg through his office at Lackland Air Force Base near San Antonio. Gregg had promised Colonel Baker a position in the Texas military once the bombs stopped flying. He and his wife could enjoy life far better for the next several years in Texas than they could inside Raven Rock.

"Yes, Captain," replied Baker.

"The final missiles will be reentering momentarily. Our weapons defense systems are ready."

Secretary Evans overheard the conversation and turned to the president. "Madam President, let's turn our attention to the monitors, if you please," started Evans. "We have live feeds from Washington and New York."

The president, with the assistance of Acton, made her way to the back row of the theater-style situation room. Members of Baker's team were intently focused on their monitors, only periodically looking up at the large screens as if to confirm their work was being shown for all to see.

"Also, Madam President," started Colonel Baker, "we have birds with eyes on the Korean Peninsula. The South Koreans are holding their own against the short-range missiles and armaments fired against them from the bunkers on the North's side of the DMZ. Thus far, none of the nukes have been pointed in their direction."

Secretary Evans was quick to add, "Frankly, Madam President, Kim's response to the initial South Korean attack has been muted. It could have been a lot worse. Either he has no intention of engaging the South Koreans further, or he's incapable for some reason. The return fire from the North has been designed to repel an invasion, not annihilate the enemy, as he has always boasted he could do."

"Here we go," exclaimed Baker, focusing everyone's attention on the monitor.

"Omaha has been hit!" declared one of the service members at a computer terminal.

"Toledo also!" shouted another.

The president cupped her hand over her mouth to stifle a reaction.

"More incoming, two directed toward New York City."

The cameras switched rapidly from scene to scene as the military's hardened wiring enabled those in the situation room to study the live feeds from various cameras scattered throughout the city.

"We took out one of 'em," said a young woman with a heavy Southern accent.

The group continued to watch the monitors as they scanned Manhattan, Queens, the Bronx, and Brooklyn.

Suddenly, an intense flash of bright white filled two of the screens followed by static.

"Which boroughs?" asked the president.

After a brief delay, one of the technicians replied, "The Bronx and Manhattan, ma'am."

"Cameras are down in Brooklyn Heights, Astoria, and at College Point."

President Harman turned to Acton for clarification.

"Those are neighborhoods along the East River, Madam President," said Acton. "Manhattan is only thirteen miles wide. The blast radius and fallout will overtake Queens and Brooklyn."

She gasped and muttered aloud, "My god, millions will die."

"Philly and Pittsburg are hit!" shouted a lieutenant from the front of the room. "Three missiles inbound for Washington."

The room became still and quiet. The tapping on the keyboards ceased, and all eyes were directed to the large monitors mounted on the curved wall at the bottom of the room.

"What's happening?" asked the president.

"Madam President," Secretary Evans began to respond, "there are six ground-based midcourse intercepts dedicated to these last three missiles. They have been tracking the inbound ICBMs. They are designed to intercept the warheads after the burned-out boosters fall away. The computer systems will have to differentiate between the boosters, the cloud of debris associated with separation, and also the decoys."

"Decoys?" asked President Harman.

"Yes, ma'am," Secretary Evans responded. "Assuming the North Koreans are following the Russian design, the missile can deploy simple aluminized Mylar balloons outside the Earth's atmosphere. Because they will be in a condition of weightlessness, they become an effective countermeasure potentially leading our kill vehicles astray."

Once the booster rockets of the ICBM intercepts burned out, they separated and left a five-foot-long bullet-shaped device known as a *kill vehicle*. This tracker was designed to hunt down its prey—the nuclear-tipped warhead. Using its sensors as well as guidance from satellites and ultrasensitive ground radar, the kill vehicle attempted to distinguish between the warhead and any decoys or debris.

"Then what?" she asked.

"Onboard thrusters will steer the kill vehicle into the path of the nuclear warhead, shattering it on impact in the upper atmosphere before the bomb has a chance to detonate."

"How do we know if these kill vehicles are successful?"

Secretary Evans sighed and turned away, choosing to focus on the cameras panning throughout Washington. He responded in a hushed, faint voice.

"The cameras will tell the story."

CHAPTER 14

December 1
Los Angeles, California

The three-hundred-kiloton nuclear warhead burst in the air just above downtown Los Angeles, as directed by the computers deep underground in Pyongyang. Had it not been for the EMP attack of a week ago, the Los Angeles Coliseum, home to the University of Southern California Trojans, would have been packed with ninety-three thousand football fans for a rare season-ending Thursday night game with crosstown rival UCLA. Chinatown would be teeming with tourists while Koreatown filled bellies with dining delights. Wine would have been consumed at gLAnce and the BottleRock. The Killers rock band was scheduled to perform at the Staples Center to thousands of adoring fans. Families would have packed the Walt Disney Concert Hall to hear the Los Angeles Philharmonic perform Christmas music.

In any given twenty-four-hour period, there might be approximately two-point-eight million people in downtown LA. At night, it became the epicenter of cultural events, entertainment, and nightlife. But after the EMP, much of the population had escaped downtown LA and headed toward the perceived safety of the Angeles National Forest toward the north.

Those who remained lived in a lawless society in which gangs moved in and preyed upon the weak. Downtown LA was their turf now. The wars taking place in the inner city raged as the California National Guard and the U.S. military ceded the once vibrant downtown to the criminals and opportunists.

However, on this night, the inhabitants of downtown LA would face a threat far greater than the bands of roving marauders written about in post-apocalyptic fiction. It was ground zero for the final journey of the Hwasong-15 missile that had left North Korea thirty-five minutes ago.

There were no warnings. The power grid failure had destroyed the civil defense system set up years ago during World War II. For the gangs and seedy side of a post-EMP world, it was simply business as usual until the nuclear warhead performed an airburst detonation a mile above LA.

Within seconds, the several hundred thousand residents remaining in the city were killed instantly. Those who weren't eviscerated suffered third-degree burns, which are eerily painless because the depth of the burns destroyed the pain nerves, throughout the layers of their skin. The depth of the burn went beyond the layers of the skin, but also affected deeper tissues and muscles. The skin became blackened and charred, resulting in infections that, if left untreated, would result in death within hours or days.

Those who weren't burned received a massive five-hundred-rem radiation dose. Without immediate medical treatment, ninety percent of those exposed would die a painful death within days.

The overpressure of the nuclear blast, at five pounds per square inch, caused most buildings to collapse, crushing or burying those who sought shelter inside. Injuries to anyone seeking shelter in the buildings would be universal, and fatalities were widespread.

Even with much of the population evacuated as a result of the collapse of the power grid, the death toll would rival the casualty rate the U.S. military suffered in World War II, the wars in the Middle East, and the terrorist attack on 9/11 combined. From Beverly Hills, to Pasadena, to South Central LA, very few lives remained unaffected.

The City of Angels had become a wasteland that would last for decades.

CHAPTER 15

December 1
Kingsbury Colony, Montana

"Man, these guys are serious," said Riley. "I can see why the government doesn't like them. They're organized, prepared, and independent."

"They're hell-raisers," quipped Palmer. "Did you hear all that talk about setting up their own roadblocks? They have no use for FEMA either."

Riley leaned back in his chair and clasped his hands behind his head. With a shrug, he responded, "Look, the president ordered martial law, which includes things like confiscating guns and excess food. If FEMA guys came to Momma's door demanding her guns and food, she'd fill their backsides with buckshot."

Palmer continued to raise concerns about the Montana militia group. "The guy doing the broadcast talked like they have groups all over the country, including Texas. Doesn't the government have enough to deal with already without these guys getting in the way?"

Riley disagreed. "I think they're just tryin' to protect our rights. We're not the bad guys in all this, the North Koreans are."

"That part was weird, too," Palmer shot back. "He said there are North Korean soldiers on American soil. C'mon, Riley, that's nuts. We probably just blasted them to high heaven. They'd be idiots to try to attack America."

"Sis, they have eyewitnesses, and they saw—" started Riley before his older brother calmed the conversation down.

Cooper intervened. "Listen, y'all. Don't make too much of all that talk. They're just tryin' to get their guys fired up. It sounds like the guys who patrolled the border when we were in high school. Duncan didn't like them too much 'cause he said it wasn't their job and they were too over the top. This group is no different."

"Well," interrupted Palmer, after giving Riley another *look*, "back then, he was a rule follower. Dallas's dyin' changed all of that. Duncan is, um, hardened. It's almost like he's too serious."

"He feels guilty, I think," said Cooper, who hung his head. "I sure as heck didn't make it any easier on him. It's crazy, y'all, but I've thought about him a lot since this whole thing happened. Where do you reckon he is?"

Riley turned off the radio and pushed it into the middle of the table. "I sure hope it's a long ways from here. Did you hear the list of cities that got hit? They nuked G-Town."

"Yeah, Coop," started Palmer. "Why would North Korea wanna send a bomb to Galveston?"

Cooper shrugged but provided his best guess. "I bet the target was Houston. They were probably trying to take out the refineries and overshot their target."

"Whatever, no loss," mumbled Riley. "Place is overrated anyway. Whadya think about Denver gettin' hit?"

"Colorado Springs, but same thing," replied Cooper. "Well, besides the fact our military is run from there right now, that ain't good. For us, we just need to steer clear of Denver. It's probably a nuclear wasteland."

Palmer leaned in to whisper, "It's right on our route home. Maybe we should wait for the smoke to clear?"

"Radiation, you mean, but I get it," said Cooper. "Here's the problem. The other route we have as an option takes us straight through the heart of the Rockies. While I appreciate the use of Red Rover, that old truck can't climb the steep inclines through Butte, Idaho Falls, and Salt Lake City. Albuquerque, too. Stayin' on the eastern side of the Rockies is relatively flat."

"What about the radiation?" asked Palmer.

Cooper had considered the risks. He wished he knew more about the fallout and how long it lingered. He thought the winds helped move the stuff out, and from what he recalled from the times they'd attended rodeos in Denver, the wind screamed off the eastern slope of the Rockies like a banshee, especially in the winter.

"We have the RAD stickers and the IOSAT tablets," he replied. "I hate to put it this way, but Denver was the city that concerned me the most between here and home. Big cities equate to big chaos. Those folks got a lot of problems to deal with now, which means they might leave us alone as we drive by."

"What if we drive a little farther east than we planned, like when we were gonna be on horseback?" asked Riley. "The car saves us all this time. We can afford to be safe and avoid gettin' fried by radiation."

"Or we could wait another couple of days," added Palmer.

"I don't know, sis," said Riley. "I'm with Coop on this one. Let's get rollin' while the bad guys are distracted."

"Riley, I thought we were gonna sleep on it," said Cooper.

"Nah. I say let's go first thing unless more bombs come flyin' by."

"Okay, then," said Palmer. "It's settled. Off to bed, boys. I'll stay up with Fiorella for a while."

Riley and Cooper pushed their chairs away and headed for the living room.

"I call first shift on drivin'," Riley whispered as they headed for the couch. The Rodeo Kids were ready to head home.

CHAPTER 16

December 1
Raven Rock Mountain Complex
Liberty Township, Pennsylvania

Fights typically begin with an aggressor. Aggression could be a social or physical behavior that intended to harm another individual or nation. The aggressor would identify a target and was not only willing to harm the target, but also undertake actions that the target dislikes. In most instances, no matter how hateful the aggressor acts, it has no impact on the other party unless it was deemed to be hurtful.

President Harman sat alone in the conference room as she considered human behavior and how it related to the advent of this nuclear war. Her mind wandered to her younger days when she'd attended an outdoor rock concert with a girlfriend.

During a break in between bands, she and her friend acknowledged an inherent problem with large crowds at an event such as the one they were attending—a lack of bathrooms. Add excessive use of alcohol and a potential chaotic situation was in the making.

They made their way through a crowd toward a row of forty port-o-potties, which had dozens of people lined up in front of each. She and her friend each chose a line and hoped one would reach the front sooner than the other, at which time they'd join up.

Twenty minutes later, she recalled, she'd reached near the front of the line when suddenly three women appeared and forced their way in line with their boyfriends. Like several others in line, she'd grumbled about the new arrivals.

Were they really cutting in line? Everyone was *holding it*, as they say, and these women had no right to jump in front of those who'd been patient.

Soon, the crowd began chanting, "Back of the line. Back of the line."

Undeterred, the three women laughed, tossed their hair about, and hung on their boyfriends as they inched closer.

This reaction infuriated the crowd. In a flash, a drunk man rushed past her and began to urinate on one of the women. The woman's boyfriend reacted by shoving the man to the ground, where he continued to urinate, except on himself.

Now at a fever pitch, those in line behind her, fueled by alcohol and anger, rushed forward, knocking those in line to the ground in some cases. A fistfight ensued, and police moved in to tamp down the hostilities by using pepper spray and threats of arrest. In the end, everyone in line was delayed, and the stench of people urinating at will filled the air.

President Harman had learned about aggression and societal collapse on that day. She learned that tense situations could get out of control, resulting in a breakdown of morals and values.

On this first day of December 2022, a date which would be remembered for centuries, she learned that the war of words could raise tensions between nations to a fever pitch, one that could result in aggressive behavior that couldn't be tamped down.

Secretary of Defense Evans had just left her with the *good news* that the war was over. The so-called *good news* was the annihilation of North Korea's nuclear capabilities and much of its infrastructure. The *good news* was that they could no longer attack the U.S., and America could breathe a sigh of relief.

A sigh of relief? She repeated the names of the cities of America that would not be able to breathe a sigh of relief, much less breathe. Washington, New York, Philadelphia, Pittsburgh, Toledo, Omaha, Galveston, Shreveport, Colorado Springs, San Diego, San Francisco, and Los Angeles.

A dozen American cities. Already gone, in a span of hours. The bulk of the nation was without power. Anarchy in the streets made her experience at a rock concert decades ago look like a birthday party for a bunch of not-yet-potty-trained two-year-olds.

The President of the United States buried her head in her hands. She was at a loss as to where she should start first. She took a deep breath and exhaled, but it wasn't a sigh of relief that the *Twelve-Hour War* was over. It was more of a gasp for air as she tried to avoid suffocating from despair.

Part Two

Road Trips

CHAPTER 17

December 2
Kingsbury Colony, Montana

The Rodeo Kids learned early on that having an operating vehicle in a grid-down scenario was both a blessing and a curse. In America, the average age of a passenger vehicle was twelve years. Out of two hundred seventy million cars, only about twenty thousand were a 1972-model year or older. Having the ability to travel long distance was a valuable asset; however, a moving vehicle was not only a rare sight, but a much-coveted commodity. One that was worth killing for in a world without rule of law.

"Ma'am, God blessed us when He introduced us to you," started Cooper. "I can't thank you enough for what you've done to protect me and my family, not to mention what you're doing for them boys." Pacheco had already said his goodbyes and returned to his post at Morales's side.

"Don't you say another word about it, young man," said Fiorella as she gave Cooper one last hug. "It's been my pleasure to help you young folks."

Palmer, who was standing next to them, reached out to hug Fiorella again. "Are you sure you won't take a packet of these potassium iodide tablets? We calculated our drive home and are pretty sure we don't need them all."

The night before, Palmer stayed up and talked with Fiorella for an hour while they watched the Brazilian boys sleep. Palmer felt a sense of guilt over how helpful Fiorella had been, and the Armstrong kids had done nothing in return. After providing Fiorella with a RAD sticker, she offered her a fourteen-day pack of IOSAT. Palmer calculated the three of them had enough in the remaining two packets to make it back to Texas.

Fiorella smiled and patted Palmer on the back. "Honey, I've got two bottles of Lugol's Oil. It works for everything from wound treatment to upset stomachs to disinfecting drinking water. But most importantly, for our present circumstances, I can use it to protect from the radiation poisoning. With the Lugol's Oil in our bodies, the radioactive fallout has nowhere to bind as it travels to the thyroid. If the time comes, we can ingest it and I can apply it to our skin around the lymph nodes. We'll be just fine."

Palmer gave her one last hug, as did Riley, while they loaded up.

"Ma'am," started Riley, "my momma would thank you for what you've done for us. In fact, when this is all over, we'll come back to see y'all. I promise."

"Oh, dear, that would be nice, but we know how these things go. You three just be safe, and I hope the food I packed will help you along the way."

"Are you kiddin'?" said Riley with a laugh. "It's all the fuel I need to make it clear to the ranch. And thank you for those old maps too. We plan on avoiding the cities. The maps of Montana, Wyoming, and Colorado show all the small county roads, so we can try to avoid trouble."

"Well, you're welcome," Fiorella replied with a smile. "My husband and I loved to sightsee. You can't see this beautiful country sailing down an interstate at seventy miles an hour. You need to travel the back roads. I know the maps are old, but last time I checked, they haven't been digging up any of the country roads and hauling them away."

She laughed along with the group, and Riley gave her yet another hug goodbye. Cooper reached into the back of Red Rover and pulled out his rifle. He was riding *shotgun*, and in a post-apocalyptic world, that title meant something.

After warming up the diesel engine, Red Rover made its way down the driveway toward the highway, full of hope for a safe trip.

CHAPTER 18

December 2
Peach Springs, Arizona

Duncan and Sook rode in the front seat of an M35 as it made its way from the airport to the small town of Peach Springs. The town's one thousand residents consisted almost entirely of members of the Hualapai Tribe. It had no historic landmarks, claims to fame, or well-known dignitaries associated with it. Located on Route 66, which ran from east to west across the desert southwest, Peach Springs was the tribal capital of the Hualapai Tribe.

The territory had been settled by their ancestors in the 1860s following fierce battles with Americans moving toward California, as well as with the Mojave Indians. For decades, they were attacked by miners and settlers, and responded in kind. The war, however, was short, as the Americans carried diseases unknown to the Hualapai. Weakened by sickness and dysentery, they eventually surrendered and retreated into the mountains surrounding the Grand Canyon.

Finally, by an executive order issued by President Chester Arthur in 1883, the tribal lands were restored, and the Hualapai eked out an existence until Highway 66 and the airport were constructed, bringing a modicum of wealth to the community.

Unlike their more modern counterparts of Indian nations, which relied upon casino hotels for their existence, the Hualapai lived a simple, throwback lifestyle reminiscent of their ancestors'. When the power grid collapsed, they hardly noticed.

What they did notice, however, was when the military rolled up loaded with troops and assault vehicles to commandeer their airport. By the executive order of 1883, the Hualapai Tribe was declared to be a sovereign nation and governed by an executive and judicial branch, plus a tribal council made up of seasoned, knowledgeable elders.

The passage of time had not erased the memories of the elders, who'd been told of the American invasion of their lands in the late nineteenth century. When the military had arrived three days prior, the tribal leaders closed their eyes and harkened back to the 1860s, when men with similar attitudes had arrived on horseback and wagons rather than in M35s and Humvees.

As the convoy arrived from the airport, the passengers were told to disembark at the entrance to the Peach Springs School directly across the street from the Hualapai Tribe government building.

Dr. Clay Bravo, a council member, and Deputy Chief John Banda of the Hualapai Police Department stood on the sidewalk of the government building, watching the vehicles unload.

"The plane arrived last night," said Dr. Bravo.

"Looks like more soldiers and a couple of civilians," Banda commented. "Where are they from?"

"I don't know. They tell us nothing. But I have a better question. Just where do they think they're going? We can't let them stay here."

Banda began to walk across the parking lot to get a better look. He adjusted his belt and made sure his service weapon was readily available. He didn't expect trouble, but a group of a hundred plus had just descended upon Peach Springs with little more than the clothes on their back and a knapsack.

Dr. Bravo arrived by the police officer's side when shouting broke out between two soldiers and one of the civilians. The civilian was being pushed by the men as he shielded a young Asian woman behind his arms. Dr. Bravo and Banda slowly crossed the street to get a better look.

"You shouldn't have brought her here, pal!" shouted one of the men, who suddenly dropped his duffle bag to the gravel parking lot. "She and her people just nuked the hell out of us. We ought to take our revenge on her, right here, right now!"

The man dressed as a civilian was showing remarkable restraint, in

Banda's mind. Rather than fighting back, the young man tried to diffuse the situation. Now, however, a crowd was gathering around, which led to an escalation of the argument.

"Listen up, buddy," the civilian shouted. "A lot has happened, but it's not this girl's fault. You and your buddy need to back off!"

"No, buddy," the soldier said sarcastically. "You should never have brought her on our plane to begin with. She could be a spy or somethin'. Why don't you be a good boy and get out of our way so we can deal with this?"

"I'm from South Korea," the young woman shouted, which only served to make matters worse.

"Big f'n deal!" the other man shouted. "You're all the same. You're probably in cahoots with them anyway. I think it's time to teach a few lessons, what do you guys think?"

A few shouts of yeah could be heard while others egged the two bullies on. The crowd was angry over what they'd witnessed and were ready to lash out at the first available target.

Out of habit, Banda reached for the microphone attached to his vest, intending to call the Hualapai PD dispatch and ask for backup. Then he remembered their electronics were fried.

When the man continued taunting the civilian and poked his finger in the man's chest, Banda knew his hopes for a peaceful resolution were dashed.

In a lightning-fast maneuver, the civilian grabbed the man's arm and forcibly pulled him towards his body. He yanked the soldier's arm behind his back until a loud snap occurred, dislocating the man's shoulder. The soldier groaned in pain as he fell to his knees.

Banda ran to where the men were fighting but not before the other man bum-rushed the civilian in an attempt to tackle the man to the ground. It was a bad decision. The civilian got into a fighting stance and kicked his front foot forward, catching the man in the chin, forcing his face upward.

Unfortunately, this did not end the fight, as one of the soldiers grabbed at the young woman from behind. She quickly swung around on one leg, with her raised leg kicking the man in the ribs. As he doubled over in pain, she jumped and kicked him with both legs in the side, sending him tumbling into the crowd. Just as Banda was about to pull his sidearm and fire a warning shot into the sky, the fight was over, as three men lay on the ground battered from the defensive tactics of the two civilians.

The two triumphant fighters stood back-to-back as the man yelled, "Anybody else? Come on, now. Y'all scared? Who else has a big mouth like these fools?"

The group gathered up the injured soldiers and retreated to the other side of the M35s. Banda and Dr. Bravo walked up to them, and the two relaxed somewhat.

The young man spoke first. "Hey, that was self-defense. We don't want any trouble."

"We know," replied Banda. "We caught most of it, starting with the yelling and the accusations."

"Don't worry, friends," said the elderly Dr. Bravo. "Our people understand what it's like to be the brunt of hostilities such as these. Why don't you gather your things, and let's go inside? We don't have much to offer in the way of hospitality, but it will be better than what you experienced from those men."

"We'd be much obliged. My name is Duncan Armstrong, and this is my friend Sook. We've been through an awful lot to get back to the States. The last thing we needed was a fight from guys like them."

Banda picked up Duncan's bag and handed it to him. "Feels heavy, Mr. Armstrong. More than just clothing, I suspect."

"The world has changed," said Duncan.

"Indeed it has," said Dr. Bravo. He smiled as he hooked his arm through Sook's. "Would you mind helping an old man across the street, young lady?"

"Yes, sir," she replied with a smile and a wink to Duncan. "Thank you. You are the second American to be nice to me."

Dr. Bravo laughed. "Well, I've said something similar once. Let me tell you a story as we walk inside."

The group walked toward the governmental building, unaware they were being watched from afar by a man with one eye.

CHAPTER 19

December 2
Texas Homeland Security Operations Center
Austin, Texas

Former Texas governor and now Texas President Marion Burnett had just completed recording a series of announcements to be broadcast over any operating Texas radio stations and the Texas Emergency Broadcast System. It had been seventeen hours since the first missiles were launched by North Korea. After the initial barrage and the retaliatory strike ordered by the president, the threat subsided. Nonetheless, the former governor urged Texans to be mindful and pay attention to news reports in the event tensions flared up from another source.

She departed the Fusion Center and returned to the Governor's mansion under heavy guard. Despite the nuclear threat, the rising sun brought out protestors to the mansion grounds, protesting the lack of food. The Texas president was beginning to feel the effect of the catastrophic event and the impact it had on the state's food supply.

While Texas had done an admirable job of protecting its power grid and remaining fiscally responsible, the former state's politicians failed to take into account that much of their foods were brought in from California and the Midwest. This weighed heavily on her mind as she entered a conference room filled with her top advisors. President Burnett mumbled to herself, "Man cannot survive on beef alone," a phrase that would be decried as blasphemy in Texas.

"Good morning, everyone," she announced as she arrived. "Please, stay seated. This will be a long meeting, so we should all get comfortable."

"Coffee, Madam President?" asked her aide.

"Wow, that sounded, well, different." President Burnett chuckled. "Needless to say, the start of our transitional government from a state to a nation is on today's agenda. Forming a new country is difficult enough, but the circumstances we face make it dang near the stuff of movies."

She reached for the coffee mug and took a quick sip of the black brew. Amidst the nuclear war and food shortages, her mind wandered to coffee availability, of all things. Then, in a brief moment of compassion for President Harman, she wondered how another new president was coping with the magnitude of the collapse. These events would test everyone's mettle.

"Thank you. Now, let's get started. Let me have a damage report on Galveston and how Texas was affected by the blast near Shreveport. Kregg, you're first."

Kregg Deur, who held the position of adjutant general and the head of the Texas National Guard, stood and moved to the front of the room near two wall-mounted monitors.

"Thank you, Madam President," started Deur. "As you know, some of the world's largest refineries are located in the area of Galveston Bay. Baytown produced six hundred thousand barrels per day, pre-collapse. Marathon locations in Texas City and Pasadena, together with the Valero facilities in that area combine to produce just over a million barrels a day. It was a logical target for our enemies."

"But they missed, right?" asked the new president.

"Yes, ma'am, although the point of impact has resulted in a devastating loss of life. The missile struck a few hundred yards off Stewart Beach at the east of the island. The underwater explosion created a tsunami that covered Galveston Island clear down to San Luis Pass nearly ten miles away. The force of the impact caused the sand comprising the east end of the island to push into the bay, filling the entrance to Galveston Bay. It's unknown at this time whether the relocation of the island will rectify itself, or if we'll need to undertake a massive dredging project."

"What about the people of Galveston?"

"Ma'am, a thirty-foot wave swept across the entire island," replied Deur. "By the time the wave, coupled with debris, hit the historic district at the Strand, it was too late for anyone to seek shelter. Most who went underground to avoid the nuclear blast drowned. Those who climbed to the highest points of the buildings may have survived. We're sending choppers filled with search and rescue crews there now."

"Kregg, casualty estimates?"

"Ma'am, most of the tourists left after the EMP attack in an attempt to go home. That's a plus. The residents remained, choosing to stick together and live off fishing resources. The population of the island is around fifty thousand. My guess is that most perished."

"Were any of the refineries damaged?" she asked.

"We're waiting on a damage assessment from ExxonMobil and BP facilities in Texas City, which was closest to the point of impact."

President Burnett's aide slipped her a note, and she grimaced. Monty Gregg needed to speak with her urgently. She needed to address the food matter before she called him.

"Continue, Kregg."

"Yes, ma'am. Well, Texas was spared in the bomb blast that struck the Shreveport area. Barksdale Air Force Base on the east side of the city took a direct hit. The mushroom cloud rose into the air but quickly dissipated to the east as a result of a strong wind. The problem that affects us the most are the masses of people attempting to cross our border from Bethany up to Caddo Lake. We need more personnel to hold them out."

President Burnett stood and whispered to her aide. Then she addressed the group. "Everyone, please wait here while I make a quick phone call. I may have a solution."

She and her aide hustled out of the conference room and found an empty office down the hall. She handed her aide the phone and instructed her to get Montgomery Gregg on the phone.

President Burnett walked aimlessly through the room as she considered the ramifications of her next actions. The nuclear attacks would drive even more refugees toward Texas. The only way to keep them out was through the use of force. The nuclear explosion near Shreveport had created a humanitarian crisis. There would be people with radiation poisoning seeking medical treatment and refuge in Texas.

"I have him on the phone, ma'am," announced her aide.

"Good morning, Monty."

"Marion, I have some news for you," was his curt reply. Monty Gregg was a man who got to the point.

"Okay," said President Burnett hesitantly.

"Our recon choppers know of your problems at Shreveport. The pressure is growing along other sections of the Texas border as well. I'm sending men to provide a show of force, but I think you need to double your border fencing."

"Tell Kregg Deur what you need and we'll round it up. Monty, I can't leave those people in Shreveport suffering. They need immediate medical attention. The ones who weren't injured need to start a potassium iodide regimen to block the radiation from entering their systems. We both know Washington, or wherever they are, can't move as fast as we can."

"Marion, I hate to be callous, but they're not your problem now, remember? That said, I might have a solution that can gain you favor with Harman, take the heat off your secession play, and feed Texans in the process."

President Burnett sat down and gestured for her aide to join her. "Go ahead, Monty. I'm all ears, as our buddy Ross Perot once said."

"Yeah, of course. Marion, I think you should contact President Harman with a proposal. The primary purpose of your call will be the crisis in Shreveport. Like you, she can't turn her back on her citizens who are suffering, even if she doesn't like your proposal."

"What is my proposal?"

"Number one, she must formally recognize the Republic of Texas as a sovereign nation. This will prevent any future political fights as Texas gets on its feet as a new nation and the U.S. recovers from this nuclear war."

"Okay, what else?" she asked.

"Second, tell her Texas will treat the ill at Shreveport, but in order to do so, you'll need access to the Strategic National Stockpile locations in Texas."

"Do you know where they are?"

"Not precisely," Gregg responded, before adding, "I suspect they are in Dallas and Houston based upon my calculations. The locations were protected by statute with only a few members of government aside from the president having that knowledge."

"Within these stockpile locations, will there be radiation drugs or conventional medications?"

"Absolutely," Gregg replied. "My understanding is there are large amounts of prepackaged, individual ten-to-fourteen-day regimens for over three hundred thousand people per location. You'll have access to large quantities of IV drugs, chemical antidotes, and medical supplies. Plus, there are pallets of MREs, bottled water, and ordinary household cleaning supplies. You can't feed every household, but you can certainly help the hardest hit in large population areas."

President Burnett smiled. "This could help me solve a couple of problems. Thank you for the suggestion, Monty. I'll make the call shortly. Anything else?"

He waited a moment before responding. President Burnett knew him to be a very calculating man. As a general and a master chess player, Gregg was known to think through every move and troop deployment.

"Marion, Harman's going to want more than what you're offering."

"Like what?"

"Opening the borders."

"Monty, that's not gonna happen. If we do that, we'll be overrun."

"I know, and I'm not suggesting you capitulate on this issue at all. Promise her you will consider a merit-based immigration system giving deference to family ties to Texas. However, each immigrant will come with a price, in gold or equivalent, that meets the needs of your new nation."

President Harman chuckled. "You want me to set up a barter system for new residents?"

"Absolutely. It's just like setting up a trade agreement with any nation. Marion, Texas is its own country now. You've got to start acting like one."

CHAPTER 20

December 2
The Armstrong Ranch
Borden County, Texas

Major huddled in the corner with Lucy and Preacher. They'd stayed up all night monitoring the radio broadcasts and, frankly, waiting for more bombs to drop. The aftermath of any military bombing or attack was likely to make people feel vulnerable and fearful. As the U.S. and Texas went on alert for a second time because of the threats of nuclear Armageddon, the mental stability of those affected was put under an incredible strain.

Major and Lucy had had extensive discussions during their adoption of a prepper lifestyle regarding the state of mind necessary to survive. Not everyone, they acknowledged, was willing to make the sacrifices to prepare for a catastrophic event. For those who did undertake to prep, many were not able to withstand the intense pressure associated with the life-and-death decision-making. Even fewer anticipated a nuclear attack on America.

Everyone within their bunker appreciated what Major and Lucy had done to protect them, but it didn't diminish the intense feeling of anxiety they experienced when the thought of a nuclear attack invaded their minds.

President Burnett had issued an all-clear announcement, and therefore it was time for everyone to return to their homes. However, unlike their first use of the bunker following the EMP, when the group couldn't climb out fast enough, this time around, nobody was ready to leave.

"Maybe we shouldn't have given them access to the radio," started Lucy. "Even the limited amount of media coverage that came out of Dallas and Mexico frightened them. Seriously, I've never seen post-traumatic stress disorder, but it sure seems like some of our people are exhibiting symptoms."

"Well, the first thing we can do is get everyone back to a normal routine," said Major. "It's a shame that they witnessed the nukes flying over our heads. Thank goodness they don't have access to television, which would force them to relive the attacks over and over."

Preacher nodded. "I agree. Fear is natural in folks, and their reactions to it will vary. I think their behavior might change, at least for a little while."

"Let's do this. They all look up to Antonio. Preacher, bring him in here, and let's discuss how we should approach this."

While Preacher left to fetch Antonio, his number one ranch hand, Major spoke to Lucy. "Honey, we can't lose our people. If they get scared and try to head for Mexico because they think it's safer, we won't be able to protect the ranch."

"I know," said Lucy. "Let's get Antonio's input, but I think the four of us need to be very active in the daily activities around here. Not only because it's prudent, but it also shows that we're not afraid to be out on the ranch with them in the midst of all of this."

"Good idea. I'll focus on security. I'll have Preacher and Antonio implement our plan to cut down the size of the ranch. You can focus on the barnyard and feeding everyone."

Lucy nodded and then leaned into Major to whisper, "I'm going to start issuing meals on a daily basis. I don't want them stockpiling too much, giving them the courage to hit the road."

"Okay, but don't make it obvious. I really believe their apprehension will subside over time, with a return to normalcy. Being down here can make you nuts anyway. I don't know how people do it for long periods of time."

She patted him on the chest and kissed him on the cheek. "Thank you for making this investment for all of us. Without it, all of them would have left screamin' into the night. I, for one, would be worried out of my mind as well."

"You're welcome, honey. It's hard to put a price tag or value on peace of mind."

After confirming their plan with Antonio and identifying those families most likely to make a rash decision, Major and Preacher followed the same procedure as the day after the EMP attack. They tested the atmosphere for radiation and retrieved the RAD sticker to confirm it was safe. Unlike before, they went to great lengths to show everyone in the bunker the sticker. This seemed to have a positive effect on the families' attitudes.

Then Major, Lucy, and Preacher emerged first through the bunker's hatch to a clear, crisp Texas morning. Reluctantly, the families emerged, with several women and children jockeying to be the last to emerge. It took about ten minutes to help the group out of the shelter, and in just that short period of time, fear and anxiety diminished.

By the time Preacher and Antonio assigned tasks, coupled with the Armstrongs providing hugs to the wives and children, the images of the rockets soaring past had disappeared from most minds.

Today was a new day.

CHAPTER 21

December 2
Near Winslow, Arizona

There was no more famous town along historic Route 66 than Winslow, Arizona. Referenced in the popular song from the early seventies performed by the Eagles, the town flourished economically until Interstate 40 bypassed the town in the late seventies. Today, its inhabitants were starving and in dire need of fresh water.

In the days following the EMP attack, small towns in Northern Arizona sent envoys to one another in an attempt to strike deals with civic leaders. Unlike the major cities, towns like Winslow and Holbrook didn't experience the same levels of societal collapse. While it was true that lawlessness occurred, it was quickly tamped down by the citizens in that first week.

But then the lack of critical infrastructure in this arid part of the U.S. took its toll. The region had been experiencing an El Nino-induced drought for months. The Little Colorado River had begun to dry up. Reservoirs to the west in the Coconino National Forest had potable water safe for drinking in its lakes, but there was no efficient way to pump the water into tankers, even if the small towns had the capability.

Nearby Flagstaff had reached a critical stage in terms of its water supply. Smaller towns like Holbrook and Winslow were on the brink of being totally dry after just one week.

Deputy Chief Banda knew of Winslow's water shortages. As he discussed travel options with Duncan, he came up with a solution. Every other day since the collapse of the grid, the town had sent their early seventies model gasoline tanker to Winslow to receive gasoline.

In trade, they dispatched an antique milk-hauling truck filled with potable water from their gravity-fed tank atop a hill in the center of Peach Springs.

The water tank, built by the Army Corps of Engineers years ago, was full, with enough water to last the inhabits of Peach Springs for more than a year. In dire need of gasoline to run their generators and the few operating vehicles that were available to the Hualapai Tribe, they entered into a deal with Winslow to trade two thousand gallons of water for five thousand gallons of gasoline.

Today, the trip was made by Banda and a deputy, who followed along in an old Ford Bronco II with Duncan and Sook in the back. Just west of Winslow, there was a rancher friend of Banda's. He'd fill up his friend's hundred-gallon tank with fresh water in exchange for a couple of horses. This would give the travelers a hundred-fifty-mile start on their journey, plus transportation.

The convoy pulled off the interstate about twenty miles west of Winslow at the Canyon Diablo exit. Canyon Diablo, the devil's canyon, was a true Arizona ghost town on the outskirts of the Navaho Reservation.

They slowly approached the ranch, which was nearly eighteen thousand acres. Duncan, who had never been interested in the ranching aspect of Armstrong Ranch, knew how to ride and also knew enough about horses to know that the ones racing across the scrubland on both sides of him were wild. While he appreciated the head start on their trip home, he wasn't ready to tame a mustang. He might opt for a burro instead. They were slower, but they wouldn't throw them as often.

Duncan and Sook waited by the trucks while Banda went inside to make the deal. Within minutes, he whistled to the driver of the water tanker to drive around the back of the house. Two ranch hands scurried out of the house and ran toward the barn.

Duncan managed a smile, and then he realized the task ahead. He hadn't mounted a horse in years, and he wasn't sure if Sook had ever seen one.

"Sook, have you ever seen a horse before?"

She shook her head side to side, and then her eyes grew wider as the men walked the horses closer to them. Duncan was glad to see they were saddled too.

The two young Mexicans handed over the reins to Duncan and left them alone with their new steeds. He took a deep breath as he considered the monumental task ahead of them.

Horseback riding was a combination of sport, skill, and art wrapped into one very difficult function that always looked easy on television. He remembered his grandfather saying that it didn't matter what type of horse you had, or what your plans for him were, the basics of horse handling were universal.

The first aspect was taken care of for them. The saddles and blankets provided seemed to be in good shape. He rubbed the muzzles of the horses as he walked around them and checked the straps securing the saddles. He didn't find any tears or holes in the leather, which might be uncomfortable for both horse and rider.

After confirming the bit and bridle fit the horse properly, he encouraged Sook to get to know the mare by rubbing her and talking softly in her ear. The mare wasn't in season, so she hopefully wouldn't be temperamental for her new, inexperienced rider.

He'd ride the gelding, although he was more likely to be calm and easy-going because he'd been divested of his cajones. Duncan felt the male horse could carry his weight and gear for the long trip.

"Sook, do not be afraid, okay?" began Duncan, who was always careful to avoid contractions when speaking with Sook. For someone relatively new to the English language, *do not* was understandable, the contraction *don't*, not so much.

He continued. "The horse will sense your fear. For now, we are going to get you comfortable in the saddle and make sure this horse is comfortable with you."

She continued to walk around the horse and suddenly began to cry.

"Sook, what is the matter? It will be okay. She will not hurt you."

Sook laughed and wiped her tears from her face with her hands. "No, Duncan. I am fine. I never thought I would see a horse in my lifetime. Or ride on a plane. Or come to America. Or be free. Now, I am all of those. Thank you."

She embraced him and held Duncan against her while she let out her emotions. Until this moment, she hadn't spoken much since their arrival in America, allowing him to initiate most conversations. She had turned a corner in her life.

As Sook regained her composure, Banda returned from the ranch house with a smile. "Okay, my friends, you're all set. The good people of Winslow will not notice a couple of hundred gallons of water missing from the load, and my friend here has hundreds more horses to break, if necessary."

"I don't know how to thank you for everything you've done for us," started Duncan.

"No thanks necessary," he said as he reached out to shake Duncan's hand. He then turned to Sook and reached out to shake hers.

She immediately moved forward to give him an unexpected hug. It was a genuine show of thanks.

"God bless you, Banda," she said as her eyes welled up in tears again.

"Well, young lady, God bless you too. You are an inspiration to us all."

Duncan patted Banda on the back once again and encouraged him to be safe. Banda provided him a suggested route to take as they approached Winslow, which led them along the south side of the town. He didn't expect them to run into any trouble, but why invite it?

Duncan and Sook watched as the trucks started up and continued on to Winslow. Afterwards, Duncan showed Sook how to mount her horse and the proper pressure to apply to the reins. He promised her they'd take it slow at first, and they would amble down the shoulder of the interstate. Along the way, he'd give her pointers on how to give commands to her horse, and if they found an open area free of large rocks or obstacles, he'd show her how to pick up the speed.

She was sitting high in the saddle as he asked, "Are you ready?"

"Yes."

"Okay, now I get to show you my part of the world."

Duncan strapped their bags to the rear of the saddles, and then he retrieved his Barrett rifle, which he slipped into a scabbard attached to his saddle. Despite Banda's confidence that the two riders would not run into any trouble, Duncan sensed otherwise.

CHAPTER 22

December 2
Raven Rock Mountain Complex
Liberty Township, Pennsylvania

President Harman got some much-needed rest as her surrogates assured her the Twelve-Hour War was over. The Secretary of State had personally reached out to China and Russia to confirm they had no intention of getting involved in the melee. They further confirmed they would make no military advancement into North Korea at this time, and that their massive military presence along their mutual border with the North was to prevent an influx of refugees into their countries.

Sometimes the drumbeat of war plays for an extended period of time, but once the gloves come off, the battle is over quickly. Twice in history, Israel and their Arab neighbors had engaged in wars known as the Seven-Day and Six-Day Wars. Both ended in decisive victories for Israel.

This time, the war between the U.S. and the DPRK was over in hours, with America able to declare a victory, of sorts. The U.S. success came with the annihilation of virtually everything aboveground in North Korea. It did not, however, result in the death or capture of Kim Jong-un, who remained safely tucked away deep underground in fortified bunkers.

While the shooting was over between North and South Korea, the next step in this geopolitical struggle was unclear. This evening, among other things, President Harman would address the issue of what was next.

She entered the conference room, which had become the space

she'd spent the most time in since her arrival at Raven Rock. It was cramped, the air circulation was poor, and it paled in comparison to what she was accustomed to in the White House—another issue she intended to raise during this meeting with her top people.

In attendance were Chief of Staff Acton, Secretary of State Tompkins, Homeland Secretary Pickering, acting Defense Secretary Evans, and via visual hookup, the chairman of the Joint Chiefs, Admiral Dasanti.

"Before we get started on your individual reports, I need to hear from the Secretary of State regarding the war between Israel and Iran."

Secretary Tompkins began to stand before President Harman stopped her. "Please, Jane, sit. Unless we need the whiteboard or monitor, let's keep this casual. It's going to be a long evening for us."

"Thank you, Madam President," Tompkins began. "Israel's recent enhancements to their *Iron Dome* program has proved successful since the initial attacks were launched by Pyongyang. The upgraded variant, called *David's Sling*, was designed to intercept enemy aircraft, drones, and tactical ballistic missiles. Thirty minutes after the first missile launch from North Korea was directed at Guam, the Iranians began firing mid-range rockets and cruise missiles toward Israel. They effectively repelled the attack."

"How did Israel react?" asked the president.

"Without remorse or compunction, ma'am, to be blunt," replied Tompkins. "Israel unleashed its Jericho III nuclear-armed ICBMs at Iranian targets. Reports indicate seven of the missiles hitting strategic targets within Iran, including two in Tehran. The rest of the missiles struck ports, military facilities and the Natanz Uranium Enrichment plant."

"Have you been in touch with your counterpart in Jerusalem? What is the current status of the conflict?"

"Israel is now flying sorties across Iran in their F-15 and F-16 fighters. They're conducting strategic bombing missions to destroy the remainder of Iran's military capabilities. Further, they've deployed three German-built Dolphin submarines in the Persian Gulf in an effort to back down any other players who might want to challenge the Jewish State."

President Harman leaned forward. "What about Hezbollah, Hamas, and Syria? Have they stepped up to help their allies in Iran?"

"No, ma'am. Scared out of their minds, I suspect. The overwhelming response of Jerusalem backed down all of their adversaries."

"And the Saudis?" asked the president.

"Israel has no interest in invading Iran. The much-sought-after devastation of the Iranian military and nuclear program has been accomplished. Frankly, both the new Israeli prime minister and I agree that a Saudi presence in Iran would be a stabilizing force in the Middle East. Israel plans to encourage a Saudi invasion of Iran."

"Okay, thank you, Jane," started the president. "Before we move on to the domestic situation, I want everybody's opinion on the table. Is there anyone who has a genuine concern that the Russians or the Chinese will use the occasion of our weakened condition to make a move on us?"

One by one, each of her advisors were adamant in their response—*no*.

"All right, I tend to agree. You know, the bottom line is they need us economically. Those two countries will profit substantially from our rebuilding effort. Also, we still have enough nuclear capability to cause them damage in return. I will place phone calls to both countries when we are done here, as time zones allow."

Admiral Dasanti spoke next. "Madam President, before you address domestic issues, may I ask about our intentions toward North Korea? Kim Jong-un is still alive, and our intelligence reveals that massive nuclear-protected catacombs exist throughout the country. This is a nation that has expected this moment for half a century."

"Are you suggesting we consider sending in ground troops, Admiral? I'm afraid that might draw the ire of Russia and China."

"No, Madam President, but I think we should encourage Seoul to do so. This is America's opportunity to gain a large foothold in Asia.

With a new government installed in the North under Seoul's direction, we could maintain a strong presence right across the river from China. It would allow us to keep them in check for decades."

The president exhaled and looked to her new Defense Secretary. "What do you think, Clayton?"

"Ma'am, it would be a way to make lemonade out of lemons," he replied. "Pardon my being glib. America is a resilient nation and we will rebuild. In the meantime, our allies on the Korean Peninsula can carry the burden of ensuring stability in the region. Besides, the South Koreans are the logical country to do so. I can't imagine the United Nations objecting in any way."

"Let them know, off the record, they've got the green light and our full support to go in there to clean up the mess. You know, as a *humanitarian mission*. Liberate as many of the North Koreans as they can find alive and deal with the military apparatus as they see fit."

The president looked around the room at her team. With Montgomery Gregg's departure, she was surrounded by loyalists that she could count on, with the lone exception of Admiral Dasanti. Although he never pushed back against her decisions like Gregg did, she was never quite sure of what he was thinking. It was confounding, but an admirable trait nonetheless. Thus far, he hadn't led her astray.

"Shifting gears, let's talk about our return to Washington," started the president. "With tensions easing, and the good fortune of excellent sharpshooting by the Department of Defense, the last three incoming missiles destined for our nation's capital were destroyed. I believe the first step in restoring order across the nation and confidence in our government is to return to Washington as a show of resolve and strength. Does everyone agree?"

The responses were varied, but approving.

"Absolutely!"

"It'll send a clear message that our nation is made up of survivors."

"The rebuilding effort should begin there, without question."

The president was pleased with the enthusiasm of her key

advisors. Only Admiral Dasanti failed to respond to her suggestion. This did not go unnoticed.

"Admiral, do you have a contrary opinion?" asked President Harman.

"I agree in principle, based upon the diminished nuclear threat, Madam President. However, I do not believe Kim Jong-un has been completely defeated. Like bin Laden, I want proof of his being deposed or his death. Either will suit me just fine."

President Harman appeared puzzled by his statement and looked at the others in the room to see if they had a similar reaction. She returned her attention to the admiral. "Do you think that Kim Jong-un is capable of some type of counteroffensive?"

"All I can say is the DPRK's actions were outside of our extensive war-planning scenarios," replied Admiral Dasanti. "He never attacked South Korea and Japan, as was anticipated. Further, and we haven't completed our analysis of our satellite intel, but in the days prior to the initial launch from Komdok-san, his troops appeared to be taking a defensive posture. Some even disappeared from earlier flyovers."

"Are you suggesting Kim ordered his forces to go into hiding?" asked Defense Secretary Evans.

"I'm suggesting that things may not be as they appear and that we should proceed with caution."

President Harman fell back into her chair in disgust. She wanted to have confidence that this was over. She took a deep breath and addressed the chairman of the Joint Chiefs. "Admiral, do you have any reason to believe it is unsafe for us to return to Washington due to a nuclear threat?"

"No, ma'am. I don't think the DPRK poses a nuclear threat to us any longer for so long as their nuclear-capable submarines do not reach our shores."

"Wait. Are their nuclear subs unaccounted for?"

The admiral moved closer to the camera. "Two, ma'am, that we know of. After Kim solidified his ICBM program, he turned his resources toward the KPA's Naval Unit 167. Their submarine-launched ballistic missile, or SLBM, poses a real threat at this time."

"Will our THAAD antimissile system be able to identify and destroy an inbound SLBM?"

"Our radars have been focused on long-range ICBMs coming from the Korean Peninsula. If these submarines slip in behind our radar, we wouldn't be able to react in time."

"What do you suggest, Admiral?" asked the president as she grew increasingly perturbed. She desperately wanted this meeting to have at least one high note.

"We need to recall our antisubmarine capabilities from Europe. The U.S. Atlantic Fleet needs to be redeployed immediately to our east coast and the Gulf of Mexico. I suggest we send our antisub aircraft to the west coast to supplement our existing forces."

"Why the Gulf of Mexico?" she asked.

"Because our southern coast is the least protected against nuclear attacks. Texas is especially vulnerable."

The president bristled as she threw her pen on the table. "Well, now, Texas isn't our problem anymore, is it?"

CHAPTER 23

December 2
West of Winslow, Arizona

"You are a natural!" Duncan proudly exclaimed as Sook and her horse alternated between a jogging speed and then back to a walking gait. Horse and rider were growing comfortable with one another. All horses move naturally with four basic paces ranging from a top speed of a gallop, which can approach fifty-five miles an hour, to the canter, about thirty miles an hour. Sook and her mare were not ready to run together yet, but she had mastered a jogging speed of about ten miles per hour. Duncan was confident they could pick up their pace by tomorrow.

"What is a natural?" Sook asked as Duncan eased up next to her.

He laughed as he forgot that Sook, while fairly proficient in English, was not totally familiar with the idiosyncrasies of American slang and wit.

"It means you ride like you are comfortable and have been riding for a long time."

"Yes, I like her. She is very comfortable, too."

They rode together in silence for a moment as Sook continuously surveyed the landscape. She had only known North Korea and had spent most of her life on the mountainous island of Sinmi-do. The barren American Southwest was like visiting another planet.

The bright sun accompanied a near perfect sixty-degree day as they continued to make time toward Winslow. Duncan did not intend to push them too far on this first day, opting instead to find a place to bunk down for the night, hopefully with a water source. Along the rocky, relatively flat terrain, an occasional wash cut through the soil, which might lead to a pond.

Duncan led the way as they rode up a slight incline to an elevated hill alongside the interstate. It was just past this area that Banda indicated they'd find the road to a historic meteor crater. From there, he suggested they ride toward the southwest, where they'd find themselves well beyond Winslow and the only significant population center before they entered New Mexico.

Just as they got to the top of the hill, Duncan saw the paved service road leading toward the south. He also noticed trouble in the distance. He removed his rifle from the scabbard and used the powerful Leopold Mark 4 scope to study the highway ahead.

A railroad crossed from north to south, bisecting Interstate 40 about a mile ahead of them. There were several vehicles and people milling about under the highway overpass. Duncan caught movement from the interstate above the railroad. Two men came running down the side, waving their arms.

Duncan moved his rifle to gain a better view of the westbound lanes of the interstate. Off in the distance, there were vehicles approaching from Winslow. He adjusted his focus and squinted. Two trucks. One car.

"Dang it," he muttered aloud.

"What is wrong, Duncan?" asked Sook.

Duncan lowered his rifle and weighed his options. "Sook, our friends from Peach Springs are driving into trouble. There are men who plan to attack them on the road. I have to help them."

"I will help them too."

Duncan chuckled and reached for her hand. "This might be dangerous. I need you to wait here or …" His voice trailed off as he looked through his scope again, this time attempting to find the meteor crater location Banda had suggested. He found it. A single structure stood near the crater. It might be a safe place for them to stay the night. But it also might be occupied by someone, so he couldn't send Sook down there alone.

He dreaded the thought of sending her off without his protection. Separating was not a good idea, especially for someone unfamiliar with their surroundings. He also didn't want to put her in harm's way, but if he was killed protecting Banda and his men, then Sook would likely suffer a similar fate at some time. And it wouldn't be quick or merciful.

Sook sensed his angst. "Duncan, I can help you. I am not afraid."

Duncan surveyed their surroundings. Near the road to the meteor crater, two stone monument signs flanked the entrance, which also stood on a rise overlooking the interstate. By his estimation, this would give him a clear shot to the highway overpass of about three thousand feet.

"Piece of cake," he muttered as he used the scope to sweep the killing field. He cradled his rifle in his arms and turned to Sook.

"You have to follow my instructions."

"I will."

Duncan smiled at her and nodded. "Let's go."

He started them out slow and then picked up the pace, as he could see the convoy of trucks from Peach Springs approaching the ambush. Under the overpass, a hodgepodge of vehicles ranging from motorcycles to some type of Mad Max-looking dune buggy readied for their assault.

They quickly dismounted upon reaching the stone structures, which were the perfect hide to rest his sniper rifle on top. He could steady his aim and choose his targets with ease.

Sook took the reins of the horses and began to walk them down the asphalt road toward the meteor crater as instructed. A billboard sign with several Joshua trees stood about a hundred yards from the monument sign. This would provide Sook and the horses some cover in the event the attackers returned fire.

The convoy, led by Banda's vehicles and the tanker trucks, lumbered across the overpass doing about thirty miles an hour. They were old, slow-moving machines, especially with the tanker full of gasoline.

Duncan focused on the attackers. Their plan was obvious within seconds. They waited for the convoy to cross above them, and then they would split their group in two, with each traveling up opposite sides of the embankment. When they reached the interstate just past the guardrails, they would converge on either side of the convoy, effectively creating a kill zone.

Duncan readied his Barrett rifle. As soon as the group split up and were out of each other's view, he would eliminate the threat on the side nearest to him.

The convoy passed over the bridge, and the Mad Max bunch fired up their engines. A Toyota pickup truck and two dirt bikes tore off to the back side of the interstate. A dune buggy and two more dirt bikes took the side closest to Duncan.

They spun gravel and dust into the air as they took off, speeding up the embankment at an angle. As the ground flattened, the driver of the dune buggy steadied the wheel and kept the vehicle from swerving. Duncan took aim.

BOOM!

The crack of the Barrett echoed up and down the highway. His bullet found its mark, ripping into the upper body of the dune buggy driver. He let go of the steering wheel, which forced the vehicle to careen to the left and up the embankment toward the eastbound lane of the highway. It struck the guardrail head-on, causing its front end to rise into the air, momentarily suspended on its rear-mounted engine before tipping backward onto its roll bar, battering the man inside, if he survived the gunshot.

Duncan resisted the urge to watch the entire scene unfold, focusing on his next two targets instead. The motorcyclists, shocked at what had just happened, slowed to look and then sped forward to continue with the task at hand. Their hesitation was a mistake for the lead bike.

Another shot rang out, sending the powerful round in the direction of the first rider, striking him in the leg. It wasn't a kill shot, but his day was ruined. The man writhed in pain on the ground as the last motorcycle on this side sped past. The shot was much more difficult as the rider began to approach the asphalt highway.

Duncan had practiced shooting at a moving target since he was a child. The first step was to get a good look at the target and accurately identify its path. Today, this job was made easier by a lack of obstacles. Duncan's brain was able to calculate whether the driver's speed was increasing or decreasing, and the proximate location where he would approach the convoy.

This was different from bird hunting, where your rifle follows the target before firing. Duncan likened it more to professional football in which a seasoned quarterback, like Dak Prescott of the Dallas Cowboys, made a timed throw to his receiver. He threw the ball to a location in front of the receiver, based upon speed and timing, rather than directly at the moving receiver's last location.

Duncan's mind recalled all of his training and instincts and squeezed the trigger. The shot sailed through the air, breaking through the arid atmosphere, and ripped a gaping hole in the rider's neck. The force of the round threw him off his dirt bike, over the guardrail, and tumbling over into the middle of the highway.

Duncan quickly drew his sights on the Toyota truck and the other motorbikes, which appeared over the elevated roadway. They were in pursuit of the convoy as it continued moving forward, but now Banda's truck had slowed to move to the rear of the procession. He had seen the threat.

It was impossible for Duncan to help at this point. The other three vehicles were shielded by the slope and the guardrail. It was up to Banda now, but at least it would be a fair fight.

Duncan watched the fight through his scope. Banda's partner turned around in the seat of the old Bronco II and opened fire with his automatic weapon. Bullets tore up the asphalt. One of the motorcyclists was hit, sending him and his bike sprawling to the pavement.

A passenger in the Toyota truck returned fire, but his round missed the mark. The Toyota closed on Banda's bumper but was met with several rounds, which shattered the windshield and killed the passenger.

The driver, sensing that this was a losing battle, threw his left arm out of the driver's window, made a fist and held it in the air as he pulled to a stop.

Banda and his convoy continued on to Peach Springs, having no idea who the Good Samaritan was that probably saved their lives.

CHAPTER 24

December 2
Near Winslow, Arizona

For Duncan, the battle was not necessarily over. He took a moment to look back towards Sook. She had done a fairly good job of hiding herself behind the billboard posts and the native vegetation. He was pleased to see the horses were not spooked by his gunfire. The retort of the Barrett was thunderous in this open terrain.

The driver of the Toyota pulled his dead passenger out of the cab and abandoned him on the side of the interstate as roadkill for the vultures. The other motorcycle rider was injured, but not dead. They loaded the damaged dirt bikes into the back of his pickup.

Then they returned to the area of Duncan's three kills with caution. Probably puzzled by the turn of events, the survivors appeared to be uncertain who had caused their plans to go astray. They were carrying AK-47s, from Duncan's best estimate, and pointed them in all directions as they searched both sides of the highway for any movement.

Duncan was well-concealed behind the monument sign, and at nearly a mile away, he wasn't readily visible to the naked eye.

Satisfied that the assault on his group was over, the leader ordered the other dirt bikes to be loaded into the pickup. The man Duncan had shot in the leg was placed in the cab after his leg was wrapped with a jacket.

The hulk of a man, who was obviously the leader, walked up to the dune buggy, which had been totaled by the impact of hitting the guardrail. After rearing back and kicking one of the front tires, he reached into the demolished dune buggy, grabbed the dead man's rifle and stormed back to his truck.

Then he suddenly stopped. He removed a scarf wrapped around his neck and took off his camouflaged baseball cap, revealing a shiny bald head. He allowed the scarf to blow in the wind, and Duncan recalled seeing something similar in his past.

It was a shemagh, a scarf often worn in the Arab world as a simple way to protect your neck and face from the sun. In areas of snow or strong winds, it was used as headwear. In the military, Duncan, like many others, chose an olive drab or desert sand camo design as part of their uniform.

"He's military," said Duncan aloud as he trained his sights on the man. He considered taking him out, but the remaining riders could give chase on their dirt bikes from different directions, making it near impossible for Duncan to defend himself and Sook at the same time.

Instead he studied the man, who sensed he was being observed. He slowly turned around and shielded his face in an attempt to look toward Duncan's position to his west. The setting sun made it impossible for him to see Duncan, but Duncan could make out his facial features more clearly through his scope.

His face was rugged, hardened by battle. It bore a scar that stretched from his right eye down to his chin. And his left eye was gone. The socket was not protected by a black patch or a round piece of gauze. The man's eye socket lay open for all to see, gruesome and menacing. Duncan was looking at evil, a man whose face he'd never forget.

Duncan held his position as the one-eyed man gathered his remaining marauders and headed east toward Winslow. When they were well out of sight, Duncan trotted down the hill toward Sook.

She saw him coming and bolted from behind the billboard's posts. She crashed into him with a hug and laughter. "Three shots! You beat the enemy with three shots!"

It was the oddest reaction that Duncan could imagine. There were no tears of joy and happiness for his safe return. No congratulations for his success. She provided him accolades instead—on ammunition management, of all things.

"Well, thank you, Sook," said Duncan with a laugh. "So you know, I did not miss."

"You are a great soldier, Duncan!"

This drew another laugh from Duncan, who was still taken aback by her girlish enthusiasm. Sook was the most intriguing woman he'd ever met. She was clearly a woman, as her natural beauty proved. Mentally, she could transition from attentive nurse, to girlish hero-worshipper, to a ninja. They say you should find a lifelong mate who keeps a relationship interesting. Duncan held Sook for another moment and realized he'd never get bored with her.

He broke their embrace and smiled. "Sook, it will be dark soon. I need to go down to the highway and check the bodies to see if there is anything of value. A knife, a forgotten gun, or a cigarette lighter can all be useful to us."

"I will go with you," she said happily. "The horses are ready for a ride."

"You do not have to go, Sook. The bodies are, um, very dead."

"I know. There will be many more."

She turned to retrieve the horses, and Duncan looked toward the west. They had just enough time to look for anything of value, and then they could return to the meteor crater. He hoped the small building that was located there would be suitable for shelter and was uninhabited.

The two arrived at the scene. First, they approached the dune buggy and found the driver suspended in the front seat, hanging upside down with his seat harness still intact. Duncan pulled a dark blue ski mask off his face to get a look at his kill.

Sook noticed it first. "He's Korean! Duncan, this man is a Korean."

This surprised Duncan. A Korean man was out of place in this part of Arizona. He searched his pockets and found a stiletto-style switchblade. There was also a set of brass knuckles in the other pocket.

The two walked their horses to the dead motorcyclist in the middle of the road. He was also Korean.

"Sook, this is very odd. This is not a part of America where Koreans live. They are primarily found in large cities, especially in California."

Without hesitation, Sook rolled the body over and studied it. "Duncan, this man has many tattoos like the other man. See this one? It is the same."

Duncan studied the tattoo, which matched the other man's. "They might be part of a gang."

He gathered a lighter out of the man's pocket and another switchblade before leading Sook to the third body. The third dead man was also Korean, but he didn't have any tattoos or anything of value in his possession.

Duncan stood in the middle of Interstate 40 with his hands on his hips. He slowly turned in a complete circle as he studied the vast desert around them.

What is a gang of Koreans doing in the Arizona desert? And why were they following a bald guy, most likely an American, with one eye, as their leader?

He looked at the quickly setting sun and helped Sook mount her horse. They began their ride to the meteor crater and, hopefully, a safe place to sleep for the night, albeit a restless one.

CHAPTER 25

December 2
Meteor Crater Natural Landmark
Winslow, Arizona

Duncan held Sook back while he approached the meteor crater visitors' center alone. The parking lot was empty, and there didn't appear to be any sign of forced entry as he walked around the large contemporary-style building. The EMP had struck when the visitors' center was closed for the day, and it didn't appear that any wayward travelers or Winslow locals had thought about gaining access to the building. Duncan smiled as he realized this building was more than a place to rest for the night. It also provided an excellent opportunity to forage for much-needed supplies for their ride home.

He chose a window on the back side of the complex, which wasn't readily accessible to anyone who might wander upon the place during the night. Most likely, an intruder during the evening would break out one of the large plate-glass windows at the front entry, which would act as an alarm for Duncan.

After carefully breaking out the glass to give them easy entry, he returned for Sook and the horses. He found an oversized fenced utility area that held a small forty-yard dumpster on wheels. After he easily rolled the dumpster out of the pen, there was plenty of room for the horses to lie down. He removed their saddles and spread out their blankets to provide some semblance of bedding. Then he and Sook promised their most valuable assets they'd return with water and something to eat.

Once inside, Sook followed Duncan as he systematically cleared every room just to make sure they were alone. As they walked through the building, he made mental notes of potentially useful items, although none were more valuable than the stacks of bottled water and cans of food in the kitchen of the Subway restaurant.

Duncan gathered up some large pots from the kitchen and filled them with bottled water for their horses. He located some bread that hadn't molded yet and used that for feed. He then made his way to the front of the building and began pulling out the tall grasses used as landscape material. This was not what the horses were accustomed to, but by the same token, they had most likely been raised in the wild and later tamed to allow riders. Their survival instincts had not been tamed.

When Duncan returned to the Subway dining area where he'd left Sook in the dark, he found her walking back and forth to the kitchen, wearing a children's miner's helmet that had a light attached.

She greeted him by shining the light into his eyes. "Look at my hat! It is for mining. Now it is for making a meal."

She turned her head so Duncan could see how busy she'd been, and then she focused on one of the tables, where a variety of snacks and two bottled Cokes sat on the table ready for them to partake.

"Wow, you have been busy!" Duncan exclaimed after he saw all of the canned foods spread out around the room.

She handed him a helmet, which was way too small for his head. "For you, Mr. Miner."

Duncan let out a heartfelt laugh. Once again, her childlike playfulness amazed him. He played along and put the ill-fitting child's helmet on his head. Then he turned on the light. Despite how silly he thought he might look, the helmet served its purpose.

The two enjoyed a snack of Cheetos, peanut butter and crackers, and warm Coca-Cola. Sook admitted she'd never had a real Coke before. She knew the brand, however. There were only two countries in the world that did not sell Coca-Cola—Cuba and North Korea. The North had attempted to copy it, but she said it was flat and too sweet. Completely unaware of the slogan adopted by the Coca-Cola brand, she raised her glass and said, "This is the real thing."

After taking a moment to relax, the two visitors, mining hats fully illuminated, began to search the rest of the building for items of use. Duncan focused on the administrative offices and the building maintenance department located down the hall from the eighty-seat movie theater.

The offices didn't yield much except for some small notepads, pens, and several bottles of hand sanitizer. The building's maintenance department was a different story, as it provided them quite a few things.

First, Duncan found two large and two pocket-size Maglite flashlights. There were also batteries stored in the same cabinet. Now that their lighting was better, he was able to look in more detail. He found a variety of tools, a first aid kit, toiletries and paper goods for the restrooms, and a fold-up Rand McNally map entitled Four Corners. The Four Corners was an area where Arizona, New Mexico, Colorado, and Utah intersected. The map included detailed roads of all four states, a great find as they continued to work their way to Texas.

Sook found a duffle bag pushed under a desk in the maintenance office. Inside, there were some extra clothes, a Bowie-style knife, a small Coleman lantern, a compass, a multi-tool and an unopened bundle of paracord.

The two filled the duffle bag with the items they'd discovered and a cloth tarp that Duncan found in the tool room. After they'd gone through every nook and cranny of these two areas, they reentered the darkened hallway and considered their next move. Sook's yawn caused Duncan to do the same, and he thought it might be best to bed down for the night. If they woke up early the next day, he'd give the place one more look before they headed east.

The biggest decision he had to make was what to take. The horses were healthy and strong, but the amount of weight they could carry was limited. Fortunately, Sook appeared to be a hundred and ten pounds soaking wet. If they could find another duffle bag and a way to secure it, each of them could carry food and water to last for many days. The tarp and paracord would help them with shelter. The tools he found could help them with shelter and fire.

As they searched the building for a comfortable place to sleep for the night, they came upon a gift shop, which sold tee shirts and sweatshirts. Not only was there sufficient inventory to create a soft spot on the floor, but they now had sweatshirts with the Meteor Crater logo emblazoned across the front in yellow, orange, and red.

As the two of them got settled and said their good nights, Duncan thought of all the things he'd taken for granted before that fateful day when he'd attempted to assassinate Kim Jong-un. Things like clothing, food, water, and transportation were all expected to be available to him. After his days in North Korea, he realized even the simple things, like the sweet smile of someone he cared for, would be appreciated.

CHAPTER 26

December 3
The Armstrong Ranch
Borden County, Texas

Major and Lucy were sitting at the kitchen table, going over their food plan for the next two months. Typically, December and January were their coldest months with average low temperatures near freezing and highs reaching into the mid-fifties. The cattle would have to rely entirely upon feed hay they'd gathered in the fall, but it wasn't enough to sustain the size of the herd they'd retained. The steers they'd slaughtered for beef after the EMP attack would provide a critical source of meat and protein for the group through mid-March, but Major's concern was they'd run out of hay before the growth season started up.

"Should we go ahead and butcher steers now to be used as food?" asked Lucy. "We could save the meat from the slaughterhouse for down the road."

"I thought about that, but I need to think ahead," replied Major with a sigh. "It's not gonna be like normal in the spring. I don't know if they'll have the big auctions in Abilene or Big Spring like in the past. If we start slaughterin' the herd too early, we may not be able to buy replacements. The breeders may hold onto their stock, or realistically, some may not have the fuel to transport them to the auction."

"Have you heard something about gas and diesel shortages?"

"No, but I'm guessin' there might be if that nuke hit any refineries down south. Plus, most of these folks didn't store regular food like we did. They may be eating up their herds to stay alive."

Lucy shook her head and set her pencil down. "So whadya think?"

Before he could respond, someone began pounding on the front door. Major, as a former lawman, knew there was a difference between a polite *hello-is-anybody-home* knock on the front door and a pounding *police-officer-open-up-or-I'll-kick-the-door-in* knock. This knock resembled the latter.

"Major! We've got company."

It was Preacher. Major checked to make sure his sidearm was still on his hip, and he rushed toward the door, grabbing his shotgun as he opened the door.

Two of his ranch hands were leading a group down the driveway toward the house. A horse-drawn wagon carried a couple, and they were followed by two more couples walking behind, leading their horses by the reins.

"What've we got, Preach?" asked Major as he cradled his shotgun in his right arm. There didn't appear to be a threat, only the excitement of other human contact.

Major walked toward the visitors and shielded his eyes from the setting sun. He immediately recognized them as they pulled their wagon to a halt. It was the Slaughter family from the Lazy S Ranch over in Vealmoor.

Back in the 1880s, Christopher Columbus Slaughter, or C.C. to his many friends, moved to West Texas after serving in the Confederate States Army during the Civil War. Over the next several decades, he acquired nearly a million acres around Howard County, and at one time the Lazy S Ranch was home to forty thousand cattle.

His legacy was short lived when C.C. died without a will in 1919. His family fought over his estate. His son, Bob, accused C.C.'s brother, Bill, of mismanagement of the ranch and its holdings. The argument escalated until Bob, in a fit of anger, shot his uncle Bill. Bill survived and sued Bob for slander, eventually winning a three-million-dollar judgment in 1920.

By 1921, the family was torn in many directions, and the heirs eventually split apart the ranch. Bob went on to found the town of Vealmoor, where the family continued to operate a ranch for several generations. Over time, however, the once great Lazy S Ranch, which had earned C.C. Slaughter the title Cattle King of Texas, became a shadow of itself.

Standing before Major was the last of the original Slaughter bloodline, a family who now appeared broken and defeated.

Lucy joined Major and immediately recognized Adele Slaughter, an old high-school friend of hers. She ran to the wagon, and Adele lowered herself to accept Lucy's embrace. Adele immediately began crying.

Major helped her husband off the wagon. "Chris, are you folks all right?"

Chris Slaughter, who was named after his great-grandfather, shook hands with Major and then dusted himself off. "No, Major, not so good. It's all my fault. I take full blame for what happened."

Major noticed that Adele was still crying, and everyone around was staring at her. He decided to invite the Slaughters inside so they could hear their story.

"Preacher, would you mind taking care of their people? Get some hay and water for their horses. We'll fix supper in a little while for our guests."

"Okay, boss," replied Preacher as he approached the other visitors.

Major invited their guests inside, where Lucy fixed a pot of coffee. They sat around the kitchen table, which had a calming effect on the couple's nerves. Although they'd fallen out of touch over the past few years, the two couples used to get together to share a meal when the Slaughters' two sons were in high school with Duncan and Dallas. Like so many West Texas kids, when they grew up, they'd left for the big city, hoping to find their way in the world. The Slaughters' sons had moved to Atlanta, where they both worked for Delta Air Lines.

"The other night," Chris began the story after taking a deep breath, "I saw the rocket fly over our heads. Did y'all see it too?"

"Yeah," replied Major. He didn't elaborate because he wanted their old friend to tell his story.

"Anyway, when the second one flew to the south, I knew we were under attack. I gathered everyone up and headed for our large root cellar by the milk barns. That whole thing was built on a large slab of concrete back in the sixties.

"Well, you remember, at the time, we were all afraid the Soviets were gonna nuke us to smithereens. My parents built a nuclear fallout shelter under the slab, but it eventually became a nice root cellar 'cause the temperatures never got above fifty degrees down there.

"Anyway, I got everyone down in there, and we shut the door behind us. Major, I'm ashamed to admit this, but I was too afraid to come out of there. I didn't know what was happening aboveground, so I made everyone stay until this morning."

Chris started to speak again, and then his eyes welled up in tears. He took a moment to gather himself with the assistance of Adele, who squeezed his hands. Major looked to Lucy, who was also getting emotional from the sight of their friends in pain.

Chris continued. "Anyway, while we were underground, somebody must've come across the ranch house. Major, they burned us out. I don't know why, or how it started. But I began to smell smoke through the air vents of the root cellar, and it forced me to go topside. I hit the ground running and fell to my knees when I saw our family's home, which had stood for nearly a hundred and fifty years, burned to the ground."

He buried his face in his hands as reliving the moment brought him to emotional rock bottom. Adele hugged her husband of thirty-one years and continued relaying the story.

"Y'all, we lost everything except what was in our barns, the horses, and our dairy cows. I don't know who did this, but they took nearly everything we have."

Lucy reached across the table for her friend's hand. "At least you're safe. God protected you both, and now you're alive. Be thankful for that."

"Oh, we are, but now we're at a loss. We went to the DeWitts' ranch, hoping they'd put us up, at least temporarily."

"Mickey turned us away," interrupted Chris. "He wasn't even man enough to do it himself. He sent one of his men to their gate to deliver the compassionate news."

Major began to process the Slaughters' predicament. He knew what was coming next. Chris and Adele had traveled the thirty miles from their ranch in hopes he'd take them in. There were many factors to consider before the subject was put on the table. Also, he needed to discuss it with Preacher and Lucy first.

Major abruptly stood and excused himself from the table. "Folks, forgive me for a moment. I need to holler at Preacher for a second regarding the barnyard."

As he walked past Chris, he patted his friend on the shoulder and smiled. He then looked past the Slaughters and made eye contact with Lucy, who returned a puzzled look because there would be no reason to send Preacher to the barnyard. Major nodded his head toward to the door with a wink. He hoped she picked up on the message.

Major exited onto the porch and yelled, "Preacher, can I borrow you? I need a favor."

Preacher trotted toward the porch, and Major swung around to see Lucy shuffling through the front door to join them. Major took her by the hand and pulled Preacher to the side where they couldn't be seen through the still-open front door.

"What's wrong, boss? You look nervous."

"It's okay, Preach. They were burned out by someone while they were riding out the attack."

"Yeah, I heard. They lost everything."

Lucy added, "Guys, they've got no place to go."

"Which is exactly what Chris and Adele plan on talking about next," said Major. "We haven't talked about takin' in strays before."

"They're not strays," admonished Lucy. "They're our friends. I believe they'd do the same for us."

"It's six more mouths to feed," said Preacher. "But there is a potential upside if we can figure out where to house them all."

"What's that?" asked Major.

"From what I understand, they've got sixty head of dairy cows that their hands continue to milk. They've got milk stored, and they know how to make cheese. I'm told they dip it in wax and it's good for a long time."

"Okay, the dairy cows would be a big plus, but we can't milk that many by hand," said Major.

Preacher rubbed his chin as he considered a few options. "Well, I think we can dismantle enough of their equipment and set up a dairy station over at the Reinecke Unit. We can take a look at converting the buildings to housing too. Short-term, we could put up the two married couples that work for the Slaughters out at the house on our western boundary."

"Chris and Adele can stay in our guest room until their new place is built," Lucy chimed in as her spirits lifted, something Major immediately noticed. The thought of having Adele around might help Lucy through those times when she was missing their kids.

"How are we gonna feed them? Not the people, the cows?" asked Major.

"More good news," said Preacher. "They've got an old International truck and flatbed combo. Their hands told me the Lazy S barns are filled with rolled hay, enough to feed our cattle too. We can add dairy cows to the mix, feed our cattle into spring, plus more warm bodies to protect our perimeter. This solves a lot of our problems, boss."

Major rubbed the stubble on his face, a reminder that he'd better lean up against a razor soon or Miss Lucy would have him sleeping with the horses. He shrugged and smiled. "Miss Lucy, I don't need to even ask you for your vote. It's written all over your face."

"Major, they're good people. Heck, I've known Adele for as long as I've known you."

Major turned to Preacher. "How do you feel about their people?"

"Good. Both couples are young, but stable. Two local high school sweethearts from Howard County, and the other two grew up in Big Spring. I can work with them."

Major nodded. "It's unanimous. Frankly, I can't see any negatives other than the logistics of expanding our ranch over onto Reinecke property. Their management team was in Houston before they sold out to MarkWest Energy in Denver. I suspect the last thing on their mind is this little old gas well operation."

"Can I tell them the good news?" asked Lucy.

Major looked over her shoulder and saw that the Slaughters had emerged onto the front porch. Their arms were wrapped around each other's waists, awkwardly waiting for the Armstrongs to return.

"Absolutely, but we need to make it clear what's expected of them," replied Major. "Everyone contributes here, and we're asking them to share the rest of what they own to join us. It's the only way."

CHAPTER 27

December 3
Near Bridger, Montana

"Coop, up ahead on the left. That looks like a pretty good possibility." Riley had reluctantly relinquished driver's duties on the second day of their journey to allow Cooper a turn. All three were now on a frantic hunt for another precious commodity of the apocalypse—fuel.

Having a diesel-powered vehicle during a grid-down scenario had a few advantages over their gasoline-powered counterparts, the most important of which was availability. Finding supplies of gasoline would be limited mostly to stalled vehicles and gas cans stored for operating lawn equipment.

Siphoning fuel out of newer model vehicles was nearly impossible without the right equipment. Those who attempted to punch a hole in the bottom of the tank using a sharp object, like a screwdriver and a hammer, were in for a rude surprise if a spark ignited the gas.

Within the many garages across America, fuel cans were stored with gasoline, many of which might have been mixed with small-engine oil, tainting its effectiveness in combustion engines. Most gasoline was stored in underground fuel tanks at gas stations, which had lost power due to the EMP. Extracting the gas from underground could be done if the station had a generator. Others had mastered a technique using a PVC well-bailer to extract the gas through its fill pipes, but the process was slow, and dangerous if seen by others.

Diesel fuel was different. In rural areas, farmers had aboveground diesel storage tanks to use for their farm equipment. Unlike road-vehicle-grade fuel, which was clear, some diesel was dyed red for use in off-road vehicles and farm implements.

There was no difference between the effectiveness of the two types of diesel. The only reason farm diesel was dyed red had to do with taxation. Farm diesel wasn't taxed while clear, street-legal diesel was.

The Rodeo Kids knew this, having grown up around diesel vehicles on the ranch, and it was a consideration as they chose their route south. However, the large, spacious ranches of Montana proved to be a problem as they searched for a spot to refill Red Rover's tank. It was Riley who first noticed a possible solution to the slowly descending fuel needle.

"Let me pull over," said Cooper. "Palmer, check it out through the binoculars. Do you see any signs of activity?"

Palmer studied the small farmhouse and the neighboring barn. The three of them sat in silence, giving her plenty of time to watch for signs of life. She handed the binoculars to Riley, who took a turn.

"This might work, guys," said Palmer, not waiting for Riley's opinion. "There's a broken window on the side of the house, and the front door was left open. Looks like someone broke in, took what they could find, and left."

"Looters," Cooper said under his breath.

"Yeah, but there is a chance for some fuel," added Riley, who continued to look through the binoculars. "There's a barn with what looks like a blue and white Ford tractor sitting in it. If we can find a water hose, at least we can siphon the diesel out of the tractor."

Palmer nodded as Riley handed the Bushnell back to her. "I'll betcha there's a diesel tank around back, or at least a can or two of fuel. This thing doesn't drink much."

Cooper started up the truck and headed for the house as the sun began to set over the Rockies. The night before, they were unable to find a suitable place to sleep for the night, so they'd slept in the truck, taking alternating shifts to guard their perimeter. Cooper's hopes were high at the prospect of sleeping in a real bed for the night.

He stopped a thousand yards short of the house. Riley and Cooper grabbed their rifles and approached the house on foot, spreading out on both sides of the driveway so as to allow plenty of space between them. Palmer took the wheel and waited with the motor running in case she had to move in to pull her brothers out of harm's way.

It took the guys five minutes to clear the house and the barn. They emerged from the side of the barn, waving Palmer forward with smiles and a thumbs-up. They'd found fuel.

Riley pulled Red Rover around the back side of the barn and squeezed every drop of red diesel into the apple red Landy he could. Inside the barn were three yellow five-gallon fuel cans, which were filled, and he secured them to another find—a steel cargo carrier they attached to their hitch. The attachment was strong enough to hold the diesel and some tools they found in the barn. A silver/brown tarp and bungee cords were used to conceal the contents of the crate.

Their spirits were high when they began to look through the kitchen for food. The house, which appeared to be a hundred years old or more, creaked and cracked as they walked across the old wood floors. Whoever had arrived before them had cleaned out the cupboards of anything edible, including spices. Nary a crumb was left behind for man or mouse.

But that was okay for the Rodeo Kids, as they still had leftovers provided by Fiorella for the road. They built a fire in the woodstove, which occupied a corner of the open floor plan in which kitchen, dining, and family room were all one room.

Two back bedrooms provided comfortable king-sized beds with ample covers in the form of goose-down-filled duvets and feather pillows. Cooper joked the accommodations were like a five-star hotel.

After they ate and agreed upon their sleeping and security routine for the night, they settled into the family room and turned on the shortwave radio given to them by Fiorella. Riley, who had mastered the operation of the device, quickly found the broadcast channel used by the Three Percenter Montana militia.

"This is a call to arms, fellow patriots," the broadcast began. "Our great nation faces an existential threat from beyond our borders, as well as within them."

"Existential?" asked Riley with a laugh. "That's a fifty-dollar word."

"Eighteen points on the Scrabble board," quipped Palmer, who enjoyed playing the famous board game but could rarely find any takers in the family because she always won. Perhaps it was because she could calculate the word value in just seconds.

The man continued. "This president has declared war on our freedoms. At a time when she should be calling on us to help her defeat the enemy from Korea, instead she is using her military resources to take up arms against law-abiding citizens in violation of our Second Amendment rights."

"Sounds like the same old, same old," said Palmer.

"I'm calling on my fellow Three Percenters who can hear my voice to join me as we free those of us who have been unlawfully detained by the FEMA thugs who've descended upon a free Montana and Wyoming. Our part of this great country is not in turmoil. We are not killing one another in the streets. We continued to adhere to the rule of law and the principles of God."

Riley turned down the volume slightly. "What do you think they're talking about, Coop?"

"Sounds like martial law is being enforced around here. You know, I've always wondered if society would collapse like you see in the movies. People freak out over nothing nowadays. Imagine what it's like in the big cities."

"Remember, Fiorella said Great Falls was dangerous," added Palmer. "That's not exactly a big city."

"Heck, the small towns ain't exactly friendly," Riley said with a chuckle as he stuffed a pinch of Skoal between his cheek and gum. The unopened can of tobacco had been left behind by the looters. "They were shooting at us on day three."

Cooper smiled as he reached out for the tobacco. He stuffed it in his pocket before admonishing his younger brother. "You're not starting up on this stuff again. Momma will shoot at you too. One dip, and only because you're takin' first shift tonight. You can spit that stuff outside."

"Whatever, Coop," said Riley with a frown. "So what's the militia up to?"

"It sounds like FEMA is rounding up the militia," he replied. "You gotta wonder why they'd bother with folks up here. Denver area got nuked. You'd think they'd focus on saving folks rather than round up the militia."

"I don't care," said Palmer. "As long as they stay out of our way, we'll stay out of theirs. Let's take a look at the map and plan out our day tomorrow. I, for one, want to get in that comfy bed back there."

They opened up the map and spread it on the table. The candles they'd found in the kitchen pantry provided more than ample light to view their route options. Palmer quickly found their location just south of Bridger, Montana. She retrieved a lighter from her pocket and set it upright to represent where they were.

Cooper studied the map and used his index finger to gauge the distance against the map's legend. "It looks like we could pick up Route 310 again and head into Wyoming. It's only about fifteen miles or so."

"Hopefully, there's not a border crossing at the Wyoming line," added Riley.

"Riley, we've all got pieces of crazy in us, but yours are bigger than others," said Palmer with a laugh. "They're not gonna have border crossings goin' from one state to another. That's nonsense."

"You never know, sis," he responded defensively. "Things are weird with what's goin' on."

Cooper sensed another row brewing between his siblings, so he stepped in quickly to bring them back to focusing on the plan for tomorrow. Besides, he was ready to hit the sack too. "C'mon, y'all. Focus. We've traveled two hundred fifty miles these first two days. Now we have a full tank of gas and enough to refill a second time. That's pert near five hundred miles of fuel. That'll get us into Colorado unless we have a problem."

"All right, Coop," said Palmer. "What's the plan?"

Cooper pulled the candle closer to the map and ran his finger along the route. "We pick up US 310 through Lovell, down to Greybull, here, and beyond toward Worland. At that point, we'll get a lay of the land and see if Worland will have roadblocks and such. Okay?"

"Sounds good," said Riley as he got up from the table in search of a spit cup for his chew. "I'll patrol the outside. It's not that cold tonight, thankfully, but I'll keep the fire goin' in the stove. Coop, you'll be up next in three hours."

After Riley went outside, Cooper asked Palmer to help him with something.

"Palmer, I'm not saying every farmhouse in Montana should have a gun rack, but it kinda surprises me that they don't have one."

"What are you sayin'?" she asked.

"Well, it seems these folks are kinda conspiratorial up here, you know? If they're like that fella on the radio broadcast, chances are they hide their weapons, keeping them out of plain sight from FEMA goons, or whatever."

After the two shared a hearty laugh at Cooper's characterization, Palmer stood up and reached for the small flashlight in her pocket. She powered it up and began to scan the walls and cabinets in the kitchen. As she slowly walked around, her feet caused the pine board floors to squeak. It drew her attention downward.

"Coop, you might be right," said Palmer. "If you were gonna hide guns and ammo, where would you do it?"

"Better question is where would I start lookin'? The logical place for most is to look for a secret panel in the walls, probably behind a heavy piece of furniture. From what I've seen, there are only a few parts of the house where that would make sense."

"Good thought, but if these people truly believe in using their guns for defending their homes, or fighting the *guvment*," started Palmer, purposefully mocking the way some are portrayed on television shows when they say *government*, "they would want quick, easy access to their weapons. They wouldn't store them behind heavy furniture. Let's think outside the box."

"Gawd," Cooper moaned. "I hate that phrase."

"Okay, Coop. How's this? Don't think like the *guvment.* Think like Momma and Daddy. Have you noticed the floors?"

"Yeah, they squeak everywhere. Did they not nail 'em down good?"

Palmer laughed. "Or maybe they did it on purpose. They're like that throughout the house, which means they wouldn't necessarily stand out as unusual."

"I get it. Let's try the floor first, probably in the bedrooms."

"Yup, under an area rug or a chair."

Palmer found the utensil drawer and pulled out two butter knives. She gave one to Coop. "If we work together, we can check each room faster. It's just a hunch, but I'll give up an hour of sleep to find some more guns, how about you?"

Cooper took the knife and high-fived his little sister. He was impressed with the mindset and thought processes she'd adopted after the collapse. Palmer was a survivor.

It took them only five minutes to find their first hidden treasure. Near the nightstand of the master bedroom, there was a small bistro chair that the homeowners probably used to remove their shoes and socks at night. They moved the chair aside and noticed a finger-sized knothole in the pine flooring.

First, Palmer shined her light into the hole to make sure a mouse wasn't peering back, then she stuck her pinky finger in and pulled upward.

She was rewarded with two Smith & Wesson nine-millimeter handguns and three hundred rounds of ammunition. They quickly retrieved their treasure and ran the loot into the kitchen to be laid out on the table. Energized by their success, the two began tearing the floor up, not bothering to place the boards back where they belonged in some cases.

Two Remington shotguns were discovered under a cocktail table and a Southwestern-style jute rug in the family room. Two hundred forty double-ought buck shells were nestled between the floor joists next to them.

But the big prize was discovered last in an unexpected location. They'd just about called off their search when Cooper suggested the bathroom. He'd noticed earlier that the bathroom had been renovated to cover the pine floors with tile throughout. The threshold transition from the hallway to the bath had caused him to stumble slightly when he and Riley were clearing the home. This meant the tile was installed over the wood flooring.

He shined the light onto the floor and saw hairline cracks in the twelve-inch tile, meaning the tile hadn't been set properly. He crawled on his hands and knees to the claw-foot tub, which sat under a small window. With the knife, he tapped on the tiles under the tub and found them to be loose. Excited, he quickly pried the tiles up and set them out of the way.

Then he tapped on the pine boards underneath. They were loose as well and easily removed. Lying flat on his stomach, Cooper stretched his arm under the tub and reached into the void between the floor joists. He began laughing when his hands found the grand prize.

"Coop, what?" asked Palmer, anxious to see what had her brother giddy with delight.

He slid the AR-15 from under the tub, and Palmer quickly grabbed it.

"Wait, there's more," said Cooper as he strained to reach around the space. He began sliding box after box after box of NATO 5.56 rounds. When he was satisfied he'd found everything, he pushed himself out from under the tub and sat with his back leaning against the wall.

"This is unbelievable," started Palmer. "An AR-15, four extra magazines, and twenty-five boxes of ammo with twenty rounds each. Five hundred rounds total. Coop, we could start our own army!"

Cooper stood and took the rifle from his sister. He noticed the switch on the left side. It had fully automatic firing capability. He felt the weight in his hands and smiled. They now had the most efficient weapon made at their disposal. Somehow, Cooper knew they might need it.

CHAPTER 28

December 4
The Governor's Mansion
Austin, Texas

Montgomery Gregg walked into the governor's mansion as a man without a title for the first time in his adult life. Like the mansion in which he now stood, his existence had undergone a tremendous upheaval. The Texas Governor's Mansion was no longer the home of the governor of Texas, but rather, the President of the Republic of Texas. If Monty Gregg were making a media appearance, he'd be referred to as General Gregg, or former Secretary of Defense Gregg. Although those former titles were still a part of his history on this planet, this was his day to solidify his role within the new nation and earn a new title within the Texas power structure.

He wore a dark gray, pin-striped suit, typical for his former days within the Billings-Harman cabinet. His former military uniforms now hung proudly in a closet within his study at home, a reminder of his ascension to the highest level of the U.S. armed forces.

When acting-President Burnett summoned him to Austin for a private meeting, he sensed an opportunity. Much had happened following the EMP and the secession of Texas from the United States. The nuclear attack provided Gregg an opportunity to advise Marion on several matters, both as it related to the defense of Texas and international relations, as odd as that might sound, with the United States.

He had not been provided the details of the teleconference between the two presidents, but he assumed they had taken place, as he'd been asked to deploy troops to the Shreveport area to assist in the medical treatment of victims of the nuclear attack.

With an apprehension he hadn't experienced since he was awarded the Medal of Honor, he followed his escort into President Burnett's office. She was finishing up her conversation with her ever-present chief of staff, who was more executive assistant than she was an advisor to a new president.

"Good morning, Monty," greeted President Burnett, who immediately stood and the two shook hands. She picked up her Texas Rangers coffee mug and walked over to a buffet, which held a tray of coffee. "Please, sit down. Would you like some coffee?"

"No, thank you, Madam President."

President Burnett's chief of staff exited and closed the door behind her. As the president stirred in cream and sugar, she laughed. She held up her mug and studied it.

"W gave this to me nearly twenty years ago," she began. "I was labeled a rising star in the Texas legislature at the time because, believe it or not, I was quite a looker back in the day. My appearance got me noticed, but I wanna believe it was what I said on the floor of the State House that earned me respect. You know, Monty, I've never wavered on my core principles since I entered public life. The people of Texas always know what to expect from Marion Burnett."

Gregg adjusted his posture and crossed his legs. He was trying to read the president, hoping to get a sense of where she was headed with the conversation.

President Burnett continued after she sat in her dark leather chair. She casually swiveled from side to side as she spoke. "I rode the coattails of the Bush political dynasty like many others attempted to do, but like a determined race car driver, I took a chance to pass them by on the last lap. Folks thought I was *el loco* to challenge George P. in the Republican primary for governor. But I saw an opening after Jeb's drubbin' in his attempt to be president. George P. thought he could run around Texas, speaking Spanish, and cater to the Hispanic vote. All he did was alienate the core conservatives, which turned out heavily in my favor."

Gregg interrupted. "Madam President, you did an excellent job of reading the political tea leaves and ignoring the media pundits."

The president laughed. "Thank you, Monty, but please, when we're in private like this, call me Marion. We are old friends, right?"

"Yes, of course, Marion. I'm a military man who has the concept of protocol and respect embedded in my brain. Formality is what I know best."

"Well, those are admirable qualities, but I've asked you to visit with me about our relationship going forward."

Uh-oh. Sounds ominous.

"I'm available to help in any way that I can," said Gregg.

"Monty, you were spot-on with your advice on how to deal with Alani," the president began. "You anticipated exactly how she would react, and what she'd be looking for in return. You mentioned political tea leaves. You have experience in the swamp of DC that I don't have."

Gregg laughed. "I'm battle tested, to be sure."

"No doubt, navigating those shark-infested waters requires many talents," added President Burnett. She took another sip of coffee and moved her mug in a circular motion, momentarily mesmerized by the swirls created by the creamer. "Amidst all of this chaos, the likes of which modern man has never witnessed, we have the monumental task of forming a government and establishing a new nation. I need someone who can perform many functions, wear many hats."

Gregg's heart leapt with excitement. He was about to be offered something—*official.* He was no longer in limbo as to what the remainder of his storied career would look like.

"How can I help, Marion?"

"Through my negotiations with President Harman, and after following your suggestion, Texas now has a standing army. We will be retaining Fort Bliss and Fort Hood, as well as Lackland and other military bases within our borders. In exchange, we will immediately enter into a mutual protection treaty, much like the ones between the U.S. and Canada. If North America is attacked by a foreign enemy, we will work together to repel the threat."

"Similar to NATO," suggested Gregg.

"Exactly, but not one-sided," said the president with a nod of approval. "I expect Mexico and Canada to join us and contribute in a meaningful way. I need someone like you to establish this relationship between our countries to get it started on the right footing."

"I'm glad to spearhead the effort on behalf of Texas. In what capacity will I be representing us?"

"We'll get to that in a moment," she replied dismissively. "In addition, other agreements will need to be negotiated between Washington and Austin, which necessarily falls under the purview of a Secretary of State, a Secretary of Commerce, and Secretary of Defense. All of these cabinet members will have to be seasoned Washington veterans, well-versed in the ways DC operates."

"That's a lot of hats, Marion. I'm sure there are many Texans who can fill those roles."

President Burnett swiveled her chair around to look out the window onto the lawn of the mansion. Another day of protests had begun in earnest as Texans continued to look to her for answers for their ever-increasing food shortage.

"No one person can fill them all," she began after turning her attention back to Gregg. "But one man can ensure that the positions are properly filled. Monty, I want you to be my vice president and assist me in transitioning Texas from state to nation-state. Are you up for it?"

Gregg stood at attention. "It would be my honor, Madam President."

President Burnett stood and shook Gregg's hand. "Then it's settled. We'll make the formal announcement today and announce state, um, I mean nationwide elections in the coming days. In the meantime, we'll continue to operate under the provisional laws established by the Texas legislature in the articles of secession. Monty, we have a lot of work to do, my friend. If you can help our new government get established and find its place within the international community, I will focus on helping Texans survive this extraordinary crisis."

Well done, Monty. You got a seat at the head of the table.

CHAPTER 29

December 4
Lovell, Wyoming

The Department of the Interior made a push to preserve forestry land in the Western U.S. during the end of the nineteenth century. During the late 1920s, as unemployment became a problem across the country, Forestry was thought to be a solution through various reforestation projects. States like California had already implemented programs to hire unemployed workers for this purpose.

As part of President Roosevelt's New Deal designed to bring America out of the Great Depression, the Civilian Conservation Corps was established as a work relief program. Young families in particular benefitted from the employment of the heads of household. As part of their compensation, the families were provided shelter, clothing, and food in newly constructed camps dedicated to reforestation, but also to provide work for those in need.

Near Lovell, Wyoming, one such camp, known as Civilian Corps Camp BR-7, was constructed. Small towns like Lovell lobbied the Forest Service because communities near the camps benefited economically when the CCC members ventured into town to purchase provisions.

Over time, the camps were abandoned as America went to war following Pearl Harbor, but the permanent structures remained behind. Owned by the federal government, many of these Civilian Corps Camps became identified by conspiracy theorists as so-called FEMA camps, locations where those who opposed the government in a time of martial law were whisked away, never to be seen again.

After the EMP struck and martial law was declared by President Harman, FEMA camps were established around the country on federal lands like Camp BR-7. They were not, however, intended to be used as prison camps, but rather as a safe haven for those who couldn't take care of themselves. They were intended to be places where Americans could voluntarily take refuge.

Sometimes, things look good on paper, but once implementation is undertaken, potential for abuses can become prevalent. FEMA's use of their camps was one such example.

Montana and Wyoming residents of all political affiliations were proud gun owners. Some were more vocal in their support of the Second Amendment than others. Those who let their views be known publicly were the first targets of the military's gun-confiscation program. Using a combination of gun registries, NRA membership rolls, and social media postings, the FBI database computers—which were located at Quantico, Virginia, and protected from the effects of the EMP—the government quickly compiled a list of gun owners to be targeted under martial law. The National Guard units of both states were supplemented with active-duty military from the region.

Although the guardsmen had sworn an oath to the Constitution and supported the right to bear arms, they were also being fed and their families kept safe as payment for performing their duties. They didn't like confiscating weapons from law-abiding citizens, but it was just part of their job.

In the first hours of the door-to-door confiscations, problems arose for the guardsmen. Gun-owner compliance was near zero. The commanders in the field discussed their options at the end of the first day and elected to distribute flyers warning residents in Southern Montana and Northern Wyoming about the consequences of noncompliance. The threats included, among other things, property confiscations and imprisonment.

This inflamed the local population, who pushed back with vocal, well-attended demonstrations in the town of Lovell, which was nearest to Camp BR-7. The majority of the population of twenty-four hundred citizens had remained home following the EMP and subsequent nuclear attacks. It was a close-knit community that took care of one another.

When the FEMA notifications made their way throughout the region, people descended into town and began to hold rallies at the Lovell High School located on the westernmost end of Main Street.

With each passing day, the guardsmen were stymied in their efforts and began to be greeted with open hostility. One homeowner fired upon the guardsmen as they drove up his driveway.

The local commander of Camp BR-7 was a hard-nosed combat veteran who refused to allow his troops to be put in danger. He issued orders to search the homes of those who were on the confiscation list but who had denied gun ownership previously. Anyone resisting this directive could be taken into custody and imprisoned at a newly established holding facility within Camp BR-7.

The day the nuclear attacks stopped, guardsmen conducted surprise raids on known gun owners who also were cross-matched with local militias like the Three Percenters. The commander determined that the militia members were emboldening the local citizens to mount a resistance in the name of the Second Amendment. His assumption was right, and raids conducted on December second and third filled Camp BR-7's new stockade to capacity.

On this morning, the few residents that had voluntarily entered Camp BR-7 were transported to another FEMA facility outside Malmstrom Air Force Base in Montana. Security fencing was quickly erected to quadruple the camp's detention capabilities.

Just after dawn, armed members of the Three Percenters from Montana and Wyoming descended upon Lovell High School. This time they had no plans for a pro-gun rally. Instead, the school became a rally point for an armed militia operation on Camp BR-7 to free their patriot brothers.

The commanders at Camp BR-7 got wind of the militia's intentions. Rather than wait for them to attack the camp, they deployed a convoy of troop transports and Humvees with fifty-caliber machine guns mounted on their turrets. As they drove up Highway 9 toward Foster Gulch, the commander commented that it was time to crush this uprising so the guardsmen could get back to the business of helping people through these difficult times.

For the militia, they were armed and ready. Spirits were high as they departed Lovell in a variety of old cars and trucks and headed west on US 310, which intersected at Route 9, at Foster Gulch. They thought they had the element of surprise on their side and that they'd roll right into Camp BR-7 as liberators.

Two armies, hell-bent on destroying the other, were on a collision course, at Foster Gulch.

CHAPTER 30

December 4
Foster Gulch
Near Lovell, Wyoming

"Okay, we're doin' pretty good today so far," said Cooper. The flat terrain agreed with Red Rover, and the forty-year-old truck kept a steady pace down the highway. They hadn't seen another car since they left the house. "What's the next town or intersection?"

Palmer, who didn't really care for driving Red Rover with its right-hand steering wheel and four-speed manual transmission, nominated herself as the full-time navigator. Besides, the front seat of the truck was too small to squeeze the two guys together.

"The town of Lovell shouldn't be that far ahead. Route 14 is the next side road on our right followed by Route 9. Both of those roads lead back to the southwest, so they're not a great option. Just as we approach town, there are several roads that lead to the south and connect back to US 301 on the other side."

"Sounds good. We'll stay the course," said Cooper.

They passed by an auto parts store, which had been looted, and a small diner, Debbie's Junction, which had been partially burned down at some point.

Cooper added a little more pressure on the pedal as Red Rover climbed up a slight incline and continued over a bridge that crossed Sage Creek. At the apex of the bridge, all three of them saw oncoming vehicles at the same time.

"Oh no, Coop!" exclaimed Palmer.

"We can't run head-on into that bunch," said Riley. "There must be a dozen cars coming our way."

"What about over there on the left?" asked Cooper.

"Yeah, it's a construction trailer, kinda like a mobile home."

Cooper pressed down on the gas and raced toward a narrow entrance, which took him into a large gravel parking area. In the middle of the lot stood a twenty-four-foot-long construction trailer.

As he made the left turn, Red Rover, which was slightly top heavy because of its short wheel base, leaned heavily to the right, forcing Palmer and Riley to slide into him. He lost his grip on the wheel, which jerked the truck back to the right, but Cooper corrected the skid and slid to a stop. He jammed the gear shift into first gear and lurched forward until they were hidden behind the trailer.

"Now we wait until they pass," said Cooper after he shut off the motor. "This shouldn't take long. At least we know they don't have any vehicles left in town to chase us. That was a heckuva a caravan."

"It looked like they were practicing for a parade," said Riley with a chuckle. "Did you see all those flags flying in the wind?"

Palmer fidgeted in her seat. "Do you think we can sneak out and stretch our legs? Sitting on the middle gives me a butt cramp."

Riley tried to pick at her earlobe. "Aww, don't get butt hurt over your butt cramp."

Cooper and Riley had a good laugh at Palmer's expense as they opened their doors in unison and exited the truck. They stretched their legs until Cooper stopped to listen.

"Guys, get down," he instructed. "They've stopped. Listen."

Riley dropped to the ground and crawled on his belly under the trailer to get a better look.

"You're right, Coop. It looks like they've stopped right in the middle—"

Riley's words were drowned out by the roar of gunfire. He scrambled in reverse to get out from under the trailer, gashing his head open on the rusty steel frame of the trailer in the process.

As he emerged, blood was streaming out of his scalp and down his face.

"My God, were you shot?" asked Palmer as she studied Riley's face.

"No, hit it on the trailer. These guys opened fire on something down that way."

Riley pointed due south, abandoning any effort to talk due to the noise created by the rapid gunfire. He wiped the blood off his face and onto his jeans. Palmer ran to the truck and retrieved a towel, which she used to apply pressure on his scalp.

THUMP-THUMP-THUMP!

"What is that?" yelled Palmer. "A cannon?"

Screams could be heard from the men in the vehicles barely a hundred yards from them. Suddenly, the heavy-caliber bullets ripped through the flimsy aluminum trailer, leaving gaping holes as they flew over their heads into the creek behind them.

"Holy crap, get down," shouted Cooper.

Riley was slowest to drop to his knees as he began to show signs of blood loss. He managed to ask, "Should we shoot back?"

"Are you kidding?" responded Cooper. "That must be the military on the other side of that heavy machine gun. This battle is gonna be over soon enough."

Cooper crawled under the trailer but used the tires as cover. He peered between the twin axles to get a better view. He was about to crawl back when suddenly Palmer and Riley crawled on both sides of him. The family was gonna stick together on this one.

"Whadya see, bro?" asked Riley, whose prone position helped him regain his mental acuity.

"That's gotta be the militia," he replied. "This must be the operation they were talking about last night on the shortwave. I'm afraid they've bit off more than they can chew. There are dead guys all over the place."

Tires began to squeal as two trucks took off over the creek toward Montana. Two more turned into the parking lot where they were hiding.

"Duck!" shouted Cooper.

The vehicles did a donut in the gravel, spraying limestone rocks across the front of the trailer before catching the pavement. Screeching the tires, they roared toward town but not before running over the dead bodies of their fellow militia.

A few more bursts from automatic weapons could be heard from down the road, but eventually it stopped. Still under the trailer, Cooper considered their next move. Just as he was about to suggest they get in Red Rover and get while the gettin' was good, the sound of heavy-duty trucks and their knobby, off-road tires approached.

"Crap!" Cooper muttered. "It's the dang army, and they're coming this way."

"You mean here, to the trailer," said a panicked Palmer.

"No. I guess to check out the dead guys. They don't seem interested in chasing down the others."

"Coop, what should we do?" asked Palmer.

He offered a solid suggestion. "Lie here and pray they ask questions before shooting."

CHAPTER 31

December 4
Foster Gulch
Near Lovell, Wyoming

The three Armstrong siblings lay completely still, trying not to move as the soldiers poured out of the two-and-a-half-ton transports. Their commander instructed the guardsmen to gather the dead and line them up on the highway for identification. Cooper continued to peer through the trailer's tires to observe their activities.

He counted the bodies as they were carried by the arms and legs and dropped brusquely to the pavement. The dead men were soldiers, at least in their minds. Wearing mismatched camo with lace-up boots, they tried to look the part with chest rigs, ammo pouches, and military knives strapped to their legs.

But as they died, it wasn't how they were dressed or how well they could hit a target on the gun range, it was a more powerful enemy in the form of two fifty-caliber machine guns, the famous Ma Deuce, that tore their bodies to shreds.

War is hell, and these men experienced it for less than three minutes before they died.

A man's voice said authoritatively, "All right, let's pull these vehicles off to the side of the road except for the pickup truck. Load the dead in there."

"Captain, sir."

"What is it, Sergeant?"

"Are we going to transport these bodies to the camp or return them to the town?"

"We'll take them to the town," the captain replied. "We'll park the vehicle in plain sight of the high school and leave them to be buried by their families. Idiots. What were they thinking?"

"What about these vehicles, Captain?"

"Lock them up and take the keys," he replied. "We'll confiscate them under the martial law declaration and take them back to the camp with us. They'll be useful at some point."

"Yes, sir!"

The guardsman scurried about to fulfill their captain's directives. He was joined by another officer, and the two men began to stroll toward the trailer.

Cooper instinctively ducked his head, and Riley began to speak before Cooper cupped his hand over his brother's mouth. He shook his head quickly back and forth.

"Captain, this had to be done, sadly."

"I know that, Sergeant, but our job just got more difficult. Despite the fact this foolish militia opened fire upon us first, those dead bodies over there will serve as martyrs for the regular civilians who wanted nothing to do with this fight."

"Do you think we should continue the gun confiscations?"

Cooper risked detection and looked up to get a better view of the conversation.

"Dammit, Sergeant, I don't know. This has been a complete disaster. You and I know we're just following orders, but these people up here look at us as the enemy. Heck, they hate us more than the North Koreans right now."

Out of frustration, the captain kicked a stone in the direction of the bullet-riddled trailer. The stone ricocheted off the trailer's wheel, which was inches away from Palmer's head. She jerked slightly but stifled a scream.

Cooper smiled and nodded at his sister. He looked toward Riley, who was beginning to sweat profusely, which mixed with the blood and dripped down his face. Cooper couldn't wait much longer to treat his scalp wound.

Come on, Captain. Move along!

Cooper had to check himself to make sure his thoughts didn't come out as a very vocal demand. He didn't think the guardsmen would take them into custody, but they might confiscate Red Rover and would certainly confiscate their weapons and ammunition.

He stared at Riley, who nodded in return. His brother was one tough SOB.

A voice shouted in their direction. "Ready to go, Captain, on your orders."

"Come on, Sergeant. Let's finish this up and head back to the camp. We've earned a cold one, don't you think?"

"Thirteen KIA, all on their side? I call that a win, sir."

The two men quickly returned to their vehicles, and the trio under the trailer let out a collective sigh of relief.

They scurried out from under the trailer, and Palmer retrieved some bottled water and a medical bag she'd organized at the house in Bridger last night.

"Guys, you gotta treat Riley in the truck," started Cooper. "There's no way we can travel through town now. We're gonna have to head south toward the military camp and find our way back on track through back roads. Unfortunately, we don't have time to talk about it."

"Let's roll, bro," said Riley with a laugh. "I've got enough blood left in me to make it down the road a ways."

Cooper started up the truck, and they double-checked the line of sight down both sides of the highway before crossing it. Within a minute, Palmer had the bleeding under control and was unfolding the map and looking for a way to get back on their route home.

"You know what, y'all," started Cooper as he put plenty of distance between them and the battlefield in his rearview mirror. "I'm no expert on war battles or anything, but it seems to me that a bunch of militia, even though their heart was in it, was not gonna be strong enough to beat those big machine guns that sent bullets flying in one side of a building and out the other. To fight someone more powerful than you, I'm thinkin' you gotta sneak up on them and hit 'em when they least suspect it."

Cooper's words hung in the air as the trio realized how lucky they were not to get caught in the crossfire. The travelers had dodged a bullet, or twenty.

PART THREE

Beyond Borders

CHAPTER 32

December 5
West Hobson Road
Roswell, New Mexico

The world has known many serial killers. There has been a long list of those who committed hideous, inhumane crimes, but some names garnered more notoriety than others, thanks to media and pop culture. One thing they had in common—they were all children once.

The Zodiac Killer was never captured despite leaving taunting letters with cryptic clues for law enforcement. He claimed to have killed thirty-seven fellow human beings in the San Francisco Bay Area in the sixties. He was once a child, but turned into a demented human being.

Donald Henry Gaskins tortured and mutilated ninety hitchhikers in the South during his reign of terror. As a child, he was mentally tortured by a mother whose bedroom had a revolving door for the many men in her life and by his classmates, who nicknamed him Pee Wee. Gaskins got even with society, which had dealt him a bad hand at the casino table of life.

Ted Bundy was a kidnapper, rapist, and demented necrophile. The level of depravity of this human being is unfathomable. He stood in striking contrast to one's general image of a homicidal maniac. He was attractive, self-assured, and had no problem being with women. But his dark side began as a child when he spent a considerable amount of time with a grandfather who had a penchant for child pornography and a volatile temper.

The list goes on—Aileen Wuornos, Jeffrey Dahmer, John Wayne Gacy, the Casanova Killer, the Acid Bath Murderer, the Angel of

Death, and so on. All of these infamous murderers were once children, but became notorious through their crimes.

However, there are those who hadn't made the front page of the *National Enquirer* or Yahoo! News online. One such individual was Joseph Manuel Holloway.

Holloway grew up in California with his mother, an elementary schoolteacher from Sacramento, and his father, a computer programmer of Korean descent. Their life was good and drama-free.

Like many idealistic teens, Holloway wanted to see the world. Also, like many teens, he rebelled against the plans for his future envisioned by his parents. They saw four years of college followed by a graduate degree at nearby Cal State Fullerton.

Holloway spent his days locked in his room playing *Call of Duty* and *Infinite Warfare*. Following his graduation from high school, when the time came for Holloway to enroll at Cal State, he chose to march down to North Harbor Boulevard in Fullerton and enroll in the United States Army.

Holloway became a top recruit and sailed through Army basic training at Fort Sill in Lawton, Oklahoma. Then it was off to Fort Benning for more basic training. And then it was off to war in the Middle East, where Holloway learned there was a big difference between *Call of Duty, Black Ops* and Kandahar Province.

His career in the Army was stellar. He became a U.S. Army sniper and later a senior drill sergeant. Holloway had a bald head and the build of a middle linebacker. He also had the disposition of a pit bull.

His final days in the Army were unplanned. Assigned to the Kabul Military Training Centre for the Afghan Armed Forces, he enjoyed molding these young men who risked their lives and ties with their friends to fight against the Taliban. It took intestinal fortitude to be an Afghan who joined the Army to fight in the mountains. Peer pressure stopped most from considering enlistment.

Holloway was proud of these recruits and put his heart into helping them learn to fight. But one fateful day, Holloway's heart was ripped out. One of the young Afghans in training arrived at an evening dinner commemorating the completion of basic training with a suicide bomb strapped to his torso. As Holloway read words of praise for his recruits, the man detonated the device, sending shrapnel through the air, killing dozens and taking the left eye of Holloway.

His career was over. He'd gone from killing machine, to trainer of killers, to unemployed ex-vet in Fullerton, California, seeking his way in the world—with just one eye and a scarred face.

Holloway became angry. He was irate that the Army had discharged him and refused to let him fight. He was a trained killer and that was all he knew. He began to look up some of the guys from his old unit. They, too, were having difficulty finding jobs or establishing normalcy back in the States.

The *psychobabblers*, as the guys called them, immediately diagnosed the former soldiers as having PTSD, post-traumatic stress disorder. Even though the men scoffed at the concept, they readily accepted the diagnosis, which earned them extra disability pay.

The diagnosis came with a price, however. Prospective employers shied away from hiring them. There were too many stories of PTSD-afflicted ex-soldiers committing acts of violence in the workplace. They were afraid to hire soldiers like Holloway for fear of potentially having to fire them one day.

"Can you imagine what might happen?" they'd whisper privately.

Holloway and the guys started their own business, which perfectly suited their skillset—*mercenaries for hire.* They traveled the world fighting the battles of others, and they were paid handsomely. Truth be told, they would have done it for free because it enabled them to do what they loved most—*kill.*

Prior to one such operation in Southeast Asia, Holloway's team recruited a Korean man who lived in Fullerton. The man worked on the loading docks at Kraft Foods but frequented a local hangout called The Blue Door Bar, which was a favorite of Holloway's because it was preferred by Korean women, also Holloway's favorite.

During an evening of drinks, the Korean man boasted about his elite military training in North Korea. Holloway and the guys laughed it off as the man just being drunk. Then one night, the Korean was hitting on a cute Asian girl, much to the chagrin of her three brothers. They attempted to push the man away repeatedly. After the third shove, and three minutes later, the gang of brothers lay sprawled out on the floor with a variety of broken bones to show for the altercation.

Holloway and the guys were impressed with the Korean and quickly made the decision to hustle him out of the bar before the cops arrived. The Korean, as they called him, joined their mercenary group and later introduced Holloway to more like him.

Holloway was back in his element as a leader of men and a natural-born killer. Unlike more noteworthy killers, Holloway wasn't known to the American public or law enforcement.

He quietly associated himself with the Fullerton Boyz, a gang originally formed in 1996 by Korean teens. The gang was prevalent in the Orangethorpe area of Fullerton, where Holloway grew up. He returned to Orangethorpe and struck up old acquaintances. His position was cemented as the first white leader of the Fullerton Boyz.

Holloway now had an army of his own, one that enjoyed his favorite pastime—killing. Make no mistake, he'd murdered more people than the top twenty serial killers of all time combined. The difference was he continued to kill because nobody stopped him.

Now Holloway and his North Korean associates were heading east toward Texas. But first, there was business to be done in Roswell, New Mexico.

CHAPTER 33

December 6
The Armstrong Ranch
Borden County, Texas

To the south and immediately adjacent to the Armstrong Ranch was over four thousand acres known as the Reinecke Field, which included fifteen producing oil wells, water injection wells, and natural gas wells, yielding over two hundred barrels of oil a day. Before the EMP attack, Reinecke Partners employed twelve full-time personnel at the facility, including an on-site foreman.

Major led Preacher and Chris Slaughter on horseback across the ranch. Antonio was bringing the rest of the Slaughter contingent along the roads connecting the properties. Major doubted the facility was occupied, but it was necessary to inspect the complex before exposing Chris's group to potential squatters.

They approached the caretaker's house cautiously, with each man approaching from a different angle. There were no signs of activity with only a white utility truck sitting off to the side.

Preacher moved quickly along the side of the house and reached the front door first. Major, who cleared the back of the modular home, waited at the back door. Chris covered a side entrance. It was agreed that once Preacher broke through the front door, the other two men would hold their positions and overtake anyone who attempted escape through the other entryways.

A crashing sound was heard as Preacher slammed open the solid wood front door. He wasn't attempting to be stealthy upon his entry. He hoped to frighten anyone inside to surrender and not put up a fight.

"All clear!" he shouted after a moment. "We've got a dead guy."

Major turned the handle and entered the house, finding himself in the kitchen, the stale air full of the smell of death.

"Whoa," he moaned as he quickly covered his mouth and nose. "Let's get some windows open here."

Major had been through this experience before. A decayed and decomposed body put off an unmistakable odor. The foreman who once ran the Reinecke Operating Unit had been dead for many days.

Major made his way into the living room, where he found Preacher standing over the man's body.

"No evidence of foul play, as you lawmen like to say," Preacher began his assessment. "I don't know, Major. It looks like his ticker might've quit. It's hard to tell how old he was, but he could've had a heart attack."

Chris returned from opening the windows in the house. "Everything looks normal back there. I did find this nitroglycerine bottle. It's empty."

"Coronary heart disease," mumbled Major. "It's the same thing Pops had. If he ran out of his meds, his chances of a stroke shot way up."

"That's a shame," said Preacher. "He either couldn't make it to a pharmacy in Big Spring, or they were closed. We're real lucky we don't require prescriptions."

"Yup," said Major. "Chris, find a blanket. We'll wrap him up and take him out back for a proper burial. Plus, we need to air out the house before the women show up. They're not gonna want to see this."

The three men quickly removed the man's body and set it under a scrub oak tree in the back of the house. They found a shallow spot well away from the house and respectfully laid the body in it. Chris said he'd bury it later. After paying their respects to the dead man, they mounted their horses and rode into the oil tank and pipeline area of the facility.

"Looks like the old guy shut everything down," said Preacher. "None of the wells are pumping, and I can't hear the hum of anything runnin'."

"Must be part of their protocol," Major surmised before pointing at a large solar array in a nearby field. "Look, there's enough solar panels to keep the place runnin'."

"Nice," added Preacher. "They might come in handy at the ranch, too."

They picked up the speed to a trot as they headed down a dusty road toward another set of buildings. Pipes and pumps were set in concrete throughout the fenced-in area. Two oil tanker trucks were parked in line, waiting to be filled.

"Where do you think the drivers went?" asked Chris.

Major raised his index finger to his lips, suggesting to his companions to stay quiet. He pointed to the right of the trucks, and Preacher followed his directive, slowly riding along the side of the vehicles with his rifle raised.

Chris waited at the front of the trucks while Major took the side opposite Preacher. He wanted to take every precaution after what they'd experienced in their barnyard a week prior.

The two men reached the back of the trucks at the same time and relaxed.

"Abandoned," said Major.

Preacher agreed. "Seems like it. You gotta wonder where they went, but I guess it doesn't matter."

"Major," started Chris, "I like it. It ain't glamorous, but it suits our needs. This large open field between us and the house is fenced with tall chain-link, more than sturdy enough to hold docile dairy cows. The concrete slabs on top of the underground tanks can be used to mount our milk-pumping equipment. I saw stacks of pressure-treated lumber, which can be used for cover."

"Yeah, I saw it too," said Preacher. "There's more than enough for us to build those outpost towers along our perimeter."

A cloud of dust appeared on the road to their west as Antonio drove the wagon with Adele Slaughter and their ranch hands. After they arrived, Chris took his group around the facility and showed them their new home, albeit an unusual one.

Preacher gave instructions to Antonio to get the Slaughters settled and to join them at the ranch in a couple of hours.

Then Major added a directive of his own. He reached into his saddlebag and retrieved a small notepad and a pencil. He handed it to his top ranch hand.

"Antonio, I want you to take an inventory of those building materials over there. Don't make a big deal about it either, okay."

"Yes, sir."

"I want the Slaughters to get comfortable, but we have needs regarding the security of Armstrong Ranch. Before they use up all of that lumber building milk barns, I want us to take what we need to build these outposts. Elevated structures around our perimeter will give us a sight advantage over intruders approaching the ranch."

Antonio nodded and rode toward the lumber supplies.

"Too harsh?" Major asked Preacher after Antonio rode off.

"Nah," replied Preacher. "Taking care of ourselves is not selfish. You can't give water to others from a dry well. Our job is to protect Armstrong Ranch and those who live there; then we can worry about these folks."

"Yeah. We gotta do what's best for us first."

CHAPTER 34

December 6
The Armstrong Ranch
Borden County, Texas

Major and Preacher rode along the dirt roads among the silent oil wells. The men were deep in thought as they contemplated the world in which they lived. The Armstrong Ranch continued to function as it did on a normal day. The same couldn't be said for others around Texas. Despite avoiding the devastation wrought by the EMP attack and the subsequent nuclear bombs, many of the state's residents were starting to experience food shortages and a medical crisis, as evidenced by the dead foreman at the Reinecke Operating Station.

"Pops used to talk about the days following Pearl Harbor," said Major, breaking the silence. "News wasn't readily available at the time. Folks listened to the radio, mostly. I remember studying about it in grade school. Our military was caught totally unprepared. The Japanese tore us up."

"A date that will live in infamy," said Preacher, shaking his head in disgust. "I guess they'll call the day the EMP dropped something along that line. Or will it be when the nukes started flying past? Those were both far worse than Pearl Harbor."

Major urged his horse up a slight incline, and Preacher followed close behind.

"Yeah, I suppose it's all relative," said Major as they approached Wildcat Creek, which was dry from lack of rain or snow. "We all have our own personal day of infamy, right?"

"Oh yeah, I've had mine," said Preacher dryly. They rode a little farther, through the dry creek bed, when Preacher continued. "You've known me a long time, Major."

"I have."

"Yet you've never asked me why I left the church and quit preachin'," added Preacher.

"I figured you'd get around to it when you were ready, and if you thought it was important for me to know."

Preacher blurted it out. "I killed a man."

"Okay," said Major unemotionally. "I kinda gathered that for the first time when you threatened that fellow the other night at the barnyard."

"You did?"

"Yeah, you were real angry, Preach. You said, 'I've killed before and I will kill you, God help my soul.'"

Preacher looked Major in the eyes. "I said that?"

"Yessir. Your words, not mine."

"I must've been pretty dang mad."

Major laughed. "That you were."

Preacher took a deep breath. Major sensed his old friend was troubled. At any given time before Major retired from Company C of the Texas Rangers, he could've performed an extensive background check on Preacher, but he didn't. What he might find wouldn't outweigh the things he knew about the man he trusted with his and his family's lives.

"Major, you know, when I was the preacher at Mount Zion Baptist, the congregation really liked me. They trusted me too. Too often, they'd come to me with their troubles like they were confessin' to a Catholic priest."

"I could see that," interrupted Major. "You're a pretty good listener."

"Well, I reckon I was a little too good. I would get personally involved in their troubles. I'd sit down and counsel mothers on how to deal with their kids. I'd offer to mediate disputes between business partners. Heck, I even talked a young girl out of getting an abortion and found her a family that would pay for the medical bills as well as provide her baby a good home."

"That doesn't sound so bad," said Major, who was encouraging Preacher to continue, as it seemed to weigh heavily on his friend's mind. Major didn't want the conversation to turn into an interrogation.

"One day, a little girl, just nine years old, came into my office crying after Sunday school. She wouldn't tell me what was wrong, but begged me to let her wait in the office until her mother came for her after my sermon.

"I didn't press her for answers and conducted the service. As I stood at the front of the church wishing everyone a blessed day, you know, I pulled her mother aside and told her about what had happened. She and the daughter always came to church alone. Her husband, the child's stepfather, never attended with them."

The white fencing of Armstrong Ranch came into view, so Major veered his horse to the left to approach the closest gate. He squinted his eyes and saw a car parked inside the fence where one of the hands stood guard.

"Did the mother offer any explanation?" asked Major.

"Nah, but a look of fear came over her face as she ran toward my office to retrieve her daughter. Anyway, a couple of Sundays passed and they didn't return to church. The whole thing gnawed at me for those couple of weeks, so finally, one evenin', I drove out to their farm just south of town."

"How'd that go?"

Preacher lowered his head and exhaled. "Not well, boss. Not well at all."

"Preach, you don't need to go back there if you don't want to," started Major, who felt profound sorrow for his troubled friend.

"No, I need to tell you because I've been livin' this lie for too long. Major, what happened that night was my day of infamy."

"Okay, go on," encouraged Major.

"I found the front door open and the mother lying on the floor with blood coming out of a gash in her forehead. She wasn't dead, just knocked unconscious. I heard a grunting sound coming from down the hallway, so I investigated. What I saw sickened me. The animal had tied the child to the bed and was—"

Preacher stopped his horse, and tears began to stream down his face. He wiped them away, smearing the dusty grime across his cheeks. He sniffled and tried to gain his composure.

"Preach, seriously, we don't need—" said Major as he attempted to console his distraught friend. He reached his arm out to touch Preacher's, but he shook his head no.

"Major, I lost it. I was out of my mind angry at what was happening to this innocent child. I didn't turn to God for guidance. I grabbed a table lamp and cracked the man's skull with it. He fell off the girl and rolled onto the floor.

"What happened next didn't come back to me until days later. The ceramic lamp broke into several shards of sharp glass. I took a piece and bludgeoned that child rapist over and over and over again. Major, I was insanely mad. I left his face unrecognizable. What I did to him was sadistic and against everything the Bible had taught me."

Major looked Preacher in the eye. "He had it comin'."

"Oh, believe me, I've justified killin' that beast over the years. Coverin' it up was easy too. The mother regained consciousness and found me on my knees, praying for forgiveness. After tending to that sweet child, she hugged and thanked me. She then took charge. After getting her daughter settled in her bedroom, we cleaned up the mess together. I got away with committing murder."

Major had devoted his life to law enforcement as a Texas Ranger, just like his family had done before him. He knew what murderers looked like. The man who raped that little girl had murdered her soul when he did. What Preacher did was act as judge and executioner. In Major's mind, there was a difference.

"My friend, God puts us in situations like those for a reason. Most likely, you saved two lives on that night and maybe more down the road. Sometimes, the only way we can defeat evil is to attack it head-on, without hesitation. In my eyes, and in the eyes of that mother and child, you are a hero. And no matter what, you will always be a preacher. Don't give up on God because of one *day of infamy*, right?"

Preacher smiled and nodded. He and Major grabbed hands and squeezed one another for strength. Major helped Preacher through this difficult conversation knowing full well his old friend might have to help him through one later.

CHAPTER 35

December 7
Gila National Forest
Reserve, New Mexico

The weather had changed dramatically as Duncan and Sook entered the Gila National Forest. They had traveled without incident through the remainder of Arizona, finding abandoned buildings to sleep in. The food provided to them by Banda and his friends had run out, and Duncan was beginning to get concerned. Their route took them through the heart of Gila, which meant very few dwellings or opportunities to forage, and now the much colder weather posed additional risks.

Duncan's survival training was designed for Middle Eastern climates, as the conflicts in Syria, Iraq, and Afghanistan had continued during his early years in the military. However, his transition to black-ops work for the CIA took him all over the world, so he'd studied survival techniques in all circumstances, including heavily forested, high-altitude areas like Gila.

Basic survival skills didn't change based upon location or climate. The first step was to adopt a survival mindset. More than any skill he learned, Duncan recognized a strong desire to live and the establishment of a plan were most important. Surviving a life-threatening situation required a willingness to sacrifice and suffer pain and mental anguish in order to avoid death.

Duncan learned the *SPEAR* approach to adopting a survival plan of action—**S**top, **P**lan, **E**xecute, **A**ssess and **R**e-evaluate. By creating a systematic approach to any survival situation, Duncan was constantly reaffirming his desire to live, as well as providing himself encouragement while blocking out negative thoughts or panic.

After adopting a survival frame of mind, certain basics applied. In extreme weather, a person could only survive three hours without adequate shelter. In the deserts of the Middle East, the goal was to avoid heat stroke, so planning required shelter to avoid the heat and thus minimize water loss. In the high mountains of the Rockies, for example, one would avoid hypothermia, so the goal was to minimize heat loss.

Thereafter, your body would dictate your ability to survive. The human body was composed of seventy-eight percent water. Going three days without proper hydration results in organ failure due to dehydration and then death. Oftentimes, in a fit of desperation to rehydrate, many turn to any water source they discover. The water-borne pathogens, metals, and minerals found in these water sources, if untreated, could cause dysentery. This disease exacerbates dehydration and thus hastens death.

Having left the dusty flatlands of Arizona, the dense forest was a relief. The lack of industrial plants adding to the perils of the water gave Duncan confidence that their horses could drink freely, as could he and Sook.

The next challenge for them would be finding shelter for their first night in this new environment. Half of their travels across New Mexico would involve a significant increase in elevation before they dropped down toward the plains and relative flatland of the eastern part of the state. At that point, he'd be able to smell and taste Texas.

Flurries began to float through the air, and Duncan could feel the moisture content of the atmosphere pick up. Their tarp and supplies found at the meteor crater attraction would not be enough to protect them from plunging temperatures.

As they continued to move forward, Duncan noticed a sign that read *Reserve Ranger District, three miles.*

"Sook, we must find a place soon. I believe the snow will come next."

"This is like home," she added. "Mountains and forest. Snow and cold."

Duncan chuckled as he urged his horse up the steep incline. He wondered how long it would take Sook to stop referring to Sinmi-do and North Korea as home. Then a wave of sadness overtook him. If the DPRK had fired nuclear weapons at the U.S., he was sure the U.S. had rained hellfire upon their entire country. The likelihood of Sook's family surviving that were slim.

They approached a small roadside picnic area, where a truck towing a small camper had parked. Duncan held his hand up to instruct Sook to stop. He quickly dismounted and handed the reins of his horse to Sook. He wanted to approach the camper on foot, and cautiously. The two of them on horseback made for a large desirable target.

Sook hung back as Duncan moved into the forest, taking advantage of the trees to conceal his approach. A whiff of smoke reached his nostrils, which raised him into a heightened state of awareness. Carefully, with his rifle ready, he moved from pine tree to pine tree, using their aged trunks as cover. The smell of something burning increased, and he was sure the campers were cooking on an open fire.

The flurries turned to big, fat flakes, causing Duncan to gain a sense of urgency. They needed to find shelter soon. He approached the clearing as a gust of wind forced the smell toward him. Duncan grimaced and covered his mouth and nose. He'd smelled death many times, but burnt flesh was especially rancid and unmistakable.

He scanned the perimeter of the small picnic area and the vehicle that obscured its view from the road. A smoldering campfire produced a small amount of smoke as the body that lay across it starved the flames of oxygen.

The doors to the pickup truck and the retro-style camper towed behind it had been left open. Debris was scattered about the gravel beneath the rig. With the snow falling heavier now, Duncan didn't need to waste time clearing the area.

Whoever had murdered the man lying facedown in the fire had most likely left after looting the man's belongings. Also, he didn't want Sook to see the very dark side of humanity that existed in

America, just like it did in North Korea. People could be sadistic and cruel to one another regardless of nationality. He hoped to shield Sook from that undeniable truth in her new home.

Duncan made his way back to the road and jogged on the wet shoulder until he reached Sook. She was waiting dutifully with his horse, occasionally glancing behind her to scan for threats.

"Is it safe?" she asked in a hushed tone when Duncan arrived.

He climbed on his horse and shook his head. He hoped the wind didn't draw the stench onto the road.

"C'mon," said Duncan with a sigh. He looked to the darkening sky and allowed the white flakes to land on his face. The cold, moist snow snapped him out of his funk. "Let's see if we'll have better luck at the ranger station."

Several minutes later, they found the gates to the Reserve, New Mexico, ranger station. They were locked with a heavy link chain and a padlock. Undeterred, the two riders navigated on a trail that led from the road into the woods before coming out onto the gravel road a few hundred yards up the hill.

Duncan was leery of staying anywhere near the murderous scene he'd just encountered. Based upon the smoldering fire, the man had most likely been killed the night before. Whoever was responsible might have gone to the ranger station next.

As they rode around a bend in the driveway leading up the hill, he saw two vehicles parked in front of the single-story block and brick building. Once again, out of precaution, he went ahead on foot, holding Sook back for her safety.

As Duncan quickly moved around the building, he was pleased to see there wasn't any indication of foul play, as he'd seen at the campsite. The doors and windows were locked, but also intact. It was quiet in the woods, and he took a chance to bang on the door.

He pounded it with his fist three times. "Is anyone here? We're looking for a place to sleep for the night. That's all."

Then he focused his concentration on any sounds emanating from the building. There were closed blinds obscuring his view of the interior, and he watched to see if any of them moved.

Nothing.

Duncan returned to the rear entry of the building and found a fist-sized river rock, which was used as a door stop. He heaved it through the glass of the door and then listened for a reaction inside.

Still quiet.

He entered the building, which had a very simple layout. The foyer opened up into an open space featuring maps and images of the Gila National Forest. There were two small offices, which contained desks and seating. A small kitchen with an adjacent bathroom completed the twelve-hundred-square-foot facility.

It wasn't going to yield much in the way of supplies, but it would shelter them from the elements. Pleased with that, he opened the front door to retrieve Sook. What he found surprised him.

CHAPTER 36

December 7
Gila National Forest
Reserve, New Mexico

Duncan had to make a decision. A hundred and fifty pounds of food stood before him, completely unaware that he'd opened the door. The deer was beautiful, standing in the falling snow, looking in Sook's direction. Shooting the beautiful animal would not be easy for Duncan. Frankly, as he'd grown older, he'd rather shoot an enemy than a deer. However, they were out of food, and the ranger station didn't appear to provide them any options.

There was another consideration that his mind instantly processed as he raised his rifle. The retort from the Barrett would echo throughout the forest. If the killer of the camper down the road was still around, they might descend upon the ranger station. Then again, echoes had a way of distorting sound and its source. In the wilderness, pinpointing the exact location of the gunfire would be difficult.

Duncan steadied his aim, focusing on the deer's neck. He knew from his hunting days as a teen, there were several considerations when choosing what part of the deer to shoot. Every hunter hopes for a single kill shot. Despite the act of killing itself, the majority of hunters don't want the animal to suffer unnecessarily.

He gently squeezed the trigger.

At this relatively close range for a sniper of Duncan's caliber, his bullet easily found the mark and took down the deer quickly and efficiently. As he walked through the doorway onto the covered porch, he caught a glimpse of Sook moving through the woods.

To her credit, she didn't shout to Duncan. She chose to determine the cause of the gunfire rather than expose herself to danger. Duncan wondered whether children growing up in North Korea were wired differently than American kids. *Were they more attuned to danger and the risks of confronting anyone with a weapon?*

Duncan met her halfway. "It's okay. I shot a deer. The building is safe."

Sook hugged him, and then she looked over his shoulder. "A deer," she muttered. "We no longer have them in the North. They were killed for food for the parliament members. Now they are all gone."

Duncan took her by the arm and guided her away from the dead animal. They needed to retrieve their horses, and then he'd set about field dressing the deer.

An hour later, the horses were secured in a utility fenced area behind the building, with buckets of fresh water from a nearby stream. The snow was heavier now, so Duncan pulled the tarp over the space and tied it down with paracord. Next, they set about the task of draining the deer.

Using a half-inch nylon rope he found in a closet, Duncan tied the deer up by its hind legs. Then he threw the rope over the rafters of the front porch and pulled the deer into the air before tying off the rope. It was a struggle for him to hoist the heavy animal off the ground, but Sook grabbed the deer around the waist and gave her best effort to assist. Between the two of them, the deer now hung from the rafters in a perfect position to be gutted.

"Sook, this can be messy and bloody. You can go inside now if you want."

"No, I want to help and learn. I have seen death, remember?"

Their encounter with the North Korean patrol boat flashed through Duncan's mind. Sook had been unfazed by the violence.

Duncan pulled his knife from its sheath and slowly spread the fur on the deer's stomach. He ran his forefinger along the incision point to mentally mark the spot to make his cut.

"You start at the bottom at the neck," he began to explain. He wasn't sure how much of the explanation Sook would understand, but he decided to stop underestimating her. Every step of the way, she'd surprised him. "I am cutting deep enough to get through the skin starting at the base of the neck. Blood will trickle out slowly at first."

Duncan looked at her again and decided to proceed without a warning. This part of the process was grisly. He began to cut through the animal's muscle and cartilage around the neck. He looked to Sook, who continued to shine the light of a small lantern they'd found on the process. She was unfazed.

"When I was in medical training, we dissected small animals," she said unexpectedly. "This was my favorite part of training. I could be a surgeon one day."

Duncan smiled. "What I am doing is like surgery. It requires a process of cutting through skin, then to muscle, through the ribs, and then finally the organs. This next part is the most difficult. I have to cut through the stomach muscles and the rib cage. Are you ready?"

She nodded her head and continued to focus her gaze on the deer's carcass.

Duncan took a deep breath and reached into the body of the deer. He was now covered in blood, which made him realize he'd have to switch to his backup sweatshirt with the Meteor Crater logo plastered across the front. *Or I could ride back to Texas covered in blood. That would scare the bad guys away.*

"After you cut through the belly muscle, you have to pry your knife between the ribs like this," said Duncan as he maneuvered the knife back and forth with a prying motion, causing the rib cage to break.

Sook continued to study Duncan's work, learning every step of the way. After he removed the esophagus, the remainder of the deer's internal organs came out fairly easily.

"Okay, now we allow the rest of the blood to drain out."

Duncan wiped his knife on his shirt and replaced it into its sheath tied around his leg. Despite the cold, he took off his shirt, leaving only a Grand Canyon Skywalk tee shirt on, which he'd found at the Hualapai Airport.

Sook approached him and took the bloody shirt out of his hands. "I will go to the stream and wash this for you. We can dry it over the fire while you cook the meat."

For the next hour, Sook organized their supplies and washed Duncan's shirt. He skinned the deer and began to butcher it. Initially, he feared they would not be able to take all of it with them. He lamented that the best they could do was eat well that night and the next morning.

But his foraging in the building provided him an option. In one of the offices, Duncan found a soft-sided expandable lunch cooler. He packed deer meat and snow into it for the trip. There were also a couple of large ziplock baggies in the kitchen. He thought the remainder of the deer meat would provide at least four days of meals before they'd have to forage or hunt again.

After they ate, Duncan and Sook studied the maps hanging in the visitors' area. The direct route home took them through the heart of the Gila National Forest, which consisted of hiking trails and a few dirt service roads. The paved roads led them around the forest but added over a hundred fifty miles to their journey, not to mention the likelihood of interactions with others.

"Sook, if we take this direct route, we can follow the trails and creek beds until we reach the other side at this point."

He pointed to the map at Truth or Consequences, New Mexico. The small town, originally called Hot Springs, was renamed after the popular game show from the early days of television in the 1940s. The game show was known for its format in which players would be required to perform a task correctly, or they would suffer the consequences.

In a post-apocalyptic world, the rules were the same.

CHAPTER 37

December 8
The White House
Washington, DC

President Harman and her chief of staff sat alone in the White House on their first evening following the EMP and the nuclear warhead exchange with North Korea known in the international media as the Twelve-Hour War. Most government buildings associated with the nation's defense, such as the Pentagon across the Potomac and the State Department located in the Harry S. Truman building, were running on newly restored power via large generators. As members of her cabinet and high-ranking officials returned to Washington, they were asked to come by the White House to meet with Chief of Staff Acton, and the president if deemed necessary.

"James, the outpouring of support from our allies in Europe, while appreciated, comes under a cloud of betrayal, in my opinion," started the president. "Had they stood firmly by our side after the EMP, we might have considered a first strike against North Korea in retaliation. Instead, Kim Jong-un unloaded on us first, and we're left mourning the death of millions of Americans."

"Alani," started Acton, who rarely referred to the president by her first name, "right now, we need to talk as old friends and longtime political allies. You have an opportunity to rise to historic levels among presidents."

President Harman laughed. "You mean as the only president to preside over the demise of the greatest economic and political empire in history?"

"No, hear me out. It's been said that all empires collapse

eventually, and recent events confirm that America may be no exception. What lies ahead for us is arduous, but it is also an opportunity to unite the nation under your leadership. Alani, you can mold America into your vision because, in essence, the nation is starting over in many respects."

"James, where *do* we start? Our infrastructure is in shambles. Society is collapsing before our eyes. We can't get our military to enter the major cities that weren't destroyed by the nuclear bombs, for fear of getting into a firefight with large gangs."

"First, and this proposal is controversial, which is why I'm throwing it out there among friends, so to speak," began Acton.

The president gestured for him to continue.

"We can only help those who want to help themselves. The best thing we can do for these cities in chaos is to contain them. The reports from our military commanders liken Detroit or Chicago to being in a war zone. Let's cordon these metropolitan areas off so the violence doesn't spread into the suburbs or more rural areas. Law-abiding citizens just trying to survive shouldn't have to live in fear."

President Harman leaned back in her chair and folded her arms, superficially giving herself a hug. "Aren't we sentencing a lot of people within these cities to their death?"

Acton was blunt in his response. "Sadly, yes. But we both know we can't save everyone. Why not focus on those who are willing to accept our assistance, and then also lend a hand in the recovery effort at the same time?"

She allowed an imperceptible nod of approval. "Under your proposal, at some point, the populations of major cities would thin out and, as a result, become more controllable. In the meantime, the rest of the country would sing our praises."

The president was beginning to grasp the concept. There would be some pain and suffering in some locations, but those regions were out of control anyway.

"In theory, anyway," he added.

"We still have the issue of logistics," said the president. "It could take a year or more to repair our power grid. We don't have enough operating vehicles to move supplies around, much less protect the convoys. Even in the countryside, there are reports of looters and armed thugs openly defying our military. They're ambushing convoys and stealing supplies meant for everyone."

"I have a proposal that will require a bit of détente, if you will," said Acton. The president appreciated the fact that her chief advisor had considered all of these variables.

"I'm listening."

Acton hesitated, then made his pitch. "Texas is the key."

"Of course they are," interrupted the president sarcastically. "I despise that woman, James. She took advantage of our nation in its moment of greatest weakness. Politically, at least for her constituents, it was a brilliantly orchestrated move. I don't think her now former fellow Americans would agree."

"I don't disagree with any of that, and I'm sure Burnett is well aware of the ramifications of her blindside move. Therefore, what I'm proposing will help her out of a pickle too."

"Go ahead."

Acton leaned forward and lowered his voice although the doors were closed and the White House was mostly empty. "I have sources in Austin telling me Texas is beginning to experience significant food shortages. Their borders are being overwhelmed by increasingly desperate refugees, too. With the right nudge here and there, our people, meaning the CIA, could start a revolt in which her Texans grew disillusioned with their new country and President-designate Burnett in particular."

"Don't they have elections coming up?" she asked.

"Yes, so the timing would be perfect. What I propose is using Texas as a staging area for international relief supplies and replacement parts for the power grid. Their ports are temporarily closed due to the tsunami from the nuke off of Galveston, but dredging operations are already under way to open the channel. Their commercial airports stand empty without flights coming in or out. The military bases, which they took from us, contain more than enough personnel and operating vehicles to assist in the receipt and subsequent dispersal of supplies."

The president shrugged and crossed her legs. After tapping her fingers on the chair's arms, she responded, "I don't know, James, we've already promised to leave them alone with respect to their secession. We're paying them to take in refugees. What's in it for her?"

Acton chuckled. "I'll liken it to airline travel. Have you noticed on commercial flights, all the passengers are very chatty during the flight until the flight attendants roll out the carts with drinks and snacks. Once you feed them, they quieten down."

"Do you think Burnett will use her resources to help Americans in exchange for relief supplies to feed her own?"

"Absolutely," started Acton in response. "Let me reach out to Austin and suggest a deal. If she says no, we'll turn up the heat from within her borders and from those knocking at her door."

"What does that look like?" asked the president.

Acton smiled. "We have plenty of political operatives within the state who are ready to stir up trouble for the former governor. All we have to do is give them the word. You know, the usual community activism and astroturf political rallies, which we're so good at coordinating."

The president was liking where this was going. No matter what she might say openly, she'd never forgive Texas for its betrayal. "You mentioned turning up the heat outside their borders as well. What do you mean by that?"

"I have it on good authority that a couple of days ago she asked for an assessment on their border security weaknesses around their very large territory. There are some areas, such as where the interstates enter Texas, where tens of thousands of people are amassed, demanding entry into Texas. Along the western borders, the crowds are sparse and so is the security. What we need to create is a dam break. I need to identify a point where the flood gates can be opened, and starving, desperate Americans can enter Texas looking for shelter, food, and medical treatment."

President Harman scowled. "How would she react?"

"Best case is that thousands of Americans enter Texas and find a way to survive," responded Acton.

"She'll eventually seal the breach, right?"

"Yes, most likely through force and loss of life. Once word spreads of her tactics, she'll face even more pressure, especially from the international community. We could reach out to our friends at the United Nations to declare a humanitarian crisis, for example."

The president nodded. "Okay, put it in motion, but only if she refuses. If the worst-case scenario occurs, then we'll offer to fix her problems, but then she'll need to sweeten the pot. It will be an interesting negotiation."

CHAPTER 38

December 9
The Gold Rush Byway
West of Julesburg, Colorado

"Welcome to Colorado, kids!" announced Cooper to his snoozing passengers. To make sure they were awake, he flicked the toggle switch on Red Rover and allowed the air horn a short blast. Cooper received grumbles and moans from his siblings. He understood where they were coming from. While Red Rover had proved to be reliable, steady transportation as they traveled across Wyoming and southwestern Nebraska, the front seat was tight for three adults, leaving them full of stiff limbs and cricks in necks.

Palmer appeared to come to life first, which was no surprise to Cooper. Riley had always been the last to rise in the morning. For that matter, he was always one of the first to sleep at night. The boy needed his sleep, Cooper thought to himself.

"Coop, you made great time since we looped around Sidney," said Palmer, referring to a small town near Interstate 80 and the highway they'd traveled since leaving Wyoming.

"Yeah, traffic was light," said Cooper with a chuckle. "I hated to wake y'all up, but it's time for a fuel stop, and it's also getting late in the day."

"That'll be the last of our stored diesel," said Riley.

"Yeah, I know," said Cooper. "We also have a town coming up, so I need the navigator to look at our options on how to avoid it."

Riley pointed ahead, and Cooper began to slow the truck. The highway was about to intersect with another major road. He dropped the truck into third gear and slowed as they approached the road. As they entered the three-way intersection, just ahead of them was an interesting sight.

Palmer laughed. "Are they kidding? This is their airport?"

"It appears to be their local drag strip, too," added Riley, pointing to a sign advertising Friday night racing.

"I guess that's not so far-fetched," said Cooper. "They're both built alike. Before the apocalypse, I imagine folks from all over the world traveled to Julesburg, Colorado, and on the weekend, the local good ole boys raced their hot rods."

They sat idling for a moment while Palmer studied the map. Cooper constantly checked the mirrors to make sure nobody was sneaking up on them.

Palmer looked up from the map for a moment and asked, "Do y'all know anything about airplanes?"

Cooper chuckled. "Ask Riley, he knows everything."

"Screw you, Coop," Riley shot back.

"I'm just kiddin'. Seriously, didn't you used to talk to Dallas a lot about the planes in the military?"

"Yeah, and all I learned was that only a dang fool would jump out of a perfectly good airplane with nothing but one of those parachutes attached to their back."

Palmer continued. "What I'm getting at is this. Maybe some of those crop-duster planes parked over there run on diesel. I mean, I don't know, but it's worth a try, right?"

"I agree," said Cooper. "It beats sittin' out here in the open. Worst case is we bunk down for the night in one of the hangars. Whayda think?"

"Let's take a look," mumbled Riley, who was still upset at his brother's ribbing. He was the most sensitive of the Armstrong children, but also the first to stand up in an attack upon his family.

Ten years prior, the Environmental Protection Agency had set a goal of outlawing leaded aviation gasoline by 2020. The Federal Aviation Administration had opened up testing of alternative replacement fuels, including diesel, which was widely used in Africa, South America, and Asia.

Aircraft manufacturers like Cessna led the charge toward diesel engines being placed in their smaller aircraft. Prior to the collapse, certain rural markets, like Julesburg, were approved to test the new design.

Cooper drove around the locked gates, using Red Rover's four-wheel drive to drive down into a drainage ditch, and up the other side. He slowly drove into the heart of the complex. Two large hangars flanked a double-wide trailer across from the dual-purpose stretch of asphalt.

As they drove toward the back of the property, they observed several fixed-wing airplanes parked off to the side. Three utility trucks were parked haphazardly in front of the buildings.

"Wow!" exclaimed Riley, pointing at the end of the runway. "Check it out."

A single-wing Cessna had crashed short of the runway. It had apparently hit so hard that it cracked into two pieces, with the tail section thirty yards behind the nose, which had planted into a mound of dirt and turned the cockpit upside down.

"I bet the EMP killed its power," said Cooper as he slowed to a stop. He shut off the motor. "Listen up, we need to make sure we're alone before we start sightseeing. Grab your rifles, and let's stick together. We'll take our time 'cause we can't afford any surprises."

They spent the next thirty minutes methodically clearing each building, including storage sheds. Inside the trailer, they found folded-up cots that could be taken with them when they left. Mechanics coveralls were hung inside the closets and would help them stay warm as the colder weather moved across the Rockies. Two sets of binoculars were also found, adding to their ability to conduct surveillance on the final leg of their trip.

The best find was a fenced-in utility yard containing a fuel depot. A large cylindrical tank was marked—*Aviation Diesel.*

"Yeah, buddy," exclaimed Riley, who immediately shouldered his rifle. He picked up the pace as they entered through the unlocked gate. "Let's see if there's any left."

Riley grabbed the nozzle and squeezed the handle, but nothing came out.

"Dang it. Empty!" Riley quickly voiced his frustration.

"Hang on," said Cooper. "The power is off, but it seems to have a hand pump up here."

Cooper handed his rifle to Palmer, then walked between the diesel and aviation gasoline tanks. He hopped onto a platform and gripped a steel handle that was attached to the top. He began pumping.

"Try it now," he said to Riley.

Riley squeezed the handle, and the diesel poured out.

"Awesome!" Riley shouted enthusiastically.

"It just needed the pressure built up," said Palmer. "I wonder how many other people tried to get diesel out of that tank and didn't try what Coop just did."

Riley responded, "Hopefully, if they did, they left twenty or thirty gallons for us."

Cooper jumped off the platform and rejoined the group.

"Well, now that we've found some diesel, even if it's for airplanes, will it work in our truck?" asked Palmer.

"Here's what I think we should do," replied Cooper. "Let's empty our cans and fill up Red Rover. We'll refill our cans with this stuff, but I wanna plan on dumping it if we can find auto diesel. This is high-octane and may be too rich for our truck."

"It might make him run faster," quipped Riley as he slapped Red Rover on the hood. Of the three travelers, he'd become the fondest of the old Landy. "Heck, even if we could get him up to fifty, that would get us home faster."

Cooper laughed and slapped his brother on the back. "I'm not sure it works like that, brother. Will you take care of the fuel? Palmer and I are gonna go through these abandoned trucks and see if there's anything of use."

"I'm on it," replied Riley before adding, "Hey, keep an eye out for a toolbox. You know, wrenches, screwdrivers, etcetera. Ya never know when they'll come in handy."

Cooper gave a thumbs-up and led Palmer to the stalled trucks. They were typical utility vehicles with an open-bed pickup design and toolboxes mounted on the sides. Their foraging proved successful.

They found a toolkit that would please Riley, jumper cables, a portable jack stand that Red Rover did not have, a can of Fix-a-Flat, and a variety of quart-sized automobile fluids, including oil, transmission, brake, and coolant.

Under the bench seat of one of the trucks, Palmer found a basic first aid kit, which also contained face masks, additional gauze pads, and a tourniquet.

As it turned dark, they all gathered in the trailer and assigned security shifts for the night. Inside the office was another franchise location of Palmer's new favorite grocery store—a vending machine. She'd successfully cleaned out several at the hotel the night of the EMP. Those munchies were long gone, as was the food provided to them by Fiorella.

The rodeo kids hadn't eaten in thirty-six hours. Riley was the most vocal about their lack of food, but after several bags of chips, he was feeling better about their situation.

They loaded up their truck and prepared it to leave in a hurry if necessary. As was customary, they planned out their next day before they settled in for the night.

Palmer studied the map and found a country road to bypass the small town of Julesburg. They'd experienced enough mayhem around these typically quiet hamlets to look for alternative routes, even if it took them a few extra hours.

The same thought process applied to the route they chose toward Texas. The truck enabled them to make better time and swing well to the east of the Denver area to avoid where the nuclear fallout would be the greatest. The highway they chose ran due south to Amarillo.

"Whadya think, Palmer?" asked Cooper before turning in. He'd been driving for hours and was exhausted.

She set down the map and looked in the dim light at both of her brothers.

"Straight south along Highway 385 is about three hundred fifty miles. In a perfect world, that's about ten hours in Red Rover."

"Sounds good to me," said an enthused Riley.

In a perfect world, Cooper thought to himself. *This world is far from perfect.*

CHAPTER 39

December 9
Interstate 44
The Red River Bridge
Near Burkburnett, Texas

For two weeks, first Oklahomans, and then Americans from all over the Great Plains and Rocky Mountains began to gather near the Texas border with Oklahoma. The Red River, so named for its reddish-brown color derived from the red soil over which it flowed, had become a natural barrier between those who were starving and desperate, and Texas, which was an oasis in their eyes.

The methods employed by Texas to control their borders combined man-made structures, like fencing, which included concertina wire, and natural boundaries like the Red River. However, while these border protections provided physical barriers to crossing into Texas, the heavily armed members of the Texas Military Department provided a strong mental deterrent. None of the thousands of refugees seeking entry were willing to engage in a shoot-out with the Texans, until now.

Fifteen miles north of Wichita Falls lies the small town of Burkburnett, which was the point of entry into Texas along Interstate 44. The long span of bridge across the Red River had been packed with pedestrians until this cold, below freezing night when the Texas Guardsmen moved in with two water-cannon trucks to push back the crowd.

Adjutant General Deur warned his commanders to avoid the mistakes that had occurred near Beaumont in the days following the EMP. He was keenly aware that international reporters were embedded within the refugee camps that encircled Texas. While the bridge crossing over the Red River at Burkburnett was not near as tall as Beaumont, the visual of human beings jumping into the river, fleeing the crowd-dispersing tools employed by the guardsmen, would play badly in the press and put considerable political pressure on their newly formed government.

He hesitated to undertake the measure, but he considered it necessary for their own safety. The throngs of individuals that gathered in Oklahoma were forcing the pack closer to the Texas border fencing and checkpoints. The ostensibly lucky ones closest to the checkpoint gates were now being mashed into the concrete road barriers put into place.

The people on the bridge had been living in squalor, without food or water. Sanitary conditions were horrendous as the crowds increased on the bridge. For fear of losing their place in line, not that there was one, people began defecating where they stood, emptying their bowels without shame or embarrassment. When it was time to sleep, they lay on the concrete bridge amidst urine and feces. The conditions were animalistic and inhumane.

Yet admitting them into Texas was not the answer, but something had to change. Deur's instructions to his commanding officer at Burkburnett were simple—move them all off the bridge. Execution of his commands, however, was not.

Those on the bridge had grown accustomed to vehicles coming and going on the Texas side of the border. There was an armed contingent of guardsmen who rotated in and out of guard duty near the concrete barriers and fencing.

When the two mobile water-cannon trucks slowly approached the barricades, the sleeping refugees did not pay heed. As the horde of homeless refugees slept, they were infiltrated by two dozen new arrivals. The men wearing dark clothing might have blended in with the group during the day, but at night, walking stealthily toward the barricades with their automatic weapons at low ready, they were menacing.

This contingent of fighters, assembled and dispatched to the bridge crossing the Red River, was a combination of CIA operatives and military personnel with no ties to Texas. Their orders—create a breach into Texas that could be captured on film by the media. When they asked about rules of engagement, the response they received was *the uglier, the better.*

The water cannons and the U.S. government operatives were about to collide in the center of the bridge. The first stage of *ugly* was about to begin.

CHAPTER 40

December 9
Interstate 44
The Red River Bridge
Near Burkburnett, Texas

Using silenced M4 rifles, the well-equipped operatives began to implement their plan. From their intelligence, they were aware that the Texas Guardsmen were ordered to avoid firing upon the refugees unless absolutely necessary, such as a breach of their barricades. This allowed the operatives a jump-start on their assault of the Texas border.

With the near silent spit of their rifles, they shot out the large portable lighting that illuminated the barrier system. The explosion associated with the bulbs awakened the refugees, immediately grabbing their attention like a tin can rattling down the street could pique the curiosity of the Walking Dead.

The group stumbled to their feet just as the operatives were cutting multiple holes in the chain-link fencing, allowing them entry into the maze of concrete barriers. The speed at which the operatives moved caught the Texas Guardsmen by surprise, and they became easy targets as they mistakenly showed themselves to the operatives. One by one, as they raised their heads above the protective barriers, they lost their lives.

The operatives were then caught by a surprise of their own. Change is often achieved when a confluence of events occurs. The operatives had the upper hand and would've been able to declare the operation a rousing success until the water cannons opened up on them.

Rather than being able to push forward against the unsuspecting Texas Guardsmen, they were beaten down by the water cannons. Their attempts to fire upon the armored vehicles were fruitless.

As the relentless barrage of water knocked them to the pavement or forced them behind the barricades, the seasoned operatives sensed they were outmatched. Some were badly injured, losing their weapons in the process. Others continued to maintain cover behind the concrete barricades for safety. The paid mercenaries considered themselves beaten.

However, the determination of the refugees trumped the will of the operatives. After living in the filthy and wretched conditions, hoping for the day that Texas would grant them entry, the mass of humanity moved forward.

And they took up arms as they did. They grabbed the M4s knocked from the hands of the operatives. They picked up the weapons of the dead guardsmen. They advanced against the water cannons, resolute and with a sense of purpose that would not be soon forgotten.

The first several hundred managed to avoid the intense streams of water and burst into the open clearing on the Texas side of the bridge. Sprinting to freedom, they sought dry ground in Texas, which they were sure held all the answers.

As the operators of the water cannons finally found their aim, the thousands behind this initial group got bogged down attempting to force their way through the fences, barricades, and bodies that began to clog the paths around the Texas border crossing. Frightened and desperate, Beaumont repeated itself as refugees began to jump off both sides of the bridge.

But the dam had broken, and for those on the Oklahoma side of the bridge, the proverbial flood, this crack in the Texas armor was all they needed as the bum rush for the Texas oasis began.

*****

Alarm bells rang throughout Sheppard Air Force Base in nearby

Wichita Falls. Prior to the collapse, Sheppard was primarily used as a training base for airmen and civilians of all branches of the military. Because of its proximity to the major border crossing fifteen miles to its north, it also housed a quick reaction force made up of military personnel reassigned from Fort Hood in Killeen, designated the TX-QRF.

The TX-QRF was comprised of ground-based and helicopter teams. The Texas Air National Guard contributed two Sikorsky Black Hawk helicopters to Sheppard with heavy-caliber machine guns mounted underneath. In their history, these choppers were never used to fire on Americans, or Texans, until now.

After the team assembled, the Black Hawks lifted off and raced toward the bridge, covering the fifteen miles in just minutes. Without hesitation, they began to fire warning shots upon the thousands of people attempting to climb over one another to gain a foothold in Texas, unknowing that the *wet foot, dry foot* policy, which applied to Cuban refugees entering Florida, didn't mean diddly-squat in Texas.

When the warning shots didn't produce the desired results, the fifty-caliber tracer rounds fell from the sky on the refugees in an endless barrage of death. The water cannons continued to fire until they drained their tanks nearly simultaneously. The crowd began to retreat, pushing and shoving one another to avoid the hellfire raining down upon them.

As the troop transports from Sheppard arrived, the field commanders were advised to continue with the removal of the refugees from the bridge. They ordered the mobile water cannons to fall back, and they were replaced with armored D11 bulldozers supplied by the U.S. Army.

Previously used to remove stalled vehicles from the bridge and to place the concrete barriers in position, the D11s were now ordered to clear the bridge of all debris, human or otherwise.

The nine-hundred-horsepower behemoths roared to life and awaited the mobile water cannons to clear the area. The drivers, infuriated by the demise of their fellow guardsmen at the hands of the refugees, grabbed the controls of the D11s with a death grip and silently vowed revenge. Followed by two dozen Texas Guardsmen, the one-hundred-ten-ton machines each chose a lane of the interstate and lumbered forward.

The D11s were equipped with a twenty-two-foot-wide S-U blade, known as a semi-universal blade, which had more curvature than those designed for grading. This made the military version of the D11 ideal for carrying and pushing various types of material. The bulldozer's blade was modified slightly to include a dozen sharp teeth along the top of the steel attachment to catch debris, which might cause a jam in its hydraulic mechanisms. It also contained twelve-inch-long forks spaced every foot along the bottom of the S-U blade.

The second wave of refugees had become bogged down in humanity. DO NOT CROSS tape fluttered in the breeze from the mangled chain-link fencing and the bridge's safety railings. As the D11s approached, those closest to a new life in their perceived oasis, Texas, had no chance. Some of them tried to turn and run, but they were unable to force themselves against those at the rear, who were cramming themselves onto the bridge.

They ran into the razor wire, became entangled, and flailed to pull themselves free, ripping gashes into their bodies. Blood poured onto the bridge, mixing with the feces and urine of those who had occupied the space just an hour before.

For a while, the retreating refugees got the upper hand, pushing the crowd back toward Oklahoma. Not to be deterred in their quest to cross the bridge, those at the rear gathered their strength and momentum as they continued to push toward Texas. The masses of people swayed back and forth in a series of agitated waves.

Pushing forward, the mighty machines shoved everything in their path toward Oklahoma. Concrete barriers, fencing with razor wire, and refugees, both dead and alive, were piled together like rubbish at a landfill.

Those who were older and smaller fell down and were trampled underfoot before the blades, which were the width of the highway, gathered them up. People were releasing guttural, primal screams in utter fear as the massive machines pursued them, gored them with the teeth of their steel blades, and moved relentlessly forward.

"*Look out, it's not stopping!*"

"*Run for your lives!*"

"*Go back! Go back!*"

Shouts of despair and agony filled the air as the twin dozers continued to push everything in their path back to Oklahoma. The refugees sought safety, and many chose to exit the bridge by jumping into the Red River below. Bodies landed on their backs, killing the jumpers instantly. Those who survived the leap were treated to a shower of blood flowing from the drainage scuppers from the bridge. The Red River had truly turned *red*.

Those who didn't choose the jump-off-the-bridge exit option or survive the rush back to Oklahoma became mutilated and crushed under the power of the D11 bulldozers.

By daybreak, a pile of unrecognizable corpses and body parts, mixed with concrete, wire, and debris, created a new border barricade on the other side of the Red River Bridge. A new line in the sand had been established.

In the dark and cold of that night, both sides of a political struggle accomplished their purpose. Texas cleared its bridge, and Washington created its media firestorm.

CHAPTER 41

December 9
Gila National Forest
Near Truth or Consequences, New Mexico

"In North Korea, laws were passed to provide women equality." Sook continued her conversation with Duncan as their horses trudged through the fifteen inches of snow that had fallen in the last forty-eight hours. The storm moved through quickly, and the sun provided much-needed warmth on their bodies. "With these laws, women were allowed to work at a job, we could inherit from our families, and we were free to marry and divorce."

"America is the same way," said Duncan. "But I heard that North Korea has arranged marriages."

"Yes, sometimes. Over time, arranged marriages disappeared so couples could make love matches. In the country, traditional families require children to get their parents' permission to marry. Your choice was made for you years in advance."

Duncan slowed their pace as the slope ahead of them began to decline at a steeper rate. He stopped them for a moment and studied the map he'd pulled off the wall at the ranger center. Duncan had followed trails to avoid the highest mountain peaks of the Gila National Forest, which were to his south. In order to avoid the town of Truth or Consequences, he led them parallel to the Rio Grande River toward the Mexican border.

The thinning of the forest coupled with the rougher terrain indicated they were close to the river and the much flatter plains of Eastern New Mexico. Pleased with their progress despite the snowy weather, Duncan folded up the map, and the two pressed on.

He wanted to continue the conversation with Sook, as he was just as fascinated with life for the people of North Korea as Sook was with the American way of life.

"Duncan, have you been married?"

"No. I have always been focused on my military career."

Sook rode quietly for another moment before shyly asking, "Do you have a girlfriend at home?"

Duncan began to laugh. "No. No girlfriend at home. Did you have a boyfriend?"

"No. The boys I knew from the village were all fishermen. They were destined to live their lives on Sinmi-do. I wished for more."

Duncan laughed heartily at her statement. "We have a saying in America. Be careful what you wish for."

Sook smiled. Duncan realized that she rarely allowed herself a genuine, deep from the belly laugh. She continued to be restrained. To him, it appeared North Korean women were still subjugated to the men despite the laws enacted in Pyongyang. It was part of their culture.

"I understand," she finally added. "I dreamed of plans for my life, but I learned fate does not care about my plans. I dreamed of escape to the South, but I never dreamed of going to America."

"Sook, I am a firm believer in fate. Everything happens for a reason, and sometimes, those reasons are not very clear. I think a lot about the death of my brother Dallas. I question why God would take him from our family."

Duncan stopped again near the final drop into the Rio Grande River valley and looked to Sook. He was becoming emotional. "Some people spend their whole lives seeking their fate. Others, like myself, run into their fate head-on in unexpected ways. Sook, I will never forget when I opened my eyes and saw your face. I knew that we were meant to be together. There is a reason people like you and I find each other. Maybe it is God's will, or maybe it is fate. But I know this, you have changed my life, and I thank God we are together."

Sook looked down and began to cry. Duncan didn't know what to do. He had never poured his heart out like that to a woman before. Being vulnerable had not been an option in this soldier's hardened heart.

"Duncan, I have fallen in love with you," Sook blurted out her feelings.

Duncan fought back tears that he hadn't experienced since Dallas died. "I love you too."

Suddenly, the tender moment was ruined as gunfire erupted in the valley below them, spooking Sook's horse and throwing her into the snow.

"Sook, Sook! Are you okay?" asked Duncan as he frantically dismounted and rushed to her side.

Her body didn't move as she lay in the snow. The gunfire continued, but Duncan ignored it as he dropped to his knees.

Sook groaned a little and then opened her eyes. "That was very rude."

When she smiled, Duncan began to laugh. He spontaneously kissed her, which caught her off guard. Her eyes grew larger, and then she pushed her head off the snow-covered ground. She kissed him back.

Duncan and Sook had fallen in love in the middle of the apocalypse. Unfortunately, there was no time for roses, chocolates, or romantic dinners. The gunfire continued, and Duncan, who would never stop being a soldier, knew that duty called.

"Stay here," he instructed before giving Sook another lingering kiss. He retrieved his rifle and jogged through the fresh snow toward a cliff overlooking the highway below.

CHAPTER 42

December 9
Truth or Consequences, New Mexico

The famous New York Yankee catcher, Yogi Berra, was known for creatively mangling the English language with quotes that strangely made sense, in an odd sort of way. As Duncan moved through the few remaining trees to a bluff overlooking the interstate several hundred feet below him, he caught a glimpse of the source of the gunfire and muttered aloud one of Berra's most well-known—*it's déjà vu all over again.*

This time, however, it was a military convoy under attack by gunmen. Duncan quickly assessed the situation. Three M35 deuce-and-a-half transports were being escorted by Humvees to their front and rear. The large camouflaged cargo trucks were stalled in the middle of the northbound land of Interstate 25, with their occupants huddled on the far side from Duncan's point of view.

He scanned the terrain below him, knowing the source of the gunfire was somewhere between his perch on the bluff and the interstate. Using his rifle's scope, he followed a service road adjacent to the highway. The rock outcroppings obstructed his view as he tried to pinpoint the source of the fire.

Frustrated, he moved to his right along the bluff, careful not to lose his footing in the wet snow. This was not a scenic overlook with safety rails. A slip meant a deadly tumble of three hundred feet down the rocky slope to his death.

This wasn't his fight, but it was his country under assault. Duncan ignored the risks and moved laterally along the bluff, constantly checking his position in relation to the battle. He was moving farther away, but the angle was allowing him a better view of the service road and the source of the automatic gunfire.

An explosion occurred as the left side tires of the lead Humvee were shot out. Emboldened by their success, the attackers shot out the tires on the last of the M35s in line. The convoy was now stalled and, from the looks of things, outgunned.

Duncan used his scope again to search the valley. There! Barely visible beneath the rock formations were two vehicles parked parallel to the road, nose to tail. He could make out several sets of legs lying in prone positions nestled in the thick bed of snow, using rocks and a guardrail as cover. Because the shooters had the high ground, the military personnel escorting the convoy couldn't get a good shot at them.

However, Duncan could. He eased to the edge of the bluff. He slowly lowered his body and crawled on his belly to the edge, spreading his legs wide, then used his feet to dig into the snow for stability. After wiggling his body back and forth to create a comfortable place in the snow, he steadied his rifle to begin shooting.

The angle and the obstacles did not afford him a very good shot at his targets, but the goal was not necessarily to eliminate the threat, but rather, to provide the convoy an equalizer. As far as Duncan was concerned, if he could chase off the gunmen, it would be a victory.

He began firing at the attackers' legs. The .338 Lapua Magnum rounds soared through the air, with each two-hundred-fifty grain bullet tearing up the snow and pavement as they struck around the shooters. A glancing blow wounded one of the shooters, and a mad scramble for cover ensued.

As the men sought the protection of their vehicles, Duncan sent round after round into the roofs and windshields of the old SUVs.

He switched to his fifth, and last, magazine. When he and Park had opened the rifle case to reveal the weapon intended to kill Kim Jong-un, he thought the fifty rounds of .338 ammunition would be more than sufficient to make the kill shot and get the two men to the extraction point. Circumstances changed that, and he was now down to his last ten bullets. He would need to use them wisely.

Duncan dropped his head to the ground as several rounds fired by his prey stitched the rocky face of the bluff. They were returning fire, although now the attackers were caught in a quandary of their own. The convoy's soldiers began to return fire upon the men. It was the attackers who were now pinned down between Duncan's powerful Barrett and the automatic fire of the soldiers' M4s.

The battle had reached a turning point for the attackers. Their sporadic shooting in both Duncan's and the convoy's direction indicated their heart was no longer in the fight. Duncan had a decision to make as well. *Do I spend my last ten rounds defending others?*

More bullets were sent in his direction, this time flying just over his head, tearing the bark off the pine trees behind him.

Decision made. Duncan fired back, again breaking out the glass windows of the trucks, sending bits of glass all over the men hiding behind them.

After a moment in which the attackers paused their return fire, a hail of gunfire headed toward him. Duncan pulled back from the edge of the bluff slightly to allow the bullets to whiz by. He could feel the displaced air as they flew past.

Duncan was angry now. These guys should give it up. He crawled forward and saw the men scrambling between the vehicles to wedge themselves against the bluff. He fired again and again.

This time, one of the bullets caught a body part, and the scream of agony could be heard from Duncan's position.

He decided to continue to bring the heat. His shots might not kill, but they could certainly drive home a point. *Give it up!*

Duncan fired three more times, using strategically placed shots that might ricochet off the trucks and near the hiding attackers. Then he waited.

The troops with the convoy stopped firing as well, most likely because they couldn't see the targets from their vantage point. Duncan focused, waiting for an opportunity to fire again.

The engines abruptly started on the trucks, and there was a mad scramble for the attackers to pile into them. Duncan only had a few more rounds to unleash, but he saved them. He couldn't risk giving up his final bullets to shoot at taillights.

The vehicles sped off, out of Duncan's view and away from the trailing bullets sent in their direction by the troops. The battle appeared to be over.

Duncan carefully backed away from the edge and stood on the bluff overlooking the battlefield. Several soldiers set about changing the damaged tires on their vehicles. One of them slowly walked in Duncan's direction. He was carrying a bullhorn and binoculars.

The man scanned the bluff, and Duncan raised his arm to wave. The man raised the bullhorn and shouted to Duncan, "I'd like you to come down here, friend. Allow me to personally thank you for your help!"

Duncan thought about it for a moment. While he appreciated being recognized for his efforts, he would be exposing Sook to a group of Americans who might not appreciate her being in their country. Also, Banda had warned him that martial law had been declared and weapons were being confiscated. He only had a few rounds left for the Barrett, and he couldn't afford to lose them.

"Come on down! Let me shake your hand. At the very least, let me reimburse you for the ammo you used to save our collective butts!"

Duncan felt better about approaching the convoy. He hustled back to where he'd left Sook and found her dutifully watching over the horses. The two of them would need to talk further about their kiss and how they felt about one another, but Duncan decided to put off the conversation until after they greeted the convoy.

Twenty minutes later, Duncan and Sook emerged on the interstate and slowly rode in the direction of the convoy, which had just completed replacing the damaged tires. As they drew closer, two soldiers rushed in their direction with their weapons raised.

Duncan, who had slung his rifle over his shoulder to appear nonthreatening, held his arms high and nodded to Sook, instructing her to do the same. He hoped he wouldn't regret this decision.

Two more soldiers came around the last Humvee in line and

trotted to catch up with the armed personnel. Duncan decided to speak up.

"Easy, fellas, we were invited by the officer with the bullhorn. I'm the guy from up there."

They began to lower their rifles even before they were instructed to do so by their commander.

"Lower your weapons, gentlemen. This man is one of us, a true patriot."

CHAPTER 43

December 10
Carlsbad, New Mexico

A nation-state like North Korea that spent most of its gross domestic product on its military had plenty of personnel to conduct war games and imagine various attack scenarios. A decade prior, the thought of invading the United States was considered, but discarded as a pipe dream. But as the DPRK continued to develop its nuclear weapons program until it was on par with other nations, it then focused its resources on expanding its regular army to include its special operations forces. These elite commando units were dispatched to North America to infiltrate the U.S. if the opportunity arose to wreak havoc.

With the initiation of the EMP attack, Kim Jong-un's Lightning Death Squads leapt into action. They positioned themselves throughout the U.S. to continue the DPRK's assault on their nemesis.

The nuclear attack a week later, while unexpected by the Lightning Death Squad's commanders, was uniformly welcomed by the tens of thousands of North Korean operatives who were embedded in America.

The nuclear detonations were a setback for the DPRK's plans for America. Unfortunately, thousands of their elite forces perished in the nuclear attacks. They were, however, considered heroes. Besides, their numbers were being replenished with reinforcements entering through Mexican ports and across the U.S. southern border, as well as through already established routes in Canada.

Most of the DPRK commanders in the United States were unaware of the devastation inflicted upon their homeland of North Korea by the American nuclear retaliatory strikes. Communications via satellite telephone with their superiors tucked underground near Pyongyang had ceased, but that was not unusual. There was a contingency plan for this, and a new hierarchy of commanders on the ground was established.

When Commander Kyoung-Joo Lee, the senior officer of the Lightning Death Squads in North America, left St. Louis, he was tasked with gathering together their special operations forces to infiltrate Texas.

Their first goal was to reunite with thousands of DPRK operatives located in major cities in Texas. Next, they were to do what the satellite-deployed EMPs had failed to do—take down the Texas power grid.

By the time Lee reached Carlsbad Caverns in New Mexico, a predetermined rally point for new commandos entering from Mexico, he'd been advised that he had been elevated to commander of all North Korean units within North America. He was no longer just a loyal commander of the Lightning Death Squads. Lee had been elevated to the status of a general and was now in command of the entire operation to deal the final blow to America.

Lee had received this glorious news just before his group reached Truth or Consequences, New Mexico. For the six hundred miles prior to that, he and his men had driven from St. Louis with reckless abandon. With adrenaline pumping through their veins, they murdered everyone who crossed their paths. The killing inspired his men and ensured there would be no eyewitnesses to a group of North Korean commandos on U.S. soil.

His decision to attack a military convoy at Truth or Consequences was a risky one. Lee was already behind schedule, as he had to drive farther to the west than he desired. The roads along the western border of Texas were clogged with refugees, making travel slow and burdensome. He and his handpicked team of six had just been notified of his promotion. As a result, they vowed to be cautious and not expose their new leader to a deadly bullet or a crazed mob.

When they came upon the military convoy by accident, he considered avoiding a conflict by simply pulling to the side and allowing the convoy to pass. Then he considered what a great prize this convoy might be. Not only could they commandeer any supplies and weapons being transported, but the U.S.-marked military vehicles could provide them an edge as they traveled through West Texas toward the population centers of Dallas, Austin, San Antonio, and Houston.

He'd expected a fight with the soldiers who guarded the convoy, but he had total confidence in his elite warriors. What he didn't expect was the sniper who had pinned them down during the attack.

Lee didn't think it was plausible for a military sniper to guard this convoy every mile of its travels. No, the shooter was in the wrong place at the wrong time from Lee's perspective. He and his team were lucky to escape the bullets raining down upon them.

When the shooter stopped, rather than press the fight, he decided it was time to move on and stay focused on his task. But still, he wondered who the shooter was and how he'd come to be on that ridge hovering over him.

After their escape, they descended upon the North Korean encampment southwest of Carlsbad. Located in the Carlsbad Caverns National Park near the famous caves, the location was chosen by the DPRK war planners because the one hundred plus caves would provide them cover from nuclear fallout, as well as suitable shelter while their forces regrouped.

Carlsbad Caverns was known for its deep rocky canyons, desert wildlife, and the dozens of caves formed within the limestone cliffs. Lee and his men knew nothing of the area, opting to follow road signs as they approached from the northeast. From radio communications, he knew that many of his commandos had already arrived and secured the largest of the caves as their base of operations.

Perimeter security had been established around the Big Room, as it was called by the National Park Service. The natural limestone chamber measured nearly four thousand feet long and six hundred feet wide.

He was greeted by the security team with the highest respect afforded generals in his homeland. It was an odd feeling for him at first, as he always considered himself a soldier's soldier. However, he understood the importance of hierarchy and chain of command. Every North Korean did. Yet he always considered himself on an equal level with his men, willing to kill or be killed on the battlefield alongside them.

Lee was escorted up a path by several soldiers, some of whom ran ahead of his entourage. When they reached the top of a steep incline, his team slowed their pace, allowing Lee to enter the Big Room a few paces ahead of them.

The scene shocked Lee as he stopped in awe of the reception. Hundreds of men began to rise to attention, immediately providing their new commander a snappy salute. In that moment, Lee transitioned from loyal commander of one element of the Lightning Death Squads to their new general.

He managed a smile as he returned the salute. He was up to the task.

CHAPTER 44

December 10
Office of the Adjutant General
Austin, Texas

"Madam President, they were like cockroaches," lamented Deur as he attempted to explain to the new president of Texas about his difficulties in rounding up the refugees who'd breached the border crossing. "This was a professionally coordinated attack. Our guardsmen who survived the initial stages reported the use of silenced automatic weapons and the discovery of a dozen heavy-duty bolt cutters used to breach our fencing."

"Kregg, what's done is done, and now I have to deal with the optics," interrupted President Burnett. "For now, I want to keep abreast of your progress in hunting down these lowlifes. Dead or alive, I don't care. Got it?"

Before Deur could respond, the president disconnected the call. He was frustrated because they had lost a lot of good personnel during the melee. Today, as the sun rose, the grisly scene was on full display for media cameras. His men had accomplished their goal of clearing the bridge completely, but he wondered at what cost.

His phone rang again, and he let out an audible groan, as he expected it was the president to give him another earful. He answered and was relieved that it was his TX-QRF commander from Sheppard.

"Sir, we have a situation," the commander said immediately without even so much as a hello. "A group of armed men have stormed the campus of Midwestern State University in Wichita Falls. Based upon our initial analysis, they appear to be part of the refugees who succeeded in crossing the bridge last night."

Deur fell back into his office chair and spun around to his computer terminal. He brought up a map of Wichita Falls and then zoomed in on the Midwestern State campus.

"Okay, Commander, I have a map pulled up here. Tell me what you know."

"Yes, sir, of course. The majority of students, faculty, and personnel at Midwestern are Texans. After the EMP hit and the state of emergency was declared, they returned to their homes around the state. Some of the out-of-state students accompanied their friends, but several hundred chose to remain in the dorms at the university."

Deur interrupted. "After the U.S. grid went down, didn't we order the power cut to our own nonessential government facilities like colleges?"

"Yes, sir, we did. However, at colleges where students and faculty members had no place to go, we maintained power in certain dormitories, temporarily providing housing for those from out of state, um, I mean out of country."

Deur found a campus facilities map in his archives and studied it for a moment. "Okay, Commander, tell me about the situation."

"During the early morning hours, hundreds of refugees made their way from the Red River checkpoint into Wichita Falls, largely passing by Burkburnett. We began to receive reports of—"

Deur shook his head in disbelief. "Let me interrupt you right there. How can our personnel out of Sheppard miss hundreds of people walking down the interstate to Wichita Falls? Heck, to get to Midwestern, they practically walked right past the base."

"Sir, I'm not making excuses, but our quick reaction force was focused on closing the floodgates, so to speak. We stopped the refugees from crossing first, with the intent of mopping up the rest today."

"Okay, got it. I take it this initial group disbanded as it reached Wichita Falls?"

"Yes, sir, that's correct. We are working with local law enforcement in the city to locate them now. There are reports all over Wichita Falls of break-ins, assaults, and shootings. It's incredible how a hundred desperate people can create a chaotic situation so quickly."

"Let's get back to the campus," started Deur. "What've we got?"

"A hostage situation, sir. At least a dozen or more have been observed at a dormitory named Legacy Hall. While power was shut down to all the facilities at Midwestern except for a maintenance and administration building, Legacy Hall remained open to the displaced students and a few faculty members from out of state. Well, you know what I mean."

Deur shook his head. He too was having trouble transitioning from being part of a state to a newly formed country. He had made the mistake of mischaracterizing Texas at a recent meeting with Burnett, which drew her ire afterwards. He had held his tongue during the conversation because she was aware he had misgivings about the secession push initially. Deur needed the job, and those within the Burnett administration didn't have to worry about where their next meal was coming from. His thoughts and opinions were, therefore, safely tucked inside his mind.

"How many hostages?"

"Maximum head count, according to Midwestern officials, is near two hundred thirty."

Deur recalled what he knew about the college. They had celebrated their two-hundredth anniversary earlier in the year and boasted about their proud history. Through the years, the college had been recognized as one of the top public liberal arts colleges in the U.S. It strived to attract out-of-state students with special tuition rates. Based upon this fact, Deur was somewhat surprised that the number of misplaced students still residing in Legacy Hall wasn't much larger.

He brought up an archived summary of the housing units at Midwestern. Legacy Hall was their newest co-ed dormitory, housing primarily lower classmen. Based upon the design drawings, Legacy Hall was capable of housing five hundred students.

His commander's estimates meant the building was half full, a considerable amount considering the firepower the hostage takers possessed. Between the weapons lost by their own men, coupled with automatic rifles of unknown origin found at the scene, it was likely the men who had taken control of the building were all heavily armed.

"Do you have an extraction plan?" asked Deur.

"No, sir, not as of yet. The ground level of the facility includes limited entrances, all of which appear to be barricaded and guarded. The upper levels are the residential suites, and our sniper teams stationed on the adjacent buildings report that the students are being used as human shields by their captors as they observe our maneuvers around the dorm."

"Okay, Commander," started Deur. He needed to inform President Burnett, but he wanted to get his key personnel in place first. She'd be looking to him for answers. "I'm going to deploy our units from the 71st Troop Command here at the Bee Cave Armory in Austin. As you know, they have worked closely with the feds in the past when they mobilize for large-scale social unrest situations and counterterrorist operations. They'll take the lead on the rescue mission."

"Sir, what should I do in the meantime?" asked the commander.

"Cordon off the perimeter, get your men in place in order to contain the situation, and don't do anything that'll get those kids killed. I'll be in touch after I speak with the president."

Deur disconnected the call and set the phone on his desk, which was cluttered with written reports and maps. The digital age had been placed on hold, and his job had reverted back to old-school methods, which included mounds of paperwork.

He allowed himself a moment to think. If the president was upset about last night's debacle, she'd bust a gut over two hundred plus college kids being held hostage. And what made matters worse, they were technically American citizens within her charge. Ugly didn't begin to describe it.

CHAPTER 45

December 10
Bee Caves Armory
Austin, Texas

Sitting atop a hill in the now upscale Bee Caves neighborhood of Austin was a seldom talked about, and mostly unknown, armory with roots that swirled in Cold War intrigue. The smallish, twelve-acre site located off Bee Caves Road was once simply referred to as *The Hilltop*, but was now home to the 71st Troop Command of the Texas Military Department.

Initially utilized as an outpost to provide law enforcement assistance in the event of a mass-casualty event in Austin, Bee Caves' role expanded during the cold war. Because of the importance and close proximity of Bergstrom Air Force Base, an integral part of the U.S. Tactical Air Command, the site was utilized as a fire control center and air defense facility.

During the Cold War, the suburban hilltop location had all the equipment necessary to track inbound targets and launch defensive surface-to-air missile strikes. Because of its proximity to residential areas, the Air Force chose to operate the missile defense aspect of Bee Caves under cover. The missiles were hidden in tents surrounded by large berms, protecting them from enemy attack and nosy neighbors.

As the Cold War ended, the facility's mission shifted. The missiles were removed, the 111th Area Support Group was installed, and the military operations took on a peacetime feel, except for the special operations team created to respond quickly to high-value target operations directly under the purview of the Department of Defense.

These operations varied from hostage-rescue missions, such as when the young school-age girls were captured in Somalia, to extraction of embassy personnel in potentially hostile situations. The 111th was trained for the hostage scenario under way in Wichita Falls.

When a series of military cutbacks took place ten years prior, the 111th and its personnel were absorbed into the Texas Guard and fell under the command of the 71st Troop Command. Their missions were the same, acting as an adjunct arm of the Department of Defense, but as a part of the Texas Military Department. The specialists at Bee Caves also provided material support to civil defense authorities.

Captain Doug Garland, a compactly built Irishman originally from New York, had the look of a Special Forces soldier in the sense that he did not look like a soldier at all. He was wearing khaki pants and a Vineyard Vines polo shirt, not unlike any resident of the surrounding Bee Caves community. But the thirty-nine-year-old captain had countless deployments under his belt around the globe.

Captain Garland commanded fifty-five soldiers based at the 71st. In a given year, he'd send his teams to a dozen different countries. When he received the call from Deur, he grimaced when he realized this would be the first deployment of his teams onto U.S. soil, or what used to be U.S. soil.

He summoned his top lieutenants and shared the intelligence received from Deur over the phone. He assured them that the situation at Midwestern was fluid, but that might change by the time they arrived there.

"Gentlemen, we treat this like every mission. Instructions to the teams are the same. Don't bring anything that makes you look military. We don't know what we're dealing with here in terms of the hostage takers, but we certainly don't want them to think we're juicy targets."

The extraction mission, dubbed Operation Mustangs in honor of the Midwestern school mascot, would commence as soon as the teams were on the ground and in position. They would take helicopters into Sheppard Air Force Base and ride in civilian vehicles to the campus. The captain warned his lieutenants against escalating the situation because of their mere presence.

Within an hour, the teams were assembled and loading their tactical gear into helicopters at nearby Austin-Bergstrom International Airport, where the now closed down Air Force base had existed.

When one thought of American Special Ops, they thought of SEAL teams, largely because of media mischaracterizations. In reality, the SEALs were a tiny fraction of American Special Operations. The Army dominated Special Ops, and proper references when referring to Special Forces would be directed at Green Berets.

The Green Berets under Captain Garland's command, like their counterparts in the Army, were nicknamed the Quiet Professionals, primarily at their annoyance of all the attention SEAL teams got. Captain Garland once said jokingly, "*What are two things a SEAL gets when he finishes a mission? A movie deal and a book contract.*"

While the SEALs got the glory for missions like capturing bin Laden, Army Special Forces got tasked with operations which were a lot longer, messier, and more complex. Operation Mustangs would be no different.

Garland's unit made the trip to Sheppard in just over an hour. Upon their arrival, the Air Force base was bustling with activity. Large makeshift detention facilities had been built in an open field near the runways. Armed patrols walked the perimeter, which was wholly enclosed by two rolls of concertina wire.

Dozens of people wandered aimlessly within the compound, sometimes stopping to talk, but mostly appearing to be in a daze. Captain Garland assumed these people were captured after the debacle at the Red River. Their demise briefly crossed his mind before he turned his focus back to this mission.

He was escorted into the base command offices, where he was briefed by Sean Varnell, a lieutenant colonel with the TX-QRF. The information provided by Varnell was essentially the same as Garland had received from Deur. The only thing new was a head count of the hostage takers, which now appeared to be seventeen.

Within an hour of their arrival, the TX-QRF had supplied Garland and his men with supplies and vehicles to hunker down for an extended standoff. Both commanders agreed that this standoff should be resolved by negotiation rather than gunfire, if possible.

Garland provided the lieutenant colonel these parting words as his team saddled up and headed toward Midwestern. "Victory in situations like these does not necessarily mean we engage the hostage takers in some form of combat. Despite the fact they have the upper hand, at least in their minds, at the end of the day, they are sleeping a long way from home, away from their families, and in an uncertain, dangerous environment.

"Make no mistake, my teams are made up of seasoned professionals who are just as adept at psyops as they are at killing. We will take whichever route the situation dictates, without hesitation."

Chapter 46

December 11
Near Campo, Colorado

"It's gonna be really cold tonight, Coop," said Riley, who had a knack for predicting changes in the weather based upon which of his former rodeo injuries hurt the most. The concept that aches and pains correspond with, or even predict, upcoming changes in the weather had been around since the days of ancient Greece. The typical explanation from the medical community was that the drop in barometric pressure that comes with a storm causes soft tissue and lubricating fluids around joints to expand, which in turn irritates nerves. Oftentimes, significant injuries could cause sensitivities around arthritic joints, resulting in increased pain associated with weather changes.

In any event, Riley, the Armstrong family's walking, talking barometer, was usually spot on with his predictions. Cooper looked toward the western sky and studied the clouds. The quickly forming gray cloud formations were being created by strong updrafts of air. Thus far, they'd been fortunate to travel through mild weather by December standards. The dense, towering clouds forming toward the Rockies seemed to confirm Riley's internal barometer—the pressure was dropping and a cold front was on the way.

"Palmer, let's do some quick calculations," started Cooper. "I've got enough fuel to get us to Texas. If we run out, I figured we'd look up some of our buddies in Amarillo and borrow a few horses. Heck, that red Texas soil will be so beautiful, I could run to the ranch."

"Yeah, we're gettin' closer," said Palmer, who leaned to the right and looked past Cooper toward the growing cloud formation. "But I agree with Riley, a storm's comin', and we can't outrun it."

She studied the map again and attempted to calculate the mileage. She glanced up at the fuel gauge, and then her attention was back to the map.

"I think the next town is called Ocampo, or somethin' like that," said Riley.

"Campo, not Ocampo," mumbled Palmer. "Okay, here's what we've got. Campo doesn't appear to be very large based on what I can tell, and we're only about fifty miles to the state line and another ninety miles or so to Amarillo after that."

"It's two hundred miles to the ranch from Amarillo," added Cooper. "No matter how you cut it, we're two days and two full tanks of diesel from home. How far is it to Campo?"

"Riley, what's that sign say up ahead?" asked Palmer.

Riley pulled out the binoculars and tried to hold them steady. Red Rover rode more like a hay wagon than a G-Wagon.

"Cargill, with an arrow pointing east," he replied.

"Okay, we'll be in Campo in five minutes," said Palmer.

Cooper rolled his head on his neck to release some tension. Throughout their trip, they'd exercised extreme caution as they approached any town or major road intersection. Those initial days in Canada had taught them that locals became very territorial after TEOTWAWKI—the end of the world as we know it. Every traveler was eyed with suspicion or as a source of something valuable they wanted.

As a result, a three-hundred-fifty-mile day trip, which would ordinarily take ten hours at Red Rover's pace, required three days in a hyperaware, almost paranoid, post-apocalyptic world.

"Y'all know the drill," started Cooper. "Weapons ready. Binoculars scanning for anything that can be perceived as a threat. If need be, we'll park the truck and do recon before we approach the town."

"Sis, do we have any back-road options?" asked Riley, who'd become suddenly serious. He had a way of changing from a laid-back, seemingly unexcitable guy, to one whose Spidey senses kicked in along with his adrenaline.

"No," she replied. "Just like the last hundred miles, we are in no-man's-land."

The trio continued slowly down U.S. Route 385, which had carried them from Wyoming and could take them to the highway's termination in Odessa, Texas, if conditions allowed.

"Here we go, y'all," said Cooper. "Look alive."

The live oak trees lining the two-lane highway as they entered town reminded Cooper of the Texas Hill Country. Several stalled vehicles were up ahead, and he slowed to maneuver the truck through them. Every structure, every stalled vehicle, and every out-of-place fallen tree presented a potential threat. Traveling home in this stressful environment meant they could never let their guard down. Never.

"It's a straight shot all the way through town, Coop," observed Riley as he refocused his binoculars. "I do see a couple of people standing up ahead at an intersection. I believe we've grabbed their attention."

Cooper asked, "Are they armed?"

"No rifles," replied Riley.

"Is there a bailout option in case there's trouble?" Cooper was assessing his options.

"Gravel parking lot to the right by an RV park."

"Palmer, where does the side street take us?" asked Cooper.

Palmer grabbed the map and gave it a quick check. "Don't know, Coop. It's not on the map. If we gotta use it, use it. We'll figure it out."

"All right, as Momma says, *pretty as you please*," said Cooper. "We're goin' in."

Riley lifted his rifle so he could quickly fire through the sliding passenger-side window of Red Rover. Then he let out a laugh. "Or as Pops used to say, act like you own the place."

Tensions were high as Cooper drove past the man and teenage girl standing on the side of the road. The looks they received were of astonishment and curiosity, and not hostility. The young girl waved, and Riley spontaneously waved back. *Nothing to see here, moving along.*

Riley and Cooper monitored their side-view mirrors to confirm they weren't being followed. They both exhaled a sigh of relief as they continued heading south.

"Look, Boise City, twenty-eight miles," said Palmer, pointing toward a highway sign as they left the outskirts of the small town. "That's halfway to Texas!"

Excitement began to build as they realized their long journey was almost over. Cooper thought of the number of times the three of them had returned from a long rodeo trip and high-fived one another when they crossed the Texas state line. He imagined their jubilation would be tenfold this time.

The houses became fewer and far between when Riley exclaimed, "Lookey there, if it isn't Clarence's Truck Stop. Just in time for a refuel and a hot dog."

"Very funny, goober," said Palmer, who tried to swat her brother but missed as he quickly moved his head.

Their older brother intervened. "Get serious, y'all. We're gonna see if we can top off here and fill up the cans. That'll be enough to get us home."

Riley readied his rifle, and Palmer manned the binoculars once again. Cooper pulled over to the side of the road so his navigators could surveil the truck stop.

"It's more of a gas station than a truck stop," Riley pointed out. "There are diesel pumps and large white fuel storage tanks. I see a red pickup parked at one of the pumps. Also, the plate-glass front door seems to be broken out."

A strong gust of wind swept across the open field to their right, causing Red Rover to sway back and forth despite being loaded down with passengers and gear. Cooper felt a sense of urgency. These cold fronts could move very quickly and catch them off guard.

"Gotta go for it," he announced as he rammed the gear shift into first with his left hand and slowly released the clutch. Cooper had finally gotten a knack for the right-side steering wheel. The clutch and gas pedal positioning were no different than any manual transmission vehicle.

He looked in all directions and saw that the truck stop stood alone on the highway. There were no cars, houses, or people in sight, so as he approached, he quickly cut the steering wheel to the left and hastily found his way to the back of the building.

"Hurry, and don't shoot each other," Cooper instructed as they bailed out of the truck with their rifles.

Riley and Palmer took one side of the building, and Cooper took the other. He approached two storage sheds and found them both to be locked with padlocks. When he approached the front of the building, he peered around the corner and saw Riley doing the same on the other end. Cooper held his palm up, instructing Riley to stay in position.

Crouching low beneath the windows on the front of the building, Cooper moved along the corrugated steel façade and reached the broken glass door. He nodded to Riley and motioned with his fingers for his brother to join him.

Just as Riley arrived, Cooper nodded, and the men entered the small dark building. Staying low to the ground, Cooper went right and Riley went left. They were careful not to crunch their boots on the broken glass and, once inside, walked heel to toe to avoid any noise.

The room was cleared, and next, they walked through a dark opening into a garage repair area. They couldn't see anything in the dark.

"Riley," whispered Cooper, "grab a quart of oil and hand it to me."

Riley slowly backtracked and retrieved a plastic bottle of 10W30.

Cooper took the bottle and whispered, "Ready?"

Riley patted him on the shoulder and raised his rifle to shoot at anything that moved. Cooper threw the oil across the garage, where it banged off a tool chest and ricocheted against some empty cans on a workbench. The sudden racket was designed to stir anyone hiding in the garage.

Nothing. Dead silence. Cooper took a chance and pulled out a small flashlight, which he used to illuminate the garage. It had been ransacked, but nobody was inside.

"Good deal," said Cooper as he rose out of his crouch. "Grab Palmer. We'll see about some diesel, and maybe we'll check in at the Clarence's Truck Stop motel."

CHAPTER 47

December 12
Midwestern State University
Wichita Falls, Texas

Captain Garland had to make a decision. Cries for help could be heard emanating from Legacy Hall as hostages appeared in all the windows of the upper floors. Word of the tactical team's presence must've spread through the dorm, agitating the hostages and making their captors nervous. Some could be seen being forcibly removed from the windows by the armed gunmen.

During the night, a member of local law enforcement had bravely delivered a two-way radio to the main entrance of Legacy Hall to open up lines of communication with the hostage takers. Thus far, any attempts at negotiation had been largely rebuffed. Unlike most hostage situations which involve one, in domestic cases, or just a small group of criminals, usually with a political agenda, this situation was unique.

The hostage takers weren't seeking publicity for a cause. They weren't demanding equal custody of a child, nor did they seek a ransom per se. Their demands were fairly straightforward—admittance to Texas for them and their families.

Like all hostage situations, regardless of the relative merits or sympathies associated with the demands, the hostage takers were still either terrorists or criminals and had to be stopped, then apprehended, in accordance with the law.

Garland was a skilled negotiator and experienced at diffusing hostage situations. He'd learned the most critical step in any hostage negotiation was listening. Most people were terrible listeners. Garland had a knack for it. He would listen to what they'd say without interruption, disagreement, or unsolicited evaluation of the hostage takers' position.

In the Midwestern situation, boiling down the demands of the hostage takers took all of two minutes—*let us go, and let us into Texas.*

He tried to establish a rapport with the different spokesmen designated by the hostage takers. They were unified in their response. His ability to diffuse the situation by offering to escort them back to Oklahoma without repercussions, which was a lie, fell on deaf ears.

Garland implored Deur to gain President Burnett's authority to give the hostage-taking criminals the impression a deal had been struck, only to arrest them and deport them back to Oklahoma anyway. The president refused because the international media was watching, and she didn't want the optics of using subterfuge in this delicate situation. She wanted the matter resolved quickly and with no loss of life to the hostages.

Early that morning, Garland ordered sophisticated surveillance equipment to be delivered to Wichita Falls. Both sight and sound inside Legacy Hall, even if limited, would provide him valuable insight into the hostage takers' moods and defensive positioning. There had to be an opening.

Resolution of a hostage situation was slow and tedious. The entire process required methodical logistical planning, intelligence gathering, and tactical support. Any team attempting to take control of a hostage situation had to be properly outfitted with everything from protective vests to flash-bang grenades.

A tactical assault to rescue hostages carried a high casualty rate for two interrelated reasons. First, it meant that negotiations were at an impasse or had broken down completely, leaving the hostage takers in a hopeless mindset. Second, if a firefight ensued, the resulting panic and confusion might result in hostages being inadvertently killed or wounded.

There could also be a threat of imminent harm to the hostages. After the surveillance equipment arrived, his teams quickly began the task of marking out the locations of the hostage takers inside the dorm. While it was difficult to identify whether any of the sleeping people in the dorm were hostiles, the wall-penetrating surveillance cameras could easily identify armed men stationed inside the building. Their surveillance indicated the armed men congregated near each floor's exit points—stairwells and elevators.

Captain Garland received a full set of building drawings from the university's maintenance administrator. The lower entrances as an insertion point for his teams were out of the question. They would be in plain view of the hostage takers, and the situation would erupt into a gunfight.

The roof was a much better option, but he'd need to access the top of the building without being seen. The good news was the hostage takers hadn't appeared on the roof since the beginning of the crisis. He studied the stairwell access points to the roof and was pleased they corresponded with the dorm floor entries to the stairs directly below the doors.

He had an aide retrieve the keys to the steel doors that were located on the roof while he met with his lieutenants and discussed their options. It was agreed that a top-down assault using helicopters to insert the teams was out of the question because of the noise. One of his aides pointed out the building next to Legacy Hall was slightly higher, which might enable zip-line access.

This was shaping up to be their only option, but a diversion was necessary. Garland concocted a plan. He ordered his teams to get into place on the rooftop of the adjacent building. They would launch a grappling hook over a thirty-foot alleyway to the top of Legacy Hall's roof to attach it to the parapet. Once accomplished, they could slide down the line over a two-story drop to get into position.

His job was to create a diversion. Garland needed to draw the attention of the hostage takers to the front of Legacy Hall, where he was located across the lawn. This would provide his team a precious few minutes to transfer from roof to roof, but they could do it.

Through their communications gear, the surveillance teams could keep the tactical team apprised of the hostage takers' positions during the diversion. The goal was to remove the threats using their blades or silenced weapons. Then they would descend to the next floor until they took out the leaders of the hostage takers, who constantly moved around the ground floor, alone.

After Garland received confirmation that his tactical teams were ready, he ordered the Wichita Falls emergency service vehicles to arrive with sirens blaring. They came in from every direction and arrived at the front of Legacy Hall at the same time. Their sirens wailed while Garland's team moved from one rooftop to the other.

As predicted, the surveillance team confirmed the curiosity of the armed gunmen got the better of them. They all rushed to the windows facing the front of the dorm to observe the commotion, but the cowards used human shields in the process.

Having received confirmation his teams were in place and working their way down the stairwells, Garland responded to the shouting and cursing over the two-way radio.

"I need you to calm down," started Garland. "The arrival of the ambulances is strictly protocol, as we may have a resolution coming for you. If we can come to terms, then every released hostage will need to be treated for any physical or psychological injuries."

"We didn't hurt no one, man!" screamed the hostage taker in response. "I told you that already."

"Yes, sir," said Garland politely and calmly. "Again, it's just our protocol. Now, do you want to talk about the deal or not?"

Garland released the talk button on the two-way radio and waited for a response. The hostage taker was silent, so he turned to the surveillance team coordinator and asked what was happening.

"Sir, they're scrambling back to their positions. It appears that all the gunmen are on alert. We've confirmed eighteen, actually. Four on each dorm room floor and two milling about the front entrance to the building, which is directly across from us."

"Is there any indication they're holding hostages on the ground floor?"

"No."

"What about on the other floors? Are they using the hostages as cover against our assault?"

"No, in fact, just the opposite," she replied. "The hostages all appear to be in the dorm rooms. And, I might add, there is no indication that the gunmen have entered the stairwells."

"Are our people in position?" asked the captain.

"Yes, except for the ground floor. We don't have enough personnel to cover the two—"

"Hey, man! You still there?" The lead hostage taker returned to the conversation.

"Of course, I'm waiting for you," replied Garland. "Are you ready to bring this to a head?"

"Sure am. You gonna do what we want?"

Garland looked to his tactical team commander, who provided him a nod and a thumbs-up. The surveillance team coordinator confirmed their readiness with a nod.

They were ready as Garland gave one final instruction. "Tell the tac squads in the ambulances to be ready. Instruct the stairwell teams to neutralize their targets and then descend the stairs to the bottom floor to flush out the last two vermin. They should run straight into the opening in front of us."

"Roger that, Captain," said the tactical team commander. "On your go, we'll initiate the op."

Garland took a deep breath. The hostages were out of harm's way. The gunmen had isolated themselves into distinct, easily bunched targets. He needed to make this decision quickly, but not without one last word to the leaders of this band of criminals.

The hostage taker shouted into the radio, "Hey, man, I'm growin' inpatient over here. We gotta deal, or do I need to start chuckin' these coeds out the window?"

Garland gripped the two-way until his thumb turned white. "Yeah, man," he started sarcastically as he pointed at the tactical team commander and formed his hand into a gun with his thumb and trigger finger. "You're gonna love this deal."

Garland dropped his cocked thumb, the hammer of his makeshift gun. The assault began, and just moments later it ended with the two lead hostage takers running onto the snowy front lawn of Legacy Hall, weapons raised and ready to fire, until their bodies were riddled with bullets by Garland's team.

"Don't mess with Texas," Garland mumbled to himself with a smile.

PART FOUR

All Is Not Well

CHAPTER 48

December 13
National Guard Armory
Roswell, New Mexico

Holloway and his boys had begun to wear out their welcome in Roswell, New Mexico. Former Staff Sergeant Holloway wanted to let his men blow off some steam before they joined the rest of their comrades in the Lightning Death Squads. Roswell was a stop he intended to make to hook up with an old girlfriend, but she was long gone when he arrived. Fortunately for Holloway and his crew, there were plenty of marginally willing substitutes.

During their several days of debauchery, he'd contemplated what was in store for them next. Frankly, he wasn't sure how he'd be received or utilized in what appeared to be a more structured command-and-control environment within the DPRK's commandos.

Granted, many of the North Koreans who'd entered the U.S. over the years had adopted their American surroundings as their own, some even abandoning their posts, so to speak, to lead normal American lives. The ones who had become loyal to him in Fullerton sought a criminal livelihood, but they were still beholden to the Lightning Death Squads, which had trained them for this mission.

Holloway was a leader of men. Late in his career as a drill sergeant, he'd turned the Afghans into fighting machines. He'd done the same for the Fullerton Boyz gang, most of whom were traveling to Carlsbad to reunite with him. They'd fight together, but their agenda would be different from those maniacally loyal North Koreans. He didn't have a dog in the hunt in this *us versus them* fight between North Korea and the U.S. He only cared about one thing—what was best for Holloway.

Once he arrived at Carlsbad Caverns, he intended to make a play to form his own unit, made up of his people, to enter Texas with reckless abandon. First, Holloway felt he would need to prove himself as the only Anglo amongst these Korean killers.

As they spent the last several days drinking and abusing the local women of Roswell, he also studied the National Guard Armory, which was located less than a mile from the neighborhood they'd infiltrated. Perhaps, he decided, the best way to endear himself to these North Koreans was to come bearing gifts.

The armory was located on the outskirts of town near the Roswell Airport. Two charred and destroyed aircraft lay across the field nearby, victims of the EMP attack as they attempted to land. The cockpit of a SkyWest flight from Denver landed within a hundred feet of the armory, crashing into a rental-car building.

When Holloway had observed the armory the first day of their arrival in Roswell, he thought the facility had been abandoned. There was no activity whatsoever. The grounds of the complex were simple, with only a single block-and-brick building surrounded by a chain-link fence.

Within the fence were plain white government-looking sedans and several camouflaged vehicles, including older model troop transports. Plus, there was a soft-top Jeep, which was so old, he surmised, that it could only be used for local parades. He was ready to trade in his ragtag, Mad Max fleet for something more official looking. The Roswell Armory might help in that regard.

Holloway, however, knew enough about the impact of EMPs to know that these out-of-service trucks might be the start of a Welcome Wagon package to be delivered to his new North Korean buddies. The gifts that would keep on givin', he hoped, were located inside the building.

At the end of the second day, an olive-drab green military police vehicle, an older Chevy Suburban, arrived at the facility. Two uniformed MPs entered the building, stayed about fifteen minutes, then immediately left. Holloway made a note of the time and made a point to return on day three.

Like clockwork and with typical military promptness, the MPs arrived again. They entered the building, conducted their business, and within fifteen minutes, they were locking up and on their way.

"Today is the day, gentlemen," announced Holloway early that morning as he walked through the house they'd occupied for five days. He'd studied the routine each day and was confident in his plan. "Get these skanks out of here, sober up, and get ready for our next mission. Today, at sixteen hundred, we're going shopping."

The snow had begun to melt and the skies were clearing, placing Holloway in a good mood. He missed the Southern California sunshine, although living in a nuclear wasteland was not very appealing to him.

He had plenty of men to overpower the two MPs, whom he anticipated arriving at the same time as the day before. They would still need the element of surprise; otherwise the military policemen could lock themselves in the armory until help arrived.

Holloway had noticed the MPs' demeanor during his surveillance each afternoon. They usually approached the entrance cautiously, with their weapons drawn from their holsters. But like branch managers who have a tendency to lower their guard at the end of a long day when they exit their bank, the MPs showed their vulnerability by locking up after their inspection with their weapons holstered and their backs to the parking lot. That would be his team's opportunity to pounce.

They took a circuitous route around the side of the building adjacent to the crashed airplane in order to avoid leaving footprints in the snow. Once they were there, they waited and listened for the arrival of the MPs. Holloway checked his watch, a Rolex Mariner he'd stolen from a dead man—one he'd murdered and robbed, of course. He heard the sound of their truck's exhaust system as it approached from Roswell. Moments later, it pulled to a stop in front of the building. It was four o'clock. *Right on time.*

Holloway had to be patient. He couldn't move his men into

position too soon because they might be seen by someone in the neighborhood across the street. He also had to take the MPs using their blades. They couldn't afford gunfire because, in the quiet serenity of the airport area, the retort would linger forever and draw attention to them.

He waited. It had been fourteen minutes. Too close to risk missing the opportunity to surprise them while the door was open. He motioned for his best operatives, men whom, on many occasions, he'd likened to cats stalking mice.

Silent. Quick. Deadly.

The three men waited around the corner from the covered entryway. They heard the bolt lock of the door click, and then it opened with a slight creak. The men weren't speaking, but that didn't matter. Holloway was squeezing the shoulders of his men, who were tense as they prepared to spring into action.

He released his grip on his *cats*. They raced around the corner, knives drawn, and initially undetected by the MPs. The two men were only able to turn slightly to respond to the incoming threat, but all they accomplished was to bare their necks to the trained killers.

The men held their knives in a reverse grip, punching toward their prey and ripping into their jugular veins with the serrated blades. The eyes of the MPs grew wide and stared at each other in amazement as the North Koreans shoved them inside the armory through the door, where they fell to the carpeted floor, bleeding out.

Holloway led the rest of his men through the entrance, gave a quick look around the front of the building, and smiled as he closed the door behind him.

Now let's see what we've got.

CHAPTER 49

December 15
Boise City, Oklahoma

The Rodeo Kids were stiff from sleeping on the cots found at the Julesburg airport. With nothing but rolled-up jackets for pillows and furniture pads from an abandoned U-Haul trailer as blankets, their accommodations were barely capable of fending off the cold. The snow began to fall right after dark, and the cold wind caused the chill to be well below freezing.

The cold air and the windblown snow, which forced its way through the broken door of the truck stop, did nothing to dampen their spirits. They were unable to obtain diesel from the aboveground storage tanks, but they'd found enough in two Caterpillar backhoes parked behind the building to siphon out. Red Rover was now full to the neck in diesel, not enough to make it to the ranch, but good for another day or two of travel.

It was when they were rummaging through the truck stop's contents that Riley found batteries for the shortwave radio. Riley scanned the shortwave channels for thirty minutes, searching for any broadcast, even from the Three Percenters. There was nothing.

Out of boredom, he scrolled through the FM bands and was treated to a symphony of static. Then, in a last-ditch effort to reach out to humanity, Riley gave the AM band a try. They were astonished at what he discovered.

Being close to Texas, and without any other AM band radio stations filling the airwaves, they were able to pick up AM 940 out of Amarillo. They stayed up for hours listening to the broadcast until the storm worsened and atmospheric conditions prevented them from keeping the signal. But what they heard was enough to ensure the trio was wide-eyed and bushy-tailed as the sun rose the next morning.

For the first time, the Armstrong siblings learned Texas still had power. What surprised them the most was that Texas had seceded from the United States. Their spontaneous reaction to this news said it all. They jumped off the floor and exchanged high fives. Riley and Palmer immediately jumped into a Texas two-step through the cluttered truck stop building.

One-two, one-two, slide-shuffle.

Eventually, their euphoria gave way to reality as they continued to listen to the nonstop news reporting. Details of the attack on the I-44 bridge north of Wichita Falls had reached the international community. World leaders and the United Nations were condemning the attacks on innocent Americans who were caught stranded on the bridge. President Burnett was coming under fire and heavy pressure to allow in United Nations peacekeeping forces. Calls to open the Texas borders to American refugees were coming from around the world, especially Washington.

Despite the humanitarian crisis and the new border established by Texas, the Rodeo Kids were excited that most likely their parents were safe and the ranch intact. Further, they had a real life to come home to, not one like they'd witnessed on the highway for the last few weeks.

As they approached Boise City, they began to see signs of what the newscasters alluded to during the broadcast—wayward refugees seeking normalcy in Texas.

Riley easily plowed through the three inches of snow dropped by last night's cold front. The off-road tires on Red Rover were designed for all types of weather conditions. As they drove farther south, the road began to clear somewhat but not because of a snowplow or other vehicles, but because of the shuffling of feet of people heading in the same direction as they traveled.

Cooper knew very little of the Great Depression from his studies in high school. He did recall the stories told by Pops. It was rural

America that suffered the most during those difficult economic times. Pops described children in Appalachia that were so hungry they chewed on their hands. Kids in cities would play eviction games in their living rooms, which involved piling all the furniture in one corner and then another, to simulate moving after the sheriff came to evict them.

In the suburbs, shacks and shanties were built, known as *Hoovervilles*, designed to provide shelter for destitute families. Most rural families were so poor, they couldn't afford to own a car, much less buy gasoline for one. So they walked, sometimes for many days over hundreds of miles, seeking a place of refuge until America recovered from the economic collapse.

After Pops told Cooper these stories, he left him with this thought. "Cooper, I'll never allow the Armstrong family to be poor. We'll live a life of self-reliance because know this, an economic collapse like the Great Depression happened once, and it can happen again. When it does, we'll be okay."

As the three of them rode along in silence among the shuffling feet of families, none of whom had the energy or will to attempt to stop their truck, much less wave them down, Cooper recalled his grandfather's words. Now he understood why his parents were preppers. After what he saw that morning, he vowed to carry forward the family legacy.

Palmer pointed toward the next intersection and instructed Riley to take a left back toward the south. The county roads in this part of Oklahoma traversed the state in a square grid pattern. While the highways connected towns and major cities, the country roads ran east-west and north-south. They could easily avoid populated areas as they worked their way to the Texas border.

The closer they got, however, the more people showed up on even these desolate backroads. Shuffling their feet through the snow like mindless zombies, groups ranging from a couple to several dozen walked along the road, sometimes stubbornly refusing to move as Riley approached.

The larger the group, the more emboldened they became. A few times, some of the men lashed out at their truck, slapping a fender or hurling a snowball in their direction. The closer they got to Texas, the denser the packs of refugees became, and more hostile.

Finally, Cooper had enough. "Riley, take the next right."

"Which road?" he asked.

"I don't care," Cooper gruffed. "Just get off this one for a minute so we can think this through. This is ridiculous!"

Cooper was frustrated as Riley pulled onto a county road headed toward the west. He immediately noticed the road had not been traveled upon, by car or human.

He reached down and formed a snowball and began munching on it, allowing the snow to melt in his mouth. Although after traveling past Denver, their RAD stickers no longer showed any evidence of radiation, Cooper immediately reconsidered eating snow after nuclear Armageddon. It was a bad idea and he spit it out.

Palmer emerged from the truck with the map. "I think I know what you're thinkin', Coop. All of these people have escaped Denver and Colorado Springs after the EMP attack. Somehow, word of Texas being okay got around."

"Yeah, lucky for them they left, or they'd be crispy critters," quipped Riley.

"C'mon, man, a bunch of people died back there," said Cooper, pointing to the north. "Do you remember those dead bodies when we were driving east of Denver. That's what death from radiation looks like."

Those downwind from the nuclear blast that struck Colorado Springs might have avoided death from the impact, but they were unable to avoid the radiation sickness that followed. Exposure to a large amount of radiation over a short period of time poisons the human body.

Skin that was directly exposed to high degrees of radiation will quickly produce a rash or burned appearance. Inside, the radiation invades the cells of your stomach and intestinal tract and then your bone marrow. This combination will immediately cause symptoms like vomiting, headache, disorientation and fatigue. Eventually the body's organs succumb and fail.

People lying on both sides of the highway had left an indelible mark in Cooper's mind. Not one to ordinarily worry about the harmful words people used, he drew the line at *crispy critters* under these circumstances.

Riley hung his head in shame. "Sorry, Coop. You're right."

Palmer quickly returned to the subject at hand as she studied the map spread out on the hood of the truck. "You have to figure people from major cities like Oklahoma City, Denver, and Albuquerque will take the shortest routes into Texas. They'd seek out interstates like 40, 35, and 44."

"You're right, Palmer," said Cooper, who regained his focus. "Think about what's due west of the ranch—nothing, really. Roswell in New Mexico isn't that big, and those folks would probably head straight toward Lubbock. If we could make our way south through New Mexico toward Hobbs, heck, that's straight down the highway from Gail and Lamesa. We could stroll right in."

"It's gotta be better than this," added Riley. "The farther south we go toward Amarillo, the more likely we're gonna get into it with someone, you know?"

"I agree," said Palmer. "But what about fuel? We don't have enough."

"We'll do just like we've been doin' for the last however many miles," replied Cooper. "We'll forage and keep plodding along."

Riley laughed as he put Cooper's admonishment behind him. "Y'all get me to Hobbs, and I'll carry the both of you to Momma's doorstep. Deal?"

"Deal!"

CHAPTER 50

December 14
Pecos River
North of Carlsbad, New Mexico

Duncan was not one to be philosophical but riding with Sook through another snow-filled cold front as they searched for a suitable crossing across the Pecos River was trying his soul. During his career, he learned about determination and perseverance. He had pushed through many a mission under extreme duress in adverse conditions. His survival in North Korea was his greatest test, and thanks to his new love, Sook, he'd survived it. Now, as the winds blew from the north, sending chills to their bones, Duncan and Sook had to muster all of the strength in their hearts to continue, because the true measure of anyone's soul was not shown by the strength of their bodies, but rather, by their heart.

"It's a beautiful day for a ride," shouted Sook over the noise of the wind howling through the valley.

"What?" shouted Duncan, unsure if he'd heard Sook correctly. He slowed his horse so she could pull alongside him.

Sook smiled at Duncan, although he could only see her eyes through the scarf wrapped around her face for protection. "I said it's a beautiful day for a ride."

He laughed. "Yeah, sure. Lovely."

As they pressed forward, Duncan considered stopping even though it was midday. Not having access to weather forecasts forced him to use his instincts and survival training.

The day before, the winds had shifted from being at their back, blowing from west to east, to coming from the north. He'd lived in

West Texas long enough to know that a northerly wind doesn't bode well at any time of the year.

Last night, they'd found a dilapidated fishing cabin off Route 285 near Brantley Lake. The cabin's windows had been broken out and provided little protection against the elements other than a roof. They built a fire using river rocks to contain the coals and mesquite wood, which Sook gathered from their surroundings.

Duncan observed the smoke as they huddled together to keep warm. During stable weather conditions, the high barometric pressure caused the smoke to go directly up in the air. During the hour or so that they ate their MREs provided by the soldiers they assisted, the smoke shifted and began spiraling downward, a sign that a low-pressure system was on the way.

As they awoke this morning, Duncan glanced outside the cabin and was greeted by a cloudy day, but at least the winds were calm. This was the sign that he missed. There's a reason the phrase *calm before the storm* came into existence.

They began another day of travels, thinking the biggest challenge they'd face was how to cross the Pecos River into eastern New Mexico without running into trouble. Duncan had readily accepted the hundred rounds of .338 ammo from the appreciative guardsmen he'd helped, but he was not in a mood to begin expending them in another firefight.

All of these things had run through his mind earlier as he took a deep breath and realized the air was full of moisture. That was when he muttered to himself, "It's comin'."

And come it did. The snow was light at first, almost beautiful as the two rode along the highway in silence, enjoying the flakes fall around them. Then the cold winds arrived, bone-chilling and gusty. They were caught in no-man's-land, in near-blizzard conditions, with no options but to persevere and just keep movin'.

He reached for her hand and squeezed it for a moment before the two separated again and she fell back slightly, by design. Duncan did not want the two of them to be a large easy target for anyone who might choose to shoot at them from the surrounding hills.

For the next two hours, they continued to travel slowly to the south as Duncan attempted to lead them past Brantley Lake and the dam that held back the Pecos River. Their visibility was poor, but he expected to see a side road with some type of markings indicating the location of the dam.

His heart leapt somewhat as they approached a green road marker, hoping it was their opportunity to turn due east toward Texas and the Armstrong Ranch. Instead, the sign read *Carlsbad Caverns – 12 miles.* Although disappointed, he knew they were getting closer to their turn.

"What is Carlsbad Caverns?" Sook asked from behind him. Duncan began to reconsider his strategy of riding apart. It would take one heckuva shot to nail them from a distance in a semi-blizzard. He reached his arm out and waved her forward to join him.

Sook provided her horse some pressure, and it trotted to catch up to Duncan.

"Carlsbad Caverns are ancient caves in the mountains," he replied. "Some are very large."

"Can we sleep there tonight?"

"We're not going that far south. We will turn toward the east any—"

Before Duncan could finish his sentence, Sook's horse unexpectedly dropped to its front knees in a snowdrift. A deep breath of warm air exhaled from its lungs as its eyes grew wide. Then it simply fell over in a heap, pinning Sook's right leg underneath it.

"Duncan!" she shouted, her voice mixing fright with pain from the heavy animal crushing her small body.

Duncan quickly dismounted and placed his hands over the horse's nostrils. He glanced at the beautiful animal's eyes, which remained wide open. The mare who'd carried Sook all of these miles had succumbed. She was dead.

"Try to relax, Sook. This may take a minute."

"Is she dead?" asked Sook as tears began to stream sideways off her face.

When the horse toppled over, it had fallen down a slight incline, which complicated removing the animal from Sook's leg. Duncan's mind raced. Horses could die suddenly for many reasons ranging from cardiac arrest to gastrointestinal ruptures, two likely causes because of the conditions under which they'd been traveling. Aortic or brain aneurysms were possible, both ticking time bombs within a horse that would not necessarily be triggered by the adverse circumstances. Regardless, Duncan had a problem on his hands.

The average horse weighed from nine hundred to twenty-two hundred pounds. Duncan estimated the mare to be about fifteen hands high, or sixty inches. That would put her weight around twelve hundred pounds.

As Duncan considered his options, he heard the low rumble of a vehicle approaching from the north. As the sound grew, he considered whether it was more than one vehicle.

Is it another military convoy? Maybe they can help?

He wrestled with what to do. He couldn't lift the heavy animal off Sook alone. If the approaching vehicles weren't friendly, they could both die.

There was no time to mince words. "Yes," he replied. "Is your leg broken?"

Sook hesitated before answering, "No. It is numb."

Duncan didn't waste any more time. He removed the tarp from his horse and the paracord, both of which had created shelter several evenings of their journey.

He rushed to the mare's head and neck, slid to his knees and forced the tarp underneath. The sound of the approaching vehicles grew louder, convincing Duncan there were several heavy trucks approaching. He deftly looped the paracord through the tarp's reinforced eyelets and pulled it taut. Then he attached the paracord to his horse's saddle and harness.

"Steady, big boy," he whispered into his horse's ear.

He rushed to Sook's side, glancing up the highway as the trucks' mufflers grew louder.

"Sook, I can only lift his head a little. This should give you enough room to pull yourself free. Can you do it?"

"Yes. Duncan, I hear trucks."

"I know, we have to hurry."

Duncan scrambled through the wet snow back to his horse. He grabbed the reins and patted his horse on the nose. "Okay, buddy. You gotta pull."

Duncan backed away and drew the reins toward him. His horse responded and moved forward. The slack in the paracord lines was removed, and the head of Sook's horse began to rise out of the snow.

"Yes!" shouted Sook. "A little more. More!"

The trucks came into view less than a mile away.

"Hurry!"

"I'm free!" shouted Sook.

Duncan wasted no time in pulling his blade and cutting through the paracord line. He ran around the dead mare and helped Sook to her feet. She stood but put all her weight on her left leg, favoring the right. Duncan scooped her up in his arms and rushed to his horse, which had stood steadfast throughout the ordeal.

"Grab the horn of the saddle," he instructed.

"The handle?" asked Sook.

"Yes, the handle, and hold on."

Sook grabbed the horn with both hands as Duncan hoisted her on top of his horse. He took one quick glance northward, where the blowing snow continued to minimize visibility. The trucks were coming into view.

Sook slid forward on the seat and made room for Duncan, who slid on behind her. He immediately urged his horse forward off the road and toward a rockpile a hundred feet down a slight incline toward the lake.

Just as they reached the rocks, he heard the trucks arrive at the scene. He didn't want to risk being discovered, so he hid behind the rocks and turned so they could observe the vehicles. Duncan removed his rifle from its scabbard and used his scope to get a better look.

"They are military trucks," he whispered to Sook, who was rhythmically bending her right leg to work out the pinched nerve she'd received from the fall.

Through the wind, they could make out voices shouting at one another. This grabbed Sook's attention immediately.

"Duncan, they are North Korean!" she exclaimed, causing Duncan to raise his index finger to his lips, indicating she should be quieter.

Leaning back to her, he asked, "How do you know they are from the North?"

"We speak Pyongyang dialect," she replied. "It is different from Seoul dialect."

"Are you sure?"

"Yes."

Duncan continued to study the men's movements. They were not in uniform and seemed more interested in the dead horse than their surroundings. Fortunately, the blowing snow quickly covered Duncan and Sook's escape tracks.

Puzzled, Duncan thought of their encounter on Interstate 40 with the Koreans. Now, another group, identified by Sook as being from the North, crossed their path again.

Where are these North Koreans going, and more importantly, what are they doing in U.S. military vehicles?

Duncan didn't believe in coincidences, especially this one.

CHAPTER 51

December 15
Gail, Texas

On a normal day, Gail, Texas, wasn't exactly bustling with activity. In a county that boasted only six hundred residents, with a county seat like Gail, which had all of two hundred of those Borden Countians, quiet and lack of hustle or bustle was the norm. But this was different.

After what happened to the Slaughters' ranch, Major and Preacher thought they'd notify the sheriff of the situation, even though it was in an adjacent county. If there was an organized group, or even a gang of some kind, moving through West Texas capable of destroying property, or even killing, the rest of the residents should know about it.

As soon as they passed the co-op on Willow Valley Road, they knew there was a problem. The front plate-glass windows were broken out, and the reinforced wood doors had been pulled off their hinges. The doors and the frame lay in a heap in the gravel parking lot.

"Get your rifle ready," said Major calmly as he felt for the handle of his pistol in its holster.

Buildings like the Caprock Café stood empty, as they had for years. But as they approached the county administration complex and the sheriff's office, they knew Gail had seen trouble.

Smoke was wafting out of the front door of Dorward Drug Store, a mainstay in the small town since 1901. Major had predicted pharmacies would be one of the first businesses to be looted. He'd commented to Preacher once that the drugstores would be hit by junkies looking for Oxy and preppers looking to stockpile antibiotics. The charred door frame and the billowing smoke indicated the much-sought-after drugs were out of stock during the looters' shopping days.

"Do you see anything?" asked Major. "I mean any signs of life whatsoever?"

"Not even a stray dog, boss," replied Preacher, who gripped his rifle a little more firmly. "Best be findin' the sheriff."

Major nodded and made his way to the jail. He wheeled the old Toyota feed truck through the brick monument signs identifying the Borden County Sheriff's Department and parked near the front door. They sat in silence for a moment before exiting the vehicle. If anyone was inside, they didn't make their presence known.

"Preach, let's be real careful, ya hear?"

"Oh, I sure do," replied Preacher as he moved around the passenger door of the pickup and moved quickly to the front wall of the building, pressing his back against the brick warmed by the midday sun. Preacher pointed his rifle toward the front door and nodded to Major, who immediately ran to flank the entrance on the other side.

Once in position, Major motioned for Preacher to pull the glass door open. When he did, Major rushed in with his rifle swinging from side to side in search of hostile targets.

The modest entry to the facility was empty. After Preacher joined him, the men walked together to clear each room. They found no signs of life, but clearly someone had been searching for anything of value. Desk drawers were pulled out and dumped on the floor. File cabinets were rooted through with papers strewn about. Chairs were knocked over.

The sheriff's office had taken the brunt of the search. The space had been searched and apparently trashed out of anger. The flags of the State of Texas and the United States had been shoved into a trash can. One of the looting animals had taken the time to defecate on them.

"Let's try the jail cells," suggested Major.

Leading with the barrel of his rifle and with Preacher in tow, Major made his way deeper into the dark building toward the jail holding cells. The steel door leading to the concrete and steel cells would normally be locked, but Major doubted the sheriff was holding any prisoners, so when he easily pulled the door open on its wheel and rail system, he wasn't surprised.

However, the smell of death that struck him as he entered the cell block knocked him back a step.

Major pulled his thermal undershirt up to cover his mouth and nose as he moved in. He kept his composure in order to be aware of any threats that might be lurking in the darkness, although he wondered how they could stand the stench.

"Up ahead," whispered Preacher as he walked alongside Major. They reached the last cell and discovered the source of the odor.

It was the sheriff and his chief deputy. They had been stripped naked and forced into the last cell while handcuffed. Their bodies lay facedown on the concrete floor, soaked in their own blood. The men had been shot in the back several times.

"May God rest their souls in peace," said Major as he lowered his rifle.

Preacher touched his arm and pulled him away from the gruesome scene. "C'mon, boss. Let's get out of here. We can't take any chances."

Major lingered for a moment and then left. He'd experienced the deaths of his fellow lawmen many times, but he'd never seen anything like this. Sadness and then anger overcame him as he bolted out of the cell block and through the front doors of the sheriff's department.

"Animals!" he yelled to the sky. "God, what human could do this?"

God didn't respond, but an elderly man who emerged from around the corner of the building did.

"I seen what happened."

Both Major and Preacher swung around and trained their rifles on the old guy, startled by his sudden appearance.

"Who are you?" demanded Preacher.

"My name is Cletus Cassiday. I live over on Kincaid Avenue. Sheriff locked me up for a bit 'cause I broke into the Blue Paw diner. I was just lookin' for food, but Sheriff said he had to show the folks in town that we couldn't steal from one another."

Major stepped past Preacher and reached his arm out to lower his rifle. Major did the same and then began to question the old man. "Cletus, what happened here?"

Cletus pointed over his shoulder toward the west and began. "They came into town real quick like from that away. It was *pickemup* trucks and *motorsickles*. I was back in the cell looking out the window through the bars. I seen 'em comin' and tried to warn the sheriff, but he never heard me, I guess.

"Anyhoo, before I knew it, they was shoutin' at each other out front, and I heard gunshots, so I curled up on the floor and crawled under my bunk. It sounded like they was havin' one heckuva wrastlin' match out there for a while.

"The next thing I know, the steel door was slid open, and they pushed the sheriff and his deputy into the cell doors. They was butt naked and handcuffed. These boys looked mean, mister. I mean, they was wearing leather jackets, covered with tattoos, and had lots of long hair. Real ugly types.

"I was hidin' and prayin' when they locked the sheriff and his man in the last cell. I'm guessin' the sheriff said somethin' mouthy because they started shootin'. I heard them boys laughing as the bodies hit the ground.

"Mister, I couldn't do nothin' to help, you know? I just started cryin', which gave me away. I don't know why, but they didn't kill me. They just threw the jail keys in my cell and left, laughin' all the way out the door.

"It took me thirty minutes to get the courage to let myself out."

The man fell to his knees and began to sob. Major lowered himself to the ground to comfort the old guy.

"Cletus, there wasn't anything you could've done to stop those maniacs. Thank God that you're alive, my friend, and go on home, okay?"

"Yes, sir. I was just comin' back 'cause I felt bad for not burying the sheriff and his deputy. They was good people, you know?"

Major smiled and patted the man on the back. "I tell you what, Cletus. We'll help you bury them. Can you tell me when this happened?"

"Yesterday mornin', right after sunrise."

"Do you know which way they headed when they left?" asked Major.

"Well, I'm not certain 'cause I stayed under the bunk. But I don't think it was the way they came. I would've heard them through the window."

Major stood and looked down both directions of the highway. Most likely, he hoped, they went farther east toward Snyder. There would be no way to warn them, and it was probably too late anyway. He grimaced as he reminded himself that all he could do at this point was take care of his own.

But first, he had to bury two fallen law enforcement officers who didn't deserve the fate God had dealt them.

CHAPTER 52

December 16
Near Hobbs, New Mexico

"Okay, seriously y'all, I'm gettin' tired of finding a side road that should lead us into Texas only to have to turn around 'cause there are a gazillion foreigners in our way." Riley was becoming increasingly frustrated at their efforts to return home and being thwarted by the massive crowds encamped at the Texas border.

"They're not foreigners," said Palmer. "They're Americans just like us."

"News flash, sis. We ain't Americans anymore. We're proud Texans, and these idiots are in our way. I wanna know where the loyal Texans reentry gate is located. There oughta be signs or somethin'."

Cooper rolled his eyes and continued to drive. These two had been scrappin' for the last day and a half, and it was starting to get on his nerves, but joining the fray wouldn't help matters. He had, however, given up on trying to placate Riley's frustrations. Cooper was frustrated too and concerned about their fuel levels. Their southward travels were not the issue. It was the constant five-to-ten-mile excursions toward the state line that wasted precious diesel.

As they crossed Highway 62, he saw a road sign that read *Carlsbad Caverns, 50 miles*. He remembered a class field trip he'd taken when he was in grade school to the natural attraction. His mind wandered to the tour guide, who'd told the grade school class of twenty kids that the caverns were big enough to hold two thousand classes just like theirs all at once. Cooper remembered looking deep in the Big Room and imagining it full of people.

Palmer unfolded the map again, which was now exhibiting signs of wear and tear. The edges were tattered and torn, and holes had begun to appear where the creases were made from the constant folding process.

"Highway 62 would've turned into Highway 180 at the Texas border—a straight shot into Gail. The farther south we go now, the more we'll have to backtrack to get home."

"What are our next options?" asked Cooper.

"A small town called Nadine is up ahead a couple of miles. After that, nothing in the way of roads until we hit a town called Eunice."

"Let me think a minute," said Cooper. When Dallas had turned sixteen, he and Cooper would joyride around West Texas in one of the feed trucks. Dallas loved geography, and although the younger Cooper didn't care that much about Permian Basins or the Yates Oil Field, he enjoyed hearing the older brother, whom he adored, share his local knowledge during their explorations.

"Coop, we're comin' up on the turn at Nadine. Are we gonna take it?"

Cooper shook his head. "Nah, it'll just be the same story as before. I've got a better idea."

"What's the plan?" said Riley, who suddenly came out of his funk. He was tired of the same old, same old too.

"Dallas used to call this area the *land of a thousand wells*," Cooper began to explain. "We're in the Central Basin, and the ranch is in the adjacent Midland Basin."

"Now, Coop, that's real exciting, and informative too, I might add," said Riley jokingly, which earned him a playful elbow and a chuckle from his sister.

"Yeah, yeah. Hear me out, guys. There ain't nothin' out here except oil wells and the dusty service roads that connect them. Dallas used to take me joyridin' over this way back when we were all kids."

"How does that help us?" asked Palmer.

Cooper drove past the road leading from Nadine to Texas, which indicated what his plans were. "Those service roads are not on anybody's maps. We'll turn off here in a bit, about halfway between

Nadine and Eunice. Then we'll start to work our way through the land of a thousand wells until we're in Texas."

Palmer threw the map over her shoulder into the back of Red Rover. "I don't think we'll need this anymore. This is a great idea, Coop. At least there'll be less resistance, and once we cross the border, we can find our way home with our eyes closed."

Riley responded enthusiastically. "Yeah, saddle up, y'all. We're goin' home!"

CHAPTER 53

December 17
South of Nadine, New Mexico

"Hey! Keep your hands off our truck!" Riley yelled at the refugees through his window as Cooper inched the vehicle closer to the border gate they'd found after traversing the oil fields. They'd run straight into the double rows of chain-link fencing supplemented with razor wire after heading east from the highway. They'd encountered a few refugees walking in both directions, but they chose to turn south after one group of teens yelled, "There's a gate a few miles down, but they won't let you in unless your already Texans."

That was all the Rodeo Kids needed to hear because they were genuine, born-and-raised Texans, and they had their driver's licenses to prove it. Well, at least the Texas residency part.

Approaching the gate was difficult, as the refugees surrounding the entrance were uncooperative. Cooper kept Red Rover moving, but soon some of the people became hostile.

"You can't get in!" one of them shouted.

Another yelled, "Wait in line like we are. They'll let us in eventually!"

Cooper refused to heed their complaints and kept going. Finally, Riley began to shout back at them, screaming, "We are Texans! Let us pass!"

Cooper's persistent driving coupled with Riley's allowing the barrel of his rifle to be seen did the trick, and they reached the security checkpoint. Cooper exited the vehicle and approached the guards with his hands raised.

"We're Texas citizens! We're Texans. Please let us through."

One of the guards raised his rifle and pointed it at Cooper's chest. A red dot danced around his heart as the laser sight found its mark.

"I've got my license. It's in my wallet. I also have my voter's registration."

"Real slow like, cowboy. Any sudden move and you're done, understand?"

Cooper cautiously removed his wallet and handed it to the guard through an opening in the fence. They went through its contents, even taking the time to compare the picture on his laminated Professional Bull Riders Association card to his face. Fortunately, the beard Cooper had grown didn't change his appearance that much.

The guard retained his wallet and then waved his rifle toward Red Rover. "What about those two?"

"They're my younger brother and sister, Riley and Palmer. They have ID also."

A man dressed in camo fatigues and a heavy jacket approached, studied Cooper, and then whispered with the guard.

"Do you have weapons?"

"Yes, sir."

There was more discussion, and the officer, Cooper assumed, left and walked back toward a temporary trailer used as their checkpoint headquarters. Two men immediately scrambled out of the trailer with their weapons raised and pointed at Cooper.

"Wait, hold up," said Cooper nervously as he raised his arms. "We don't want any trouble. You can have our guns. We're just tryin' to get home."

Nobody responded until there were six armed guards ready to fire if a wrong move occurred. Cooper looked back toward the truck and shrugged. He noticed the refugees had backed far away from Red Rover, hoping not to get gunned down if there was a misstep.

After a tense moment, one of the guards unlocked the gate and manually slid it open so the truck could pass through.

"Get in and drive! Hurry!"

Cooper wasted no time in getting behind the wheel of the truck and engaged the clutch. Red Rover lurched forward until it was through the gate. Cooper was somewhat astonished that the guards didn't immediately pull them out of the truck and force the trio to the ground like he imagined it would happen. Rather, the guards' focus was on the remaining refugees, who began to crowd toward the gate.

Once the gate was closed and locked, the yells came from the outsiders, but none were willing to challenge the firepower of the border guards.

The officer addressed Cooper. "Come on out, hands in the air, and leave any weapons in the truck. I need the three of you to get in the cage while we search you and check your identification."

Without saying a word, all three of the Armstrongs complied and patiently allowed the soldiers to pat them down although Palmer shot one of the men a dirty look who got a little too touchy-feely around her chest.

While they were being detained, Red Rover was searched, and all of their weapons and ammunition boxes were removed and set to the side. The officer examined their arsenal and seemed to nod his approval.

With an armed guard flanking him on both sides, he entered the holding pen and reviewed all of their identification. Comfortable with his findings, he handed them back to the Rodeo Kids.

"Where did you folks come from? The license plate is from Montana."

Palmer and Riley, who both appeared to be apprehensive, looked to Cooper to answer.

"We were at a rodeo in Calgary, up in Canada. When the EMP hit, we got on our horses and started traveling south. We were in Montana when the nukes started flyin'."

"How did you know the war started?" he asked.

"We saw 'em lift off out of the ground. There was no doubt what was happening."

The officer nodded his head and spoke to one of the guards. The men lowered their rifles and retreated out of the holding pen.

"Listen up," he began. "You don't look like trouble, but I have my orders. You know Texas is its own country now, right?"

"Yes, sir," replied Cooper.

"Burnett has issued a martial law declaration, which requires us to seize the weapons of any newcomers to the state, I mean country."

"But we're residents," protested Riley, who was given an immediate glance from Cooper.

"I understand that, son, but I have my orders," he replied. He then leaned in so he could speak in a hushed voice. "There's been some trouble in West Texas. Where do you folks live?"

"North of Big Spring," replied Cooper. "It's about a hundred miles due east from here."

The officer thought for a moment and then put his hands up to instruct them to wait there. He walked to where the guards stood and looked at the weapons spread out on the ground. He picked up the AR-15 and handed it to the guard, who immediately put it in the back of the truck along with a few boxes of ammunition.

He returned to the holding area. "You've been through too much to get hurt on the last leg of your trip home. I've left you the best defensive weapon you have plus some ammo. That should get you home. This is between us, got it?"

"Yes, sir," said Riley and Cooper in unison.

Cooper extended his hand to shake the officer's. "Thank you, sir, very much. Can we be on our way?"

"No reason not to," he replied.

"Sir," interrupted Riley, "do you happen to have any spare diesel we can have?"

The officer frowned and chuckled as he walked away. "Don't push your luck, son."

Riley decided not to press the issue, and he led the way toward Red Rover. Within a minute, they were headed east once again, through the land of a thousand wells.

CHAPTER 54

December 17
South of Nadine, New Mexico

Duncan and Sook's progress had slowed considerably. After the loss of Sook's mare, Duncan led them down toward the Pecos River until they eventually came across a one-lane bridge, which took them to the other side. With the path to the ranch clear of any other natural obstacles, Duncan immediately sought shelter to ride out the storm and recover from the trauma of the loss of her horse.

As was typical of early winter storms, within a day, the cold front blew past them and the sun was out, awakening the two travelers from a deep sleep in a toolshed they'd come across located in the middle of an oil field.

They were able to ride together for a while, with Duncan and Sook walking the horse every couple of hours to give it some relief. Duncan's gelding seemed to be strong, showing no signs of fatigue. Then again, Sook's mare didn't either. He began to think the horse had had some type of heart or brain abnormality that caused it to die. In any event, he wasn't taking chances when they were this close to Texas.

When they reached Country Road 18, Duncan noticed a highway marker, which indicated they were still in New Mexico. He became somewhat dejected, not knowing that he was only a few miles away. As nightfall approached, he focused on finding them a place to camp.

They rode along, talking about a variety of subjects related to life in America, when they crested a hill overlooking a vast open area filled with oil wells. He stopped the horse and wiped his eyes as he focused.

About a half mile before them was a pair of tall chain-link fences running parallel to one another from the north to the south. On the New Mexico side of the fence, dozens of people walked back and forth aimlessly, appearing to search for a way through the barricade.

"Wait here," said Duncan as he pulled his rifle and walked closer for a better view. When he was barely a quarter mile away from the barrier, he studied the landscape through the Barrett's scope.

"Texas has a border fence," he mumbled to himself. He squinted, trying to get a better look up and down the border. That was when he saw a commotion about a mile to their north.

Despite the recent snowfall, he could make out a road that led due east into the fence. It was near a large sand pit with a number of backhoes parked next to it. He imagined they were used to fill in gaps underneath the fencing caused by the undulating terrain.

At the sandpit was a gate with armed soldiers on the Texas side patrolling the fence line. Several dozen refugees were standing around the gate. He adjusted his sights and focused on the gate itself. There were MPs stationed there, and they appeared to be examining the credentials of the people in line.

He smiled when he saw a family of three waved through the gate and into a holding pen. "They must be Texans," he said to himself with a smile.

He continued to study the processes followed by the border guards. Within a few minutes, what appeared to be an officer with two armed guards approached the holding pen. He spoke to the family, who immediately stood and raised their arms. The officer patted the adults down and then the child. They opened their belongings for his guards to inspect. He appeared to be satisfied they were unarmed.

After some discussion, the parents provided the officer their driver's licenses. He pointed toward the child, who was immediately drawn in by his mother. After some more discussion, he reached out to shake the man's hand and instructed his guards to open the gate, granting them entry into Texas.

Excited, he jogged back to Sook as he realized their long journey was coming to an end. And then he slowed his pace as he recalled his own words. *They must be Texans.*

Sook, however, was not.

CHAPTER 55

December 19
Texas Border Checkpoint
East of Nadine, Texas

Duncan resisted the urge to rush toward the border checkpoint that afternoon. From his observations, the crowd appeared to be agitated around the gate, which might place him and Sook in danger. He opted instead to break into a block building nearby, which housed hydraulic water pumps. The pumps were not operating, and the accommodations were dark and disagreeably damp, but he and Sook enjoyed curling up in their blankets to stay warm.

The circumstances of their finding one another were certainly unusual, but their survival of the trek from Peach Springs to within a mile of Texas made them soulmates. Duncan tried not to think too far ahead about their future together. They still faced a difficult journey to the ranch with a major obstacle facing them that morning.

The sun was just peeking over the horizon when the two of them rode casually through the sleeping bodies of the refugees who were being denied entry. It was barely light when he got the attention of one of the armed guards.

"Do you have ID?" he asked gruffly. Apparently, the sleepy-eyed guard wasn't used to getting such an early start. Duncan stuffed his documentation through the gate, which included what he had been provided by the CIA officers in Seoul, the handwritten letter from Sheriff Banda in Peach Springs, and a similar letter from the commanding officer of the military convoy he had bailed out on the road the other day.

"I'm Master Chief Petty Officer Duncan Armstrong Jr., a former Navy SEAL. The paperwork I've provided you will show that I have national security interest clearance and ID confirmation provided by the Central Intelligence Agency. There are also letters of recommendations from two individuals with Arizona law enforcement and the United States Military."

The soldier studied the paperwork and then focused on Sook. "Who's she?"

"She is my liaison extracted from South Korea as part of a covert mission. She, too, has the same CIA clearance as I do."

Duncan handed Sook's paperwork through the fence. It bore the name of Min Jun Park, his beloved partner who'd died in North Korea, but most members of law enforcement or the military they encountered would not know that Park's name was masculine.

"Wait here," said the soldier as he turned. His partner at the gate moved in and lifted his rifle to low ready. He stared at Duncan and then back to Sook.

Moments later, an officer in fatigues approached the gate. Duncan recognized the sergeant stripes on his black jacket.

"Good morning, Sergeant," greeted Duncan, who wanted the officer to know he recognized the meaning of his stripes.

"Sir, you don't have any type of photo ID?" the officer asked.

"No, sir. In our line of business, we are discouraged from carrying identification of any kind. These documents were issued to us at Yongsan Garrison in Seoul before we shipped out."

The sergeant studied Duncan and Sook. He seemed skeptical, but continued his questioning. "There's also no indication that you're a Texan. Where do you live?"

"My family's ranch is due east of here, just south of a small town called Gail," replied Duncan.

The officer leaned back to whisper to the soldier behind him.

"Where's that in relation to Big Spring?"

"Our ranch is just north of Big Spring. It's known as the Armstrong Ranch."

The sergeant handed the paperwork to the soldier and then met

Duncan at the fenced gate.

"Sir, this is Texas now, and none of the paperwork means a hill of beans as far as I'm concerned. But I'm gonna give you the benefit of the doubt here."

"Thank you, Sergeant," said Duncan, who was immediately relieved.

"I have one question for you, and you better get it right."

Duncan was taken aback by his demand. He had no idea what the sergeant expected from him. He glared back and responded, "Okay, fine. What's the question?"

"Do you have any brothers or sisters, and what are their names?"

Duncan looked puzzled and then a smile came across his face. "Cooper. Riley. Palmer. My parents call them the Rodeo Kids."

The sergeant nodded and stepped back from the gate.

"Gentlemen, you know the drill. Cover the gate and let these folks into Texas."

CHAPTER 56

December 20
Land of a Thousand Wells
West Texas

"Coop, do you reckon we outsmarted ourselves?" said Palmer with a chuckle as the setting sun behind them began to cast long shadows in the land of a thousand wells.

"Whadya mean?" replied Cooper with a question of his own.

"I mean, we're surrounded by millions of gallons of oil, and not one drop of it is gonna help us get closer to home."

"We all agreed—" began Cooper defensively before Palmer calmed him down.

"Coop, I'm not second-guessin' or criticizin'. We're so far away from civilization that we'll never find diesel at this point."

"Yeah, I know," said Cooper. "It's just those military guys kinda spooked me when the officer talked about trouble around here. I thought it would be best to avoid highways and towns."

"Patricia can't be that far ahead," added Riley. "There's not a lot to it, but there are some farmers around there. We only need a few gallons to get to the ranch."

Cooper glanced down at the gauge and then leaned toward the window to catch a glimpse of the sun. It was rapidly dropping behind the mountains in New Mexico.

"All right, let's find a place to bunk in for the night. If we're gonna run out of gas, let's do it during the day. Right?"

Cooper slowed to turn the truck to the right along another dusty road connecting the pumping wells. If you tracked their path from above, it would resemble the gray line on an Etch A Sketch machine with its series of right-straight-left-straight turns, continuously advancing forward toward their destination, but using precious fuel to remain on the dirt roads.

While he continued to drive, Riley and Palmer retrieved their binoculars and began scanning the landscape. It was Palmer who first noticed an available option. She pointed to the right and nudged Riley, who focused in with his more powerful set of optics.

"Sure enough," he started. "Aboveground oil tankers. That means there's a road over there, Coop."

"I'm on it," said Cooper, who sat a little higher in the seat and began choosing right turns to make his way toward the tanks.

As they got closer, Riley got excited. "Hey, there are a couple of eighteen-wheelers parked in front. We could siphon enough to get us to the ranch, y'all."

Cooper found a service road, which took them due south, and eventually, they found their way to a long stretch of deserted highway just as nighttime arrived.

The storage tanks, which contained pure crude oil, were part of one of several hundred similar facilities located throughout West Texas. They acted as repositories for the crude pumped from the wells for further delivery to refineries.

The facilities were unmanned except for an occasional storage shed and a port-o-potty in the parking lot, although even in normal times, when mother nature called, the truck drivers most likely used the wide-open spaces surrounding the remote location.

"Riley, do you wanna clear it, or do you want me to?" asked Cooper as he stopped and shut off the motor a quarter mile from the repository. Ordinarily, the two guys would work in tandem when they found a place to bed down for the night, but the soldiers had confiscated all of their weapons and ammo at the checkpoint except one rifle.

"I got it," said Riley as he grabbed the AR-15 and jogged ahead.

While Riley headed into the dark, Cooper got out to stretch his legs. The front seat of Red Rover was cramped for a lanky young man like Cooper, especially one who'd spent most of his adult life riding bulls. After a day behind the wheel of the old Landy, he felt forty years older.

Palmer watched Riley until he was out of sight. "I can't see him anymore, Coop."

"Do you think I should've gone with him?"

"It should be—" Palmer began to answer when two gunshots rang out.

Cooper didn't hesitate as he began racing toward Riley and the oil tanks. "Bring the truck!"

Cooper's heart was beating out of his chest as he sprinted toward Riley, arriving in just a minute. His boots clomped on the asphalt road, announcing his arrival.

"Coop, we're good!" shouted Riley from the darkness.

The headlights of Red Rover illuminated the parking lot just as Cooper ran through the gravel and found Riley standing alone with his gun cradled in his arms.

"What happened?" asked Cooper as he arrived out of breath.

"I saw a wild pig and took a couple of shots at it."

As Riley replied, Palmer drove into the parking lot with too much momentum, causing her to lock up the brakes and throw gravel all over the back of an oil tanker as she skidded to a stop near its rear bumper.

"Jeez!" shouted Riley. "I didn't call for the cavalry."

Palmer spun out of the truck. "Are you okay?"

"Yeah, I'm the one with the gun, remember? I was just shootin' at a pig. I think it was a javelina."

"Really, you were hog huntin'?" Palmer was incredulous. She ran toward Riley, intent on whoopin' him for scaring her. "You dope! You can't do that in the dark and with us back there worried about you!"

Riley slumped his shoulders. "But I thought we could have a good supper. Don't you miss the taste of good Texas B-B-Q?"

Palmer slugged him again as Riley cowered. Palmer was the only person on earth, except for their Momma, who could tame Riley. Cooper had often mused that any prospective wife of his would have to hire the Armstrong women as consultants on how to keep his younger brother in line.

"Yeah, I like barbeque too, but when it's slow cooked and dripping in Daddy's sauce," said Palmer. "I'm not gonna eat some feral hog full of disease out here, half-cooked with no sauce."

"It wasn't feral, it was a javelina," Riley began to argue the point, perhaps, Cooper thought, to deflect attention from his lack of common sense at firing a rifle, which might draw attention to them.

Cooper decided to step in and play referee, as he'd done so often in his role as the oldest sibling still residing at the ranch. In that moment, he wondered if that would change once Duncan returned. *If he returned.*

"Look here, y'all. There's a difference between those feral hogs and a javelina. Javelinas are smaller and have that collar around their shoulder. Seriously, Riley, there probably aren't any around here. Are you sure it wasn't a dog?"

Palmer roared in laughter. "A dog? Did you shoot at a dog? You are such a dope!"

Riley shouldered the rifle and defended his shooting at the animal. "No, it wasn't a dog. I know the difference, even in the dark. Either way, I missed 'cause it ran off."

"Are you kiddin' me?" asked Palmer, not really expecting an answer.

Cooper walked up to them both and put his arms around them. "C'mon, y'all. Forget it. Riley, I take it we're all clear. Did you look around before you went huntin'?"

"Yeah, Coop. Nothing here except a garden-shed-looking building around back. Somebody pried the lock off and the door was open. It smells like oil inside, but we could use it for the night."

Cooper walked them toward Red Rover. They looked at the space between the passenger side and the back of the oil truck. It was about a foot.

"Well, Palmer, thanks for not wrecking the truck," said Riley.

"It would've been your fault, dork!" she shouted as she took a swipe at her brother.

Cooper rolled his eyes in the darkness and fumbled around for his flashlight in his coat pocket. He began to walk around the two big rigs parked near the oil storage tanks. The fuel caps were dangling from the chains affixing them to their diesel tanks. He shined his light inside the tanks and saw they were empty.

"Well, looks like someone beat us to it. Let's see if we can sleep in the shed for the night."

Riley climbed up on the side of the larger of the two trucks. It was a Peterbilt with a sleeper cab.

"I've got a better idea," said Riley. "This looks like it might be dee-luxe accommodations."

Cooper and Palmer joined him.

"Here's the flashlight. Take a look inside," said Palmer.

Riley shined the light inside the window. "It's empty. Let's see."

He slowly opened the truck's door, and an awful stench immediately struck him in the face.

"Whoa," groaned Palmer, who turned away in disgust.

Cooper's eyes began to water from the rancid smell. He immediately covered his mouth and nose as he spun around.

Riley jumped off the running board and ran to the side to vomit. He retched several times as Palmer patted him on the back. Cooper wasted no time in slamming the door to the rig shut.

"Somethin' is dead in there, y'all," said Riley in between heaves of vomit. The three of them moved away from the truck to join Riley, who was bent over in convulsions.

Cooper sensed this deserted part of West Texas had seen evil, and the skin crawling on the back of his neck was his body's way of agreeing.

CHAPTER 57

December 20
The Armstrong Ranch
Borden County, Texas

Major kissed Miss Lucy on the cheek as he grabbed his rifle and coat by the front door. For so many years, he'd followed a similar routine when he made the long commute into Lubbock to lead Company C of the Texas Rangers. The thought of finding a place in the city to stay during the work week never crossed his mind. For one thing, the two could never stand to be apart from one another, even for one night. Secondly, being a lawman isn't a nine-to-five, Monday-thru-Friday job. The criminal element never slept during his days as a Ranger, and Major learned they didn't rest in a post-apocalyptic world either.

Preacher was milling about at the foot of the steps leading up to the ranch house. His old friend looked concerned. Granted, that was Preacher's normal demeanor. It was only on rare occasions that Caleb O'Malley allowed his jovial Irish side to show. After their conversation the other day when they had ridden back from the Slaughters' new home at Reinecke, Major wondered if there was a Caleb O'Malley still inside his friend's body, or if that man was lost forever to one fateful night.

"Talk to me, Preach," said Major without wasting time on the usual morning formalities.

"This morning around three a.m., the hands who were assigned perimeter patrol caught a group running toward the barnyard."

"What happened?"

"The boys shouted at them to stop, but these people were bold and ignored 'em. Really, I guess desperate was the better word."

"Did they make it to the barnyard?" asked Major.

"One did," replied Preacher. "Our man fired a warning shot over his head, and the fellow fell facedown into the mud. Would you believe he kept on crawling toward the chicken coop? Our man fired again into the mud near his head, which finally got his attention. He got up and ran toward the river."

"What about the others?"

"They ran off toward the river, too," replied Preacher.

Major began walking toward the barn, where several hands were feeding the horses. "I didn't hear the gunshots. Why didn't you raise me on the radio?"

"There ain't no sense in draggin' you out of bed if we got the situation handled, boss. But we do need to make some changes. That barnyard is like a magnet to anyone who gets a whiff of or hears the chickens. We either gotta move it closer to the ranch house or add security just for that area."

Major looked around and considered the ranch's layout. The barnyard was ideally situated next to the windmill-powered well and the river's watershed. Moving it was not really an option. The better solution was security, but they were short-handed.

"We have our outpost towers constructed," started Major. "Those platforms are twenty-four feet off the ground and give us great line of sight in all directions. What if we build another one near the barn?"

Preacher put his hands in his pockets as he kicked at the last remaining snow, which had fallen a couple of days before. "We need personnel to man these posts, boss. I think it's time to call on the Slaughters to contribute to security."

"What are you thinkin'? I mean, we know nothing about their capabilities and how they would hold up if we had a gunfight on our hands. I trust our people. I'm not so sure about theirs."

Preacher patted Major on the back as he led them into the barn. "I've thought about this. Chris assures me they can handle a rifle. I say we use them during the day to man the guard towers. Their most important task will be to watch for approaching refugees and notify the rest of us. At night, we'll put our best people on perimeter security."

"Agreed. I'll speak to Chris today."

"Boss, there's one more thing," started Preacher. "This is your call, but just hear me out."

Major stopped wandering past the horse stalls and leaned up against a post. "Of course, go ahead."

"I'm not sayin' our folks are scared, okay? But here's the thing. We've told them to use warning shots and every means possible to avoid killin' these folks. Last night showed me that the level of desperation is increasing. What we found the other day in Gail gives me nightmares."

"Me too, Preach, but we still live in a society that observes the rule of law. I've gotta draw the line somewhere when it comes to shootin' folks. I've already shot one man full of bird shot just for trespassing in our barnyard."

"He had it comin'," interjected Preacher.

Major laughed. "You and I may agree on that, but the laws in Texas are still in place, the last time I looked. Deadly force can only be used when someone attempts to enter our homes, vehicles, or place of business. It's called the Castle Doctrine."

Preacher scowled. He grabbed a shovel off a hook on the post next to Major. He drew a large square in the barn's dirt floor. "All I'm sayin' is this," he began, pointing to the center of the box. "We're over here, acting like law-abiding citizens. Out here, there are desperate animals willing to do anything to survive. Major, we've been lucky so far. The people who've trespassed on Armstrong Ranch have been unorganized and unarmed. What happened to the Slaughters and the sheriff is proof all of that is changing now. It doesn't matter if Texas has electricity or not. Folks are becoming lawless."

Major considered Preacher's argument. At this moment, to his knowledge, Borden County didn't have any form of active law enforcement. In some respects, Texas had reverted back to the 1800s.

Major gave his opinion. "Okay, let's look at it this way. If I ever had to make an argument defending the activities of our people in a court of law, this is what I'd say. Armstrong Ranch is our castle. It is where we live and work. Anyone encroaching upon our land will be, under the circumstances, considered to have the intentions to use deadly force against anyone on the ranch. Therefore, everything is self-defense under the Castle Doctrine."

"You sound like a lawyer," said Preacher with a smile. "Do you think it's a stretch?"

"Maybe, but not under the circumstances. Listen, I've been around too many lawyers in my lifetime. I don't think there are any who'd argue against it, not in Texas. Anyway, Preach, tell our people we've taken the gloves off. But know this, if the last week or so is any indication, the bodies are gonna start piling up."

CHAPTER 58

December 21
Route 115
West of Patricia, Texas

Red Rover sputtered, gasped and eventually gave in as its sixteen-gallon fuel tank was emptied. Riley muscled the steering wheel to the right as their faithful steed called it a day barely ten miles from where the Rodeo Kids had spent the night in a toolshed.

"Well, that's that," said Riley as he removed the keys from the ignition. "Do we hoof it to the ranch? Or do you wanna walk up to Patricia to hunt down some diesel?"

Cooper lifted the handle and opened the passenger door. He held it open as Palmer exited and then let go, allowing the door to close itself under its own weight. The sliding-glass window rattled against the steel tracks where the truck's old rain gaskets had worn off.

Cooper laughed to himself as he looked at the vehicle, which had driven them to within sixty miles of home. They hadn't suffered as much as a scratch to the Landy's shiny red paint job. Despite traveling through snow and muddy conditions, the truck was relatively clean.

"I don't want to abandon it," he started as Riley and Palmer joined him in the middle of the road. "The sign back there said Patricia was ten miles. I guess we've traveled about five since then."

"Six," interjected Riley. "I clocked it."

"I remember Patricia," said Palmer. "I went there to visit some friends from Klondike High School when I was a senior. There's not much there, but I know there's a gas station and Patricia Farmer's Cotton gin, which was owned by my friend's family. They live up in

Lamesa, but they might have someone at the gin. I could ask them for some diesel."

Cooper shrugged and looked around again. There were no signs of life.

"Four miles will take us an hour to walk up, and an hour back, plus time to find fuel. That's three hours that we'll be separated."

Palmer volunteered. "I'll go. I know the family and can get us enough to make it home. It's only fifty miles to the ranch from Patricia. One can of diesel should do it."

"Coop, she can't go alone," said Riley. "Why don't you walk with her, and I'll hold down the fort?"

"Who gets the rifle?" asked Coop.

"Y'all take it," replied Riley. "Nobody's gonna come around here, but you might run into some folks up ahead."

"Are you sure?" asked Palmer.

"Yeah, y'all go ahead. I'll take a little siesta."

Cooper retrieved the rifle from the truck and then he put his arm around Riley. "No naps, bud. Remember what we found in the sleeper cab of that truck? I looked this morning while it was my watch. The driver had been shot in the head while he was sleeping. I don't want the same thing to happen to you."

Cooper and Palmer walked at a pretty quick pace, arriving at the cotton gin facility in less than an hour. The multibuilding facility didn't have any fuel tanks, and the only vehicles available to them were gas-powered trucks. Cooper broke into the trucks, searching for keys, and then they searched the company's offices, which had already been ransacked. There were no car keys or anything else of value. So they moved on.

They walked closer to the small town, and they found more of the same—abandoned businesses and homes, which had already been looted. Cooper and Palmer spent nearly an hour looking for any source of diesel, or signs of life, to no avail.

They finally declared their mission a failure and decided to gather up Riley for the walk home. The skies were blue and the temperatures were warming, giving them hope that they'd avoid freezing at night. The weather in West Texas could sneak up on you fast, as there weren't any significant natural impediments to fronts racing across the flatland.

After being gone four hours, much longer than anticipated, they were already showing signs of exhaustion as Red Rover came into view.

Palmer began running toward the truck.

"Coop! Riley's in trouble."

*****

They dropped the diesel cans and the siphoning hose in the middle of the road. Cooper saw a group of people pushing and shoving Riley, so he wasted no time in racing toward his brother. Whereas the night before, he'd rushed into the darkness to see if his brother might be in danger, this time he could see for himself.

"Get away from the truck!" Riley shouted as two men tried to outflank him and made their way to the back door of Red Rover.

Riley moved to stop them, but another man jumped on his back and grabbed Riley around the neck. Riley spun around and around like one of the bull's Cooper rode, attempting to throw the man off his back.

Cooper was closing the gap just as Riley backed into the side of the truck, knocking the wind out of his attacker. However, he was turned away from the other two men and didn't see the hammer that was about to strike him in the back of the head.

With the precision of a seasoned military professional, Cooper raised the AR-15, placed the hammer-wielding man in his sights and quickly pulled the trigger twice.

The bullets sailed past Riley and struck the man in the chest, throwing him backwards into his partner. Riley instinctively pressed himself against the side of the truck to avoid the gunfire because Cooper was not done yet.

The uninjured assailant rolled his dead buddy out of the way and scrambled for the hammer. Cooper didn't hesitate as he fired four shots at the man, catching him in the leg and the top of his skull. He was killed instantly.

The third attacker crawled under Red Rover and began to cry, begging for his life. Riley reached down and grabbed him by the legs and attempted to pull him out. The man, turned sniveling coward, wrapped his arms around the axle and held on for dear life.

"I've wrestled stronger animals than you!" shouted a determined Riley as he gave one more forceful tug. The man lost his grip and let go, sending Riley tumbling onto the asphalt from the momentum. The attacker considered crawling back under when he felt the barrel of the AR-15 pressed into the back of his neck.

"Get up!" ordered Cooper with a growl. He'd been mad in his life, but nothing like this. Now he knew what One-Night Stand had felt when Cooper rode him. He wanted blood.

"Don't kill me, puhleese!"

"Shut up or I will!" Cooper shouted back. He glanced over at Riley, who had finally stood up in the road and was dusting himself off. Riley nodded to his brother, indicating he was okay.

The man stood and leaned with his back against Red Rover, hands high in the air. Cooper tossed the rifle to Riley and grabbed the man by the throat. The man began to gasp for air and clutched Cooper's hands, seeking relief from the death grip.

Cooper was incensed. "This is on you! Was it worth it? You attacked my brother, and your buddy there, the one with two bullets in his chest, tried to kill him with a hammer. What's wrong with you?"

The man began to cough as he mouthed words, but Cooper didn't care what his answer was. Out of anger and frustration, he hurled the man on top of his two dead friends, causing him to flail in their blood. Without saying a word, he began walking back to where his cowboy hat had flown off in the highway.

He bent down on one knee to retrieve it, and then he stayed there. Cooper prayed for forgiveness before he retched over and over again.

CHAPTER 59

December 21
Land of a Thousand Wells
West Texas

The sound of a gunshot could carry for miles when the terrain was flat like what was typical for West Texas, especially on a clear day with little wind. Duncan and Sook had extended their travel day as they crossed through the land of a thousand wells on a nearly identical path as taken by his younger brothers and sister.

He and Sook continued their conversation with the sergeant at the border checkpoint over coffee and cellophane-wrapped cheese Danish. The food and coffee were heavenly and reenergized them both.

As did news of his family. The sergeant recounted everything he could remember from their conversation of the day before. Duncan was proud and amazed that the three of them had traveled across the continental U.S. from Canada to make it back to Texas. After allowing their horse some fresh water and to feed on some hay bales which were used for ballistic protection at the checkpoint's water tanks, Duncan and Sook took off with a new sense of purpose.

They were chatting about countries Duncan had visited during his special ops missions when they heard the gunfire. It was impossible for Duncan to gauge distance and direction under the circumstances. He immediately became apprehensive and removed the Barrett from the scabbard. He rested it in his lap as they continue to ride east.

Duncan whispered a thank-you to the sergeant for allowing him to keep the weapon, which had become a part of him since that ill-fated attempt to assassinate Kim Jong-un.

As darkness approached, Duncan saw the same oil storage facility found by his siblings the night before. He approached with caution and quickly dismounted, leaving Sook a safe distance away. After he was satisfied it was clear, except for the dead body in the back of the Peterbilt, they made a place to sleep in the toolshed.

Duncan had been warned by the sergeant that looting, assaults, and murders had grown exponentially across Texas in the last week to ten days. Lack of food and an overall loss of confidence in Austin was eroding the initial euphoria that Texas had been spared from both the EMP and nuclear attacks.

The word Duncan had used in response to the sergeant's revelations was *ungrateful*, but they both agreed that *you can never underestimate the depravity of man*. With that in mind, the execution of the truck driver sickened Duncan, but did not surprise him.

His concern immediately turned to his family. It was dark, but he felt compelled to ride on in hopes of catching up to them. He told Sook as they fell asleep that night that he could never live with himself if they were so close and might be killed or injured while just out of his protective reach.

*****

Duncan survived a night of restlessness, barely sleeping an hour or two. As soon as Sook stirred before dawn, he readied the horse so they could continue their journey. The sun was rising in front of them, and as it crested the horizon, its brightness blocked their vision somewhat.

It did not prevent a reflection from blinding him slightly. It was the shiny, apple red truck described by the sergeant as belonging to the rodeo kids.

"Hold on, Sook," Duncan said, and she responded by grabbing him firmly around the waist. He dug his heels into the gelding and shouted, "Hah!"

The horse broke into a gallop down the center stripe of the

highway, quickly closing the gap between the riders and Red Rover. As they approached, Duncan pulled his rifle and held it with one arm to study the scene through his scope. There were two bodies lying facedown next to the truck, and a third was sitting on the ground, slumped over.

Duncan stopped a hundred yards short and jumped down from the saddle, leaving Sook alone on top to slow the horse's progress. Duncan raced ahead, concerned that three bodies appeared to be dead next to the truck that had carried his three siblings so far.

As he got closer, he slowed to a fast walk and readied his rifle, scanning the road from side to side, looking for any signs of movement. He began walking as a relief swept over his body. The two dead men were not Cooper and Riley.

He moved cautiously toward the man tied to the street sign. Duncan kicked the man's leg to wake him up.

While the man stirred awake, Duncan walked backwards toward Red Rover and looked inside and underneath before carefully rolling the bodies over to confirm they were dead. He'd heard of insurgent activity used in some countries where a car accident or shooting was staged to catch anyone approaching the scene off guard. The same scheme had been used in America by carjackers. A phony two-car accident would be set up on a remote road. When a Good Samaritan came along to help, he or she would be attacked, robbed, or worse.

Satisfied they were alone, he waved Sook forward and returned to the only survivor of the attack. He grabbed the man by the hair and pulled his head up. "What happened here?"

"Hey, man. Can you cut me loose? My arms are really sore."

"First, you answer my questions, got it?"

"Yeah, sure," the man replied as he tried to raise himself up to lean against the road sign. "We came along this dude by himself and asked him for a little food or water, that's all. He told us no and, well, you know, that wasn't fair, so my buddies asked him again."

Duncan looked in the man's eyes. "Let me guess, your buddies didn't say pretty please."

"No, man. The guy wasn't sharing, you know. We've all got it tough right now. All he had to do was share and nothing would've happened."

"Back to my first question. What happened?"

The man began to cough up some mucus and attempted to wipe his mouth but forgot his arms were tied behind his back. He then attempted in vain to reach his shoulder.

"Well, I decided the guy wasn't being fair, so I kinda jumped him while my buddies over there helped themselves in the back of the truck. The next thing I knew, the guy was twirling in circles like a crazed lunatic and slammed me into the side of the truck. That's when his friends showed up."

"What did they look like?"

"Man, I dunno. It all happened so fast. I guess my buddy came at the guy with a hammer, because the next thing I knew he was falling backwards with two bullet holes in his chest. I crawled under the truck, and the guy with the rifle ran up on us. The next thing I know, my other friend had a bullet in the top of his head."

Duncan stood up and walked away from the man. His grin stretched from ear to ear. While he was concerned for their safety, he'd just learned they could hold their own. Duncan took one more glance into the back of the truck to see if there was anything left behind he could use. He turned without saying another word and shoved his rifle into its scabbard. Sook scooted back on the saddle to allow Duncan room to mount their horse.

He flicked the reins, and the gelding began walking through the human debris scattered on the highway.

The man shouted at them, "Hey, aren't you gonna cut me loose?"

Duncan replied with a smile, "Nah, man. Be glad I didn't shoot you."

CHAPTER 60

December 22
The Oval Office
The White House
Washington, DC

Former Defense Secretary Montgomery Gregg, now the vice president-designate of the new Republic of Texas, was the first representative to make an official visit to foreign soil, although there was nothing foreign about Washington or the Oval Office to him.

His arrival at the White House was met with some formality, but nothing like he'd observed other foreign dignitaries receiving. He wanted to give the president's team the benefit of the doubt that they were still finding their footing after just under two weeks of returning to DC. Or it could be they didn't think he deserved the show of respect afforded others. Either way, he didn't care. If they wanted to play hardball, he had something for them.

After he cleared security, a formality they obviously hadn't abandoned despite everyone knowing who he was, he was led to the Oval Office, where he was to meet with President Harman and her number one henchman, Acton.

As he entered, he waited for the door to be closed behind him. The president stood gazing out upon the South Lawn while Acton stood stoically, like a statue, next to the bust of Martin Luther King Jr. For an awkward moment, nobody spoke.

Monty chuckled to himself. *There seems to be a chill in the air. Trust me, I've faced tougher opponents than you two.*

The president turned toward him and approached the chair near the fireplace, which was her customary seat. "Welcome back, Monty, um, Mr. Vice President-designate." She stretched out her pronunciation of his title through gritted teeth.

"Thank you, Madam President. I'm glad to see you're well. May I sit?"

Gregg approached the chair opposite her, which left the cocktail table in between them.

"No, here," gruffed Acton, pointing to the settee closest to the president. "We still follow protocol around here."

Fine, Jimmy. Careful. This old general can still pack a punch.

"Monty, please. Sit where you'd like. I'd like to get right down to business."

To spite Acton, he sat in his customary chair opposite the president.

"Madam President, I don't want things to be awkward between us," started Gregg. "President Burnett intentionally sent me to discuss the relationship of our two nations going forward because she thought our past dealings would be conducive to an open and honest conversation."

"Honest?" asked Acton, whose attitude was getting on Gregg's nerves. "I believe the issue of treason on the part of the governor and her associates should be addressed before any conversation should commence."

President Harman raised her hand and motioned for Acton to sit. "Now, James. Marion Burnett is now the President of Texas and Vice President Gregg has come here in good faith, not under false pretenses, am I right?"

"Absolutely, Madam President," he replied, but not before shooting a glare at Acton, who finally took a seat on the settee, with a noticeable pout. "I believe we can discuss several arrangements that might be mutually beneficial to us, for starters."

"Well, Monty," she began, "may I still call you Monty? If so, I'd prefer you call me Alani."

What is this? Good cop, bad cop?

"Sure, Alani. Absolutely, when in private."

"Thank you, Monty. James reached out to President Burnett in a spirit of cooperation to arrange for the delivery of relief supplies and components necessary to rebuild our power grid to your unused airports around the state. I mean Texas. We generously offered a portion of the food supplies meant for Americans to survive as payment for this accommodation. President Burnett rejected our offer out of hand."

Gregg nodded his head to indicate he was familiar with the offer. "The deal, quite frankly, was very one-sided, and it required our military personnel to leave the state that they've sworn an oath to protect." As soon as he made the statement, Gregg immediately wished he could take it back.

"You mean like the oath you, and your military personnel, swore to the U.S. Constitution?" sniped Acton.

Gregg didn't respond, instead choosing to focus on the president. He was charged with the responsibility of opening trade channels with the U.S., and he hoped to strike a deal regarding the relief supplies to get the ball rolling. But he was damned if he'd allow Acton to pop off every chance he got.

"Listen, that was a poor choice of words, for which I apologize," said Gregg humbly. "Can we get back to the basic differences between us on your proposal so that an accord can be reached?"

"Yes, please," said the president as she frowned at her chief of staff. "I understand the need to protect your borders, especially after the debacle that happened at the Red River under your watch. However, I don't think you want us to send our military personnel into Texas to retrieve the foreign aid, do you?"

"We were thinking civilian cargo aircraft, which we'd agree to load under your representative's supervision, of course," replied Gregg.

"Fair enough," said the president. "We'd need to reach an agreement on refueling."

"Minor details that can be worked out between your staff and mine," interjected Gregg. "However, there is still the matter of the percentage of food supplies to remain in Texas for us allowing this accommodation."

Acton jumped in once again. "What? Why? You're not doing anything. The pallets are dropped off and we pick them up. Why should you get a payment?"

"There are logistical matters on our end, personnel, equipment, etcetera. We've already accepted hundreds of pallets of aid without an agreement with your government."

Acton was unconvinced. "That's like giving a tip to a waitress on a to-go order. She didn't do anything but deliver the food from the kitchen to the front door in a plastic bag."

Gregg was over his insolence. He thought about asking Harman for permission to take this outside and settle it like men, but he took a deep breath and remembered that he was a diplomat now. *Be diplomatic, at least as long as you can stand it.*

President Harman disregarded Acton's latest outburst. "Monty, can we keep the percentage the same if you'll agree to load the supplies and refuel our aircraft?"

"That's doable," he replied.

"However, there is one more thing I'd like to ask," added the president.

"Go ahead."

She sat forward in her seat and stuck her jaw out. "I'd like to seek reparations for the families that your military slaughtered on that bridge. What you did was barbaric, and frankly, Monty, I'm appalled that it happened under your watch."

Gregg chuckled and made no effort to hide it.

"Is there something funny, Mister Vice President-designate?" asked Acton sarcastically.

Gregg had had enough. "Do we have an agreement on the relief supplies?"

"Subject to your administration's agreement to pay reparations *and* issue a formal public apology," replied the president.

The old warhorse leaned back in the chair he'd occupied so many times over the years when advising the presidents of the United States. Over time, he'd learned to swim with the sharks and soon became one of the biggest, baddest sharks in the ocean.

He slowly reached into his pocket and retrieved a stack of four-by-six photographs. He reached forward and set them on the table between them. The president and Acton looked at one another, but did not move.

"What's this?" Acton finally asked.

Gregg relaxed in his chair and exhaled. "Please, take a look. Seriously. Go on now."

They picked up the photographs, and the president, repulsed by what she saw, threw them on the table.

"What's the meaning of this?" she demanded.

"Oh, Madam President, here's the meaning of this," Gregg started as he picked up several of the photos.

He pushed the photos one by one in the direction of the president and Acton. "This severed arm, identified by the fingerprint on one remaining finger, belongs to Specialist James 'Jocko' Cameron of the Defense Threat Reduction Agency at Fort Belvoir. This next one is the upper half of the body of Specialist Lawrence Klingman, also of the DTRA. This one is the severed leg of an unknown African-American operative who was wearing the exact same footwear of the aforementioned special operators, who were Caucasian. The rest of the images represent the weapons used by these operatives, which are made by Israeli Weapons Industries. When I saw these photos, I instantly recognized the Tavor carbine because I approved it for use by our black-ops people!"

"This doesn't prove—" began Acton before he was cut off by Gregg.

"It does prove something, Jimmy. Your people orchestrated this false-flag attack on the sovereign nation of Texas to disrupt our border security. It doesn't take much imagination to lead me to the conclusion that this false flag was intended to use as leverage over our new administration in some way. Well, you're both busted. You can cut the act, Acton. I'm tired of your mouth and, Madam President, from now on, we'll deal in good faith and on a level playing field. Agreed?"

As Acton sank into the settee, looking for a deeper hole to climb into, and the President of the United States cowered into her chair as her eyes avoided the gruesome pictures of the dead operatives, General Montgomery Gregg knew he'd won this battle.

CHAPTER 61

December 23
Carlsbad Caverns
Carlsbad, New Mexico

Holloway, Lee and two of his top commanders huddled around a fire built near the opening of the Big Room, the largest of the Carlsbad Caverns. Holloway, whose reputation as a leader and killer preceded him, was readily accepted by Lee upon his arrival. To solidify the newly formed relationship, Holloway graciously turned over the bounty from their raid of the National Guard Armory in Roswell. Four vehicles, including the MPs' Chevy Suburban, were added to the fleet of older model cars and trucks brought to New Mexico from around the country.

The weapons and ammunition bolstered the already impressive arsenal of the Lightning Death Squads. U.S. military uniforms, rocket launchers, grenades, and communications equipment, which had been protected from the EMP blast, were all welcomed with open arms.

The automatic weapons manufactured by the Mexican drug cartels for the commandos were impressive. The amount of ammo brought to the meeting point by the DPRK commandos filled up its own cave. The high-tech gear delivered by the new arrivals who came through Mexico on Indonesian-flagged freighters provided them the ability to fight on par with the U.S. military.

Most importantly, Holloway brought his knowledge of the American military's tactics. He'd learned of the state's secession, but he advised Lee that the military was still American trained. This made him a valuable asset under Lee's command.

There was one drawback, however. The North Koreans were reluctant to follow Holloway's lead because he was an American. He was assigned a small fighting force of twenty men who were associated with the Fullerton Boyz. Holloway, therefore, asked to be given unusual, covert assignments, which enabled him to use his skills learned as a special operator, later as a mercenary, and, ultimately, as a hardened criminal.

He explained something to Lee during those initial days together. Fighting a war was one thing, but an insurgency was another matter. A war was about power. An insurgency was about disruption. In order to fulfill their Dear Leader's directive regarding Texas, they would have to be stealthy, moving quietly and under the radar around the state.

Lee couldn't suddenly insert thousands of Koreans into the state of Texas. Holloway laughed during the conversation. *You'll be lucky if a dozen Koreans go unnoticed.* The two commanders concocted a plan that would achieve their goal, and then they could focus their attention on the larger plan.

On this day, the men sat around the fire as equals, with a common goal of advancing their interests. Lee's was to fulfill a promise to Dear Leader to destroy the rest of the North American power grid. What the EMP had failed to accomplish, his Lighting Death Squads would. Unknown to Lee, Holloway's goal was to kill, pillage, and destroy.

So the two men waited, dreaming of their future battles. As soon as the additional thousands of soldiers of the Korean People's Army arrived in Mexico, and ultimately in the Southwestern United States, the operations of the Fifth Column would begin.

CHAPTER 62

Christmas Eve
The Armstrong Ranch
Borden County, Texas

It's been said every person must experience a long journey before they could realize how wonderful home was. For the Rodeo Kids, they could've clicked their heels together like *The Wizard of Oz*'s Dorothy back in Calgary and skipped the journey part. More than once over the four weeks of travel, the three swore and promised each other that once the world was right again, they'd never leave the ranch. Forget rodeos. No trips to the mall. No rides into Lubbock with their daddy. Nope, they'd become homebodies for life.

It was late on their fourth day of walking when Cooper, Riley and Palmer began to recognize the land west of Armstrong Ranch. Even though this part of West Texas would look the same as any other to the unfamiliar eye, to the three youngest members of the Armstrong family, every mud hole and dry creek bed reminded them they were close to home.

When they reached the corner fence post marking the start of the southern boundary of the ranch, they broke out into a trot, which quickly became a jog. Cooper led the way courtesy of his lean build and long legs.

The AR-15 rifle, which had been a lifesaver to them on this long road home, bounced heavily on his back, so he removed it and cradled it in his arms like a security blanket as he jogged ahead.

"Look, y'all," said Palmer, pointing up ahead. "Daddy and Preacher built guard towers. I wonder if they built a fort and a moat with gators too?"

"Wouldn't surprise me," replied Riley as he put his right hand on Palmer's back, urging her to pick up the pace. Cooper had stretched his lead to almost twenty yards when Riley shouted to him. "Hey, Coop. Wait for—"

Riley's sentence was cut off by several gunshots fired in their direction from the newly constructed tower.

Cooper fell to the ground and rolled down a slight embankment into the fencing. Riley and Palmer continued ahead but ran into the dirt to get off the road.

Riley shouted to his brother as he crawled forward on his hands and knees to keep his body low. "Coop, are you okay? Coop?"

Cooper moaned his response. "Yeah, just tore up my hands and knees."

Palmer was furious. "Who's shooting at us? We're not lost, are we?"

"No," replied Riley. "Just some danged fool. Coop, give me that rifle. I'll let 'em know we don't appreciate the rude welcoming committee."

Cooper clutched the rifle a little tighter, not because he wanted to do the shooting, but to keep the impulsive Riley from doing something stupid.

"Keep your heads down and just wait a minute. This'll sort itself out," instructed Cooper through gritted teeth. He wiped his hands on his jeans to remove the small bits of gravel embedded in his skin.

"Hey, I hear the sounds of trucks comin'," said Palmer.

The three of them lay prone on the ground, hoping that the approaching vehicles were the cavalry and not a bunch of killers roaming West Texas that might have overtaken the family's ranch.

The first pickup to arrive was recognized by Cooper immediately. It was used by Antonio. Cooper quickly closed his eyes and prayed for safety. When he opened them, Antonio was cautiously approaching with his rifle raised, followed by another hand, who did the same.

Coop pushed himself onto his knees with his hands raised. "Antonio, you're not gonna shoot me, are you?" Antonio and

Cooper had practically grown up together and had always been close. Despite Cooper's bearded, disheveled appearance, his old friend instantly recognized him.

"Coop, seriously? Riley! Miss Palmer! Stand up. I'm so sorry they shot at you. Come here, my friends!"

The three rushed to Antonio and hugged him over the livestock fencing, which surrounded the ranch. Antonio began to help them climb over the wire fencing as a white pickup approached at a high rate of speed. Cooper dusted himself off and helped Riley do the same. Once Palmer joined them, they walked down the perimeter road and stood waiting for the truck they knew was used by Preacher.

Their daddy jumped out of the passenger side before Preacher could slide to a stop in a cloud of dust. Palmer was the first to jump in his arms, tears streaming down her beautiful, dusty face.

Major couldn't control his emotions as he began to cry. Now all three kids were in their father's arms, crying tears of joy and relief. The family reunion overtook the emotions of Preacher and Antonio as well, as tears and sniffles, followed by nervous laughter, became contagious.

"Y'all are one heckuva Christmas present," said Major through his sobs and laughter.

"Whoa, I forgot about Christmas," said Palmer, who wouldn't let go of her daddy. "When is it?"

Major looked into his only daughter's eyes and saw a younger version of Lucy staring back. "Honey, today is Christmas Eve, and you three are nothin' short of a miracle. Lord, thank you for keeping them safe." Then he began to cry again, unable to compose himself.

He tried to ask Preacher to raise Lucy on the radio, but he couldn't manage the words, not that it mattered. His old friend understood and immediately instructed Antonio's hand to drive to the ranch house to bring Miss Lucy on the double. *Tell her the Rodeo Kids are home.*

Major and their children walked arm in arm as they approached the tower. Standing at the bottom was one of the displaced Lazy S ranch hands, begging forgiveness for firing upon them. He was beside himself as he apologized. It was Cooper who eased the man's mind. He embraced him and whispered in his ear, "Don't you apologize. Let me thank you for taking care of our family while we were gone."

Feeling better, the man climbed the ladder to his post just as the pickup returned from the ranch house. All three kids immediately broke down again, knowing they'd feel the hugs of their mother after all this time.

Major and Preacher stood back as the truck approached. Miss Lucy was in the front seat with her hand covering her mouth. Her eyes were draining tears as if buckets of water had been poured over her head.

Somewhat in shock, she remained frozen in the front seat, unable to move. With smiles of joy and the floodgates of emotions pouring out of them, the Rodeo Kids went to greet their mother. She slid out of the truck and squeezed the life out of each of them.

When Major joined them, the group once again became a babbling mess of tears and snotty noses. Nobody cared. Their love passed from one to the other.

The love a parent has for their child is like nothing else on earth. This powerful bond knows no fear, no regret, and it dares anything to get in its way, ferociously crushing any obstacle.

CHAPTER 63

Christmas Eve
The Armstrong Ranch
Borden County, Texas

Once the emotions calmed, Lucy conducted the customary check of her Rodeo Kids, just as she did after every rodeo trip. She asked about bumps, bruises, and broken bones. She quickly converted from deliriously happy mother to Miss Lucy, *ruler of the roost*, and told every one of them they would hose off in the barn before being allowed to enter the house. "My horses smell better than you three," she said with a laugh. And she said, with her back bowed up, neither of her sons would be allowed at the dinner table until those beards were gone.

The conversation lingered, as none of them wanted to be apart for the short ride back to the ranch house, until the guard who'd fired upon Cooper shouted down to Preacher, "We have a rider approaching from the west."

Preacher scrambled to the trucks. "Y'all need to get behind here and stay out of sight. We'll handle this."

Major led the family to safety, and then he pulled his handgun. Preacher scrambled up to the tower to get a better look.

"Antonio, let's go," shouted Major as he ran to the driver's side.

"I'm comin' too," shouted Cooper as he grabbed his rifle, which lay across the hood of the other pickup.

After Cooper jumped in the back, Major pointed forward, urging Antonio toward the west to meet the intruders. The numbers of refugees finding their way near the Armstrong Ranch was growing more frequent, and Major intended to meet any threat head-on. Just like when he'd led his men at Company C, he would never ask anyone within his charge to do something he wasn't willing to do himself.

Cooper slid over to the driver's side of the truck and pointed his rifle in the direction of the riders.

Major hollered back to him through the sliding window of the pickup's cab, "Whadya see, Coop?"

"Looks like two riders, one horse, Daddy. Second rider is smaller, maybe a child or a girl."

"Any weapons?" asked Major.

"No, sir. The rider isn't raising a gun of any kind. He's just rollin' along like it's a Sunday stroll."

Antonio slowed the truck to avoid several potholes and to prevent Cooper from bouncing out of the bed. As he did, Cooper steadied his rifle.

"Holy smokes!" he exclaimed, which immediately drew Major's attention.

"What?"

"I don't know, Daddy. But it sure looks like a furry version of Duncan. I'd swear to it. It also looks like he's got a girl with him, a pretty one too. Not furry like him."

Major started laughing and motioned for Antonio to slow down. Cooper stood up in the back of the truck, and the rider lifted his right arm to wave.

"Daddy! It's Duncan for sure!"

Antonio slowed to a stop, and Cooper, still carrying the AR-15, rushed to greet the brother whom he'd been estranged from for so many years following the death of Dallas. At this moment, all ill feelings were erased and a clean slate established.

Duncan slid off his horse and helped Sook down as well. The two siblings crashed into each other with the fence separating them. They slapped each other on the back, pulled at each other's beards, and then started the process over again.

Major, who didn't think he had any more tears in the reservoir, opened up the spigot as he reached his oldest son. Every time

Duncan left on a mission, there was a fear that he might not return. He'd been out of touch since his last FaceTime chat with Miss Lucy back in the fall.

"Thank God you're alive, son," said Major, who was overcome with emotions once again. "I always knew you would be. You're a survivor."

"Thanks, Daddy. You have no idea. Listen, I want you and Coop to meet my friend Sook. She saved my life, Daddy. When I was destined to die, facedown in an ice-cold, North Korean river, she found me and nursed me back to health. I owe her my life."

Major smiled and reached across the fence to embrace Sook. She giggled nervously as tears streamed down her dust-covered face. Major pulled a red and white handkerchief from his pocket to gently dab her wet cheeks.

"Missy, you are adorable in so many ways. Thank you for saving our son."

Duncan helped Sook over the fence, and then he joined the group while Antonio tended to his horse. Duncan told him to treat this gelding like a king, because he'd sure earned his crown on this trip.

Antonio led the horse away as Lucy, Riley, and Palmer arrived in the second truck. The three of them raced into Duncan's arms. Major stood back as Lucy was reunited with her firstborn, alternating hugs and kisses with inspections and touches to the face to make sure he was real.

Then they were introduced to Sook and embraced her like a long-lost sister. The family was instantly mesmerized and enthralled by her command of the English language. They commented how her accent was so adorable, with Palmer warning Sook that she'd probably lose her voice as the family of Texans sought to listen to anyone that didn't sound like they were from around here.

As he admired the loves of his life, Major wasn't sure how many tears the human body could produce at a given time, but one thing was certain, the reunification of the Armstrong family, plus one, created enough to keep the ranch's wells filled for a month.

CHAPTER 64

Christmas Eve
The Armstrong Ranch
Borden County, Texas

Many Texans used the Christmas season to exhibit their Texas pride, adorning their homes with out-of-the-ordinary décor and gracing their dinner tables with nontraditional foods. The history of cowboys in Texas was on full display at the Armstrong Ranch on this extraordinary day.

Wreaths made of barbed wire centered around an old boot were hung throughout the ranch house and the barns, which were the focal point of their Christmas activities. Wreaths were also made of cactus pads strung together with rope in celebration of the vast West Texas desert. Garlands were made of spurs strung together with twine.

All the ranch hands and their families were arriving at the barns for a late afternoon worship service followed by the passing out of gifts to the handful of kids who lived on the ranch. Antonio had brought an old wagon from the barnyard down to the house, pulled by one of several Texas Longhorns in their herd. He was giving the kids a ride in a circle-eight path, which wound its way around the barns.

The Mexican connection to Christmas at the Armstrongs' was evident as well. Called *las posadas*, the celebration traditionally began on December 16 and ran through *Buena Noche*—Christmas Eve. Historically of Catholic faith, Mexicans would attend midnight mass on Christmas Eve, followed by gift giving.

For this Christmas Eve celebration, the women and children had gotten together over the last few days to make *piñatas* made of papier-mâché and cloth. Miss Lucy had bags of candy left over from past Halloween celebrations on the ranch as part of her food stores. The sweets, plus some old Hot Wheels cars, which had belonged to Cooper and Riley, were used to fill the piñatas before they were hung around the barn.

Major, Duncan, and Preacher were gathered around the front porch of the house, sipping freshly brewed coffee, when they were joined by the youngest of the Armstrong men—Cooper and Riley.

"This has turned out to be quite the Christmas, gentlemen," said Major with a smile as he took another sip of the hot coffee. Riley peeled away to fetch a couple of mugs for himself and Cooper.

"It is, Daddy," said Cooper. "Honestly, this is the first Christmas I've been really excited about since I was a kid. You know, when you grow up, the whole concept of Santa Claus kinda fades away, and soon your hopes for packages under the tree is replaced with dreams of envelopes full of greenbacks."

Everyone laughed along with Cooper's analysis. The wonder of Christmas was best seen through the eyes of a child. The meaning of Christmas, however, can only be appreciated by adults, especially those who've faced adversity and who considered the challenges in life that were in store for them.

Upon their arrival, the Armstrong children and Sook focused on cleaning up and getting ready for the evening worship service established by Preacher. Miss Lucy told them not to get bogged down in storytelling about the events of the past month. They were all keenly aware that the ability of man to destroy one another had been on full display.

The Armstrong kids had faced death and unimaginable horrors. Now they were home, surrounded by protective parents and the comradery of friendships. The battles would continue because the threats persisted, but for tonight, they promised to focus on how God had blessed them and delivered them home safely.

Duncan was the first to break his promise to his mother. "Daddy, I'm gonna need to speak to someone about what I observed out there. I'm neither paranoid nor conspiratorial. Y'all know that. I'm tellin' you, something's brewing, and it's closer to home than anybody realizes."

"I understand, son," said Major. "We'll plan on driving into Austin to see Marion as soon as we can. I met former Secretary Gregg at a Christmas party the night of the EMP. He seems like a reasonable fella. He's vice president, you know."

"Of Texas?" asked Duncan.

"Yessir. I suspect he cut ties with Washington—"

Major was interrupted by Miss Lucy's arrival on the front porch, followed by Riley with two mugs of coffee. He joined the menfolk and delivered Cooper his favorite mug bearing the PBR logo.

"Enough shoptalk, boys," she demanded. "Y'all need to line up down here in front of me and let me hand out your marching orders."

Palmer and Sook emerged from the house with big smiles on their faces. They appeared to enjoy the spectacle of Lucy barking out the orders.

"Now, Miss Lucy, before you start, I need to talk to you about security," began Major. "We can't pull all the hands off the fences. Somebody's gotta handle security while we—"

Lucy held up both hands and shook her head, providing Major a clear stop sign advising him not to say another word.

"Now you boys listen to me," she began authoritatively, to the giggles and delight of her young female charges standing behind her. "I've trusted my life to God for all of these years, and if I can't trust him to watch over this ranch for two hours while all of us enjoy this Christmas Eve service, what does that say about my faith?"

"But, Miss Lucy—" started Preacher before being cut off.

"Not another word. It's time to establish new traditions, starting with this glorious Christmas together. Preacher, I expect you'll deliver a beautiful sermon, your first in many years, but full of spirit and joy nonetheless.

"Duncan and Coop, start putting the picnic tables in place for tomorrow's Christmas dinner in the big barn. Also, put as many chairs and crates in the new barn for tonight's service as you can find. Afterwards, you can move them back to the dining barn, we'll call it.

"Major, you'll make sure everyone is present in that barn to hear this good man's words. Tomorrow, we'll serve up a fabulous Christmas dinner as we bring our big, extended family together for the first time in many years.

"After that, you can secure your fences and save the world. Agreed? Good."

Lucy didn't wait for a response before she stepped closer to each of her foot soldiers. "Preacher, go clean up. You look more like a wrangler than you do a minister. Major, you are the host of this Christmas Eve shindig. Go greet our guests and, well, just go host."

Palmer and Sook couldn't stifle their laughs any longer. Their giggles drew the attention of Miss Lucy, who turned and gave them a wink with a grin.

She continued. "Duncan, you and Coop make sure the tables are arranged and help tend to the horses of the ranch hands and their families. This is our way of saying thank you to them for being a part of our family. Let's treat them as guests."

"Okay, Momma," said Cooper.

Preacher stepped backwards and headed toward his horse. Major spun around and marched toward the barn, followed by his three sons.

Miss Lucy put her hands on her hips. "Where do you think you're going, mister?"

The boys stopped and turned back toward their mom. She was staring at Riley.

He pointed at his chest. "Me?"

"Yeah, you. Where do you think you're going?"

"Um, I figured I'd be with the guys."

"Nope, you're with me today."

"C'mon, Momma," protested Riley. "What did I do?"

"Follow me," was Miss Lucy's response as she turned and shooed her giggling girls back into the house. "And don't argue!"

*****

Preacher felt a little awkward as he approached the makeshift pulpit consisting of an overturned apple crate on top of a folding table. Miss Lucy had found an old red velvet cape, which had belonged to her mother, in a trunk full of family heirlooms. It was draped over the crate and bunched around the table to provide a more reverent feel.

The suit Preacher wore made him look like Wyatt Earp—a throwback to the nineteenth century. It was a suit he hadn't worn in many years, since the last time he'd addressed his flock in Big Spring. The long, fully lined black coat and black formal vest, over a white pleated tuxedo-style shirt, gave him an Old West look. His black wool hat topped off the imposing outfit.

Everyone crammed into the barn, most carrying their family Bibles. The Armstrong family Bible had been handed down through the generations, just as the ranch had passed from one steward to another. Notes about the family's history, records of births, deaths, baptisms, confirmations, and marriages filled its pages. The pages were loose, tattered, and sometimes torn, but it was the heart of the Armstrong family, and Major clutched it with pride.

Preacher hit his stride almost immediately, finding his footing as a man of God, one who was blessed with the ability to impart words of inspiration on the congregation.

"I am a sinner and a fallen man," he began as he hung his head for a moment. He took a deep breath and continued. "I've begged God's forgiveness and asked for the strength to put on this suit once again. With the help of all of you, my family, He gave me the courage to pull it out of the closet, and by His Grace, it still fits."

Preacher patted his stomach a few times and managed a smile.

"We have tremendously high expectations of life. We want everything to be perfect. We have pictures of children playing, people smiling, and getting along. But often, as we've learned, this perfect view of life is not always the way things are.

"Our visions of Christmas are no different. We listen to Christmas songs with lyrics like the *most wonderful time of the year* and *the happiest season of all*, but for many families, especially during this particular Christmas, that will not be the case. Their lives full of hope have been interrupted by starvation, sickness, and death.

"Life is full of interruptions. Some are insignificant and dealt with quickly. Other times, when forced upon us by evil barging into our lives, we have to adapt and face the challenges head-on.

"As I look around this barn, I see the faces of God's children and our large family. Together, a challenge lies before us—the greatest interruption of our lives. We must be careful not to react with fear. Remember, God is with us, and He will guide us in all things."

Preacher continued to remind his first congregation in many years that, as a family, they could overcome the challenges they'd face in the future. He led them by singing inspirational hymns that filled their hearts with love. Then they chose a few traditional Christmas carols that left them laughing and hugging one another.

Finally, Preacher bowed his head and prayed aloud.

"As we celebrate this most extraordinary Christmas, we thank You for Your protection from harm, misfortune and sadness. Let not any of our enemies, thieves, bandits, or evildoers approach us. We ask that You turn around their evil intent.

"In return, we will enjoy the privilege of spending time together to share joy, celebrate the addition of a new member to our family from a faraway land, and to be there for one another when we need comfort.

"Finally, Lord, thank You for the blessings You've bestowed upon Texas, our home and a new nation, as it finds a way to flourish in this troublesome world. May good health prevail for all Texans, this family, and may we find ever-present faith in Your mercy and grace. Amen."

Preacher raised his head from prayer and smiled at his new congregation, but their good feelings were replaced with a sense of foreboding as the deafening roar of two fighter jets racing low across the western horizon just barely above the high plains of West Texas interrupted their moment with God.

THANK YOU FOR READING *LINES IN THE SAND*!

If you enjoyed it, I'd be grateful if you'd take a moment to write a short review (just a few words are needed) and post it on Amazon. Amazon uses complicated algorithms to determine what books are recommended to readers. Sales are, of course, a factor, but so are the quantities of reviews my books get. By taking a few seconds to leave a review, you help me out, and also help new readers learn about my work.

And before you go…

SIGN UP for Bobby Akart's mailing list to receive special offers, bonus content, and you'll be the first to receive news about new releases in The Lone Star Series, The Pandemic series, The Blackout series, The Boston Brahmin series and The Prepping for Tomorrow series—which includes twenty Amazon #1 Bestsellers in forty fiction and non-fiction genres. Visit Bobby Akart's website for informative blog entries on preparedness, writing, and his latest contribution to the American Preppers Network.

www.BobbyAkart.com

www.ingramcontent.com/pod-product-compliance
Lightning Source LLC
Chambersburg PA
CBHW020933310726
48980CB00007B/747/J

* 9 7 8 0 6 9 2 0 8 3 4 6 8 *